"I SWOR... ...OF VEN-
GEANCE. ...OR. YOU
KNOW W... ...CKJACK,
DON'T YO...

Blackjack didn't answer. Topaz nodded slowly, her face cold and emotionless.

"Very well then. A fair fight. I will not use my esper powers. Swords only. Then, when I kill you, I will be able to savour it all the more. Pick up your weapon, mercenary. . . ."

Ace Books by Simon R. Green

The Hawk & Fisher Series

HAWK & FISHER
WINNER TAKES ALL
THE GOD KILLER
WOLF IN THE FOLD
GUARD AGAINST DISHONOR
THE BONES OF HAVEN

MISTWORLD

MISTWORLD

SIMON R. GREEN

ACE BOOKS, NEW YORK

CALL her Mary. When she sang, she could break your heart or mend it, but that was before the Empire found and used her. Now she's just another refugee, running for her life. Deep within her, madness stirs. Her name is Mary. Typhoid Mary. And nobody in Mistport will ever forget her.

CHAPTER ONE

A Ghost in the Night

A low, gusting wind came moaning out of the north, unsettling the snow-flecked mists that filled the narrow Mistport streets. Lamps and lanterns hung at every door, burning yellow and red and orange against the endless sea of grey. The mists were always at their thickest in the early hours of the morning, before the rising of Mistworld's pale sun.

A dim figure padded confidently across a slippery slate roof, his slender frame barely visible amidst the swirling snow flurries. The pure white of his thermal suit blended harmoniously into the snow and the mists, whilst its heating elements insulated him from the wind's cutting edge. The man called Cat crouched down by an outjutting attic window and pushed back his suit's cowl, revealing pale, youthful features dominated by dark watchful eyes and the pockmarks that tattooed both cheeks. He winced as the freezing air seared his bare face, and then he slid carefully down the snow-smeared tiles to bump into a gently smoking chimneystack. He took a firm hold on the uneven brickwork and leaned out from the roof to stare about him.

From his high vantage point there lay stretched out before him all the tiled and gabled rooftops of Mistport, his hunting ground and private kingdom. Cat had spent most of his twenty years learning his trade and refining his craft to become one of the finest burglars Thieves Quarter had ever produced. The ornately carved and curlicued wood and ironwork of Mistport's buildings were hand- and footholds to him, the cornices and gables his landmarks and resting places.

Cat was a roof runner.

Light from the huge half-moon shone clearly through the curling mists, reflecting brightly from the snow-covered roofs and streets and setting out the scene below in eerie starkness. To Cat's left lay the scattered glow of Thieves Quarter, sprawled in a tangle of shabby streets, where outleaning timbered buildings huddled together as though for warmth in the cold night. Its occasional lights shone crimson against the dark, like rubies set on velvet. To his right lay Tech Quarter, and the starport.

Sensor spikes blazed in the night, blue stormfire shivering up and down the slender crystal lances. Oil lamps and torches burned in regular patterns across the starport grounds, marking out the huge landing pads, each of them half a mile wide. Of all the port's buildings only the steelglass control tower, last remnant of the Empire's original Base, still boasted bright electric lights. Less than a dozen ships lay on the landing pads, mostly abandoned hulks stripped down for the high tech they possessed. A handful of smugglers' ships lay scattered across one pad, five silver needles glowing ruddy from the flickering torches. Beacons suddenly flared into life around the largest pad, like corpsefires on a newly built cairn, and Cat realised with a thrill of excitement that there was a ship coming in. Ships of any kind were growing rare these days, and any new arrival was good news. Cat turned reluctantly away, and looked down at the streets below him.

Nobody moved in the empty alleyways, and the pale blanket of freshly fallen snow remained unbroken. Only thieves and spies braved the bitter cold of Mistport's night, and they never left tracks.

Cat pulled his cowl back up to shield his face, and releasing his hold on the chimneystack, he slipped carefully over the roof's edge. He took a firm grip on the narrow drainpipe and slowly eased himself headfirst over the edge until he was hanging upside down, his feet hooked firmly under the gutter. The rusty ironwork groaned under his weight, but held firm as he thoughtfully studied the small steel-latticed window before him. The window was less than two feet square, and the grille was cast from stainless steel. *How very unhospitable,* thought Cat. *Anyone would think they were afraid of being burgled.* He looked more closely at the window frame, and smiled complacently as he spotted two slender wires attached to the upper right-hand corner of the grille, which disappeared into the brickwork to no apparent purpose. Obviously an alarm of some kind. Cat drew a pair of miniature cutters from inside his left boot, reached out to cut the wires, and then hesitated. The wires were too obvious. He checked again, and grinned wryly as he discovered a small electronic sensor fitted flush into the grille's ironwood frame. Touch the grille or the frame, and the sensor would set off an alarm. Cat slipped the cutters into his glove, and drawing a slender steel probe from his right boot, he delicately shorted out the sensor with the casual skill of long practice. He slipped the probe back into his boot, and then took the cutters and carefully snipped both of the wires, just in case. He put the cutters back in his left boot, took out a small screwdriver, and calmly set about undoing the four simple screws that held the grille in place.

Blood pounded in his head from being upside down so long, but he ignored it as best he could and refused to be hurried. He dropped three of the screws one by one into the white leather pouch at his belt, and then put away the screwdriver and tugged cautiously at the steel grille. It came easily away in his hands, and hung loosely by the one remaining screw. Cat grinned. So far, everything was going as planned. He pushed aside the grille and slipped an arm through the window. His head followed, and then he breathed gently as his chest and back scraped against the unyielding ironwood frame. He took a firm grip on the inner frame with his hand, and then, taking a deep breath, he worked his feet loose from under the gutter. His body jerked violently in the window frame as his legs fell free, but the jolt wasn't enough to pull him back out the window. He waited a moment while his breathing steadied, and then released his grip on the inner frame. Inch by inch he worked his upper torso through the narrow gap, and then his waist

and hips followed easily. Only someone as wiry and limber
as he could have managed it. Which was one of the reasons
why even Cat's rivals acknowledged him as the finest roof
runner in Mistport.

He swung lithely down from the window, and crouched
motionless in the shadows while his eyes adjusted to the
gloom. A narrow hallway stretched away before him, with a
stairway to his left and two closed doors to his right. Moonlight spilled through the open window behind him, but even
Cat's experienced eyes were hard put to make out details in
the darkness beyond the shimmering light. He took off his
gloves and tucked them into his belt, and flexed his long,
slender fingers through a quick series of exercises. To a
good burglar, the hands were just as important as the tools
they used. Cat always looked after his hands. He gingerly
pressed the tips of his fingers against the floor, and then
closed his eyes, concentrating on the feel of the polished
wood. Faint vibrations tingled under his fingertips, and Cat
frowned thoughtfully. There were sensor panels hidden in
the floor, no doubt designed to set off all kinds of alarms if a
man's weight triggered them. Still without opening his eyes,
Cat leant slowly forward and swept his fingers back and
forth across the floor in a series of widening arcs, judging
by the rise and fall of the vibrations where it was safe and
where it was not. He slowly worked his way forward, inch
by inch, until he was sure he'd located the main pattern, and
then he opened his eyes, stood up, and padded confidently
down the hallway, easily avoiding the treacherous areas.

Just like the old game, he thought dryly. *Step on a
crack, break your mother's back . . .* And then he frowned,
remembering how long it had been since Mistport could
afford to maintain paved sidewalks. The times were not
what they had been. Cat shrugged, and moved quickly on
to the lower of the two doors. The sooner this part of the
job was over, the better; the same white suit that hid him
in the snow and the mists was wildly conspicuous in a dark
deserted corridor.

He stopped before the closed lower door, and studied it
warily. His fence had briefed him as thoroughly as possible

on the house's exterior, but hadn't been able to tell him
much about the inside. The door had to be booby-trapped
in some way; it was what Cat would have done. He ran his
fingers gently over the harsh-grained wood, but couldn't
detect anything out of the ordinary. He took a pencil torch
from inside his right boot and thumbed it on. Then, leaning
closer, he ran his gaze over the door frame, inch by inch.
Sure enough there was a small, slightly raised button high
up on the frame; a simple catch that was released when the
door opened. Cat shook his head dolefully at such a meagre
testing of his talents, and taking the steel probe from his
boot, he slipped it quickly past the button to turn it off.
And then Cat frowned, and pulled back the probe. The
alarm button was already in the off position; they must
have forgotten to set it before going to bed. Cat rolled his
eyes heavenwards. This was becoming ridiculously easy.
He snapped off the pencil torch, put away both torch and
probe, and taking a firm grip on the door handle, slowly
eased the door open. He checked quickly for backup alarms,
and then peered cautiously into the bedroom.

A sparse light filtered past the bolted shutters to show
him a dim form huddled under thick blankets in the canopied bed that took up most of the small bedroom. A few
glowing coals burned redly in the fireplace to his right,
taking the chill off the air. Cat slipped into the room, closed
the door behind him and moved over to the bed, silent as
the ghost he seemed. He paused briefly as the sleeper stirred
and then lay still again. Cat didn't carry any weapons; he
didn't believe in them. He was a roof runner and an artist
at his craft, not some bully boy vandal or heartless thief in
the night. Cat had his standards. He stood motionless beside
the bed until he was sure it was safe to move again, and
then he leant forward over the sleeping shape and reached
out his hand. Judging his moment nicely, he eased his hand
under the pillow and drew out a small brass-bound casket.
The bed's occupant slept on, undisturbed. Cat stepped back
from the bed, drew a small key from the pouch at his belt,
and tried it cautiously in the casket's lock. The key turned
easily, and Cat grinned broadly as he pushed back the lid

and the crystal in the casket blazed light into the room.

As an Outlaw planet, Mistworld was cut off from Empire trade, and high tech was limited to what the smugglers could bring in on their infrequent visits. A computer's memory crystal thus became far more tempting loot than any diamond or ruby. Cat didn't know what information the crystal held, and didn't care. His fence said she had a buyer for the jewel, and that was all that mattered. Cat reached into the pouch at his belt and brought out a blank crystal, glowing twin to the jewel in the casket. He carefully substituted one crystal for the other, closed the casket lid, and locked it. He dropped the key back into his pouch, and then leaned forward and deftly replaced the casket where he'd found it. His hand had barely left the pillow when the bedroom door suddenly flew open. Light flooded the room, and a tall figure with a lantern filled the doorway.

Cat pulled the blankets from the bed and with one desperate heave threw them over the newcomer's head. The bed's occupant sat up sharply, pulling a silk nightdress about her, and Cat paused to drop her an appreciative wink. The newcomer struggled furiously on the floor, helplessly entangled in the bedclothes. The dropped lantern lay on its side in the doorway, filling the room with a flickering light. Cat decided it was time he was going. He stepped carefully round the pile of heaving blankets and made for the open door. The woman in the canopied bed opened her mouth and sang.

Cat sank to his knees as the song washed over him, scrambling his nervous system. *A Siren!* he thought wildly. *They set a Siren to guard the crystal!* The song screamed through his body, shaking in his muscles. He lurched to his feet, considered punching the woman out, decided this was no time to be heroic, and plunged for the doorway. The Siren's song washed over him in waves, numbing his hands and feet and blurring his eyesight.

Cat staggered out the door and down the passageway, paying no attention to the pressure alarms in the floor, just concentrating all his will on not giving in to the Siren song that was trying to batter him unconscious. He finally reached the window through which he'd entered, and pulled himself up into the narrow opening. He wriggled through the window with desperate speed, and then his heart missed a beat as a hand closed around his ankle, bringing him lurching to a halt. He kicked and struggled wildly, and the hand lost its grip and fell away. Cat pulled himself out the window, grabbed the drainpipe, and hauled himself up towards the roof. He scrambled over the gutter and then collapsed to lie flat on the snow-covered tiles. He lay there a while shaking in every limb, slowly relaxing as he realised he'd left the Siren's song behind. A woman whose voice and esp could combine to scramble a man's thoughts was an impressive guard. Unless, of course, the burglar happens to be a deaf mute . . .

Cat grinned, and rising quickly to his feet, he padded away into the mists. For the first time in years, he was glad not to have heard something.

CHAPTER TWO

A Gathering of Traitors

THE reception area of Leon Vertue's office was warm,
comfortable, and desperately civilised, and Jamie Royal
hated it. Much as he appreciated good living and luxury,
he resented having his nose rubbed in it. There was something decidedly smug in the office's ostentatious display of
wealth. The sign over the modestly plain front door had
said simply BLACKSMITH, but Jamie doubted that anyone
who worked in this luxurious office would know an anvil
if they fell over it. He sighed, leant back in his recliner
chair, and tried to look as though he was used to such
comforts. He surreptitiously trailed his fingers across the
slick, shining surface of the chair's arms. Plastic. Now that
was real luxury. Jamie could count the number of times he'd
seen plastic on the fingers of one hand. More and more, he
felt that he was very much out of his depth.

He crossed one leg over the other, and tried to at least
look relaxed. He glanced casually about the office, hoping
to find a lapse in taste so he could sneer at it. The wood-
en wall panels gleamed dully in the light of the banked
fire, and the single great window was closed and shuttered against the night cold. The main light came from
a single overhead lightsphere set into the ceiling. Jamie
didn't care much for the electric light. It was brighter
than he was used to, and he didn't like its unwavering
intensity. There was something cold about electric light,
cold and . . . unnatural. Jamie put the thought firmly from
his mind, and concentrated his attention on the gorgeous
redheaded secretary sitting behind her desk. Her flawless

8

skin had a rich peaches-and-cream glow, even under the harsh electric light, and her features had a sharp, classical perfection. Her figure was simply spectacular. Jamie cleared his throat loudly, and gave her his most charming smile. She didn't look particularly impressed. Jamie sighed, and went back to looking around the office.

Papers and magazines lay scattered across the coffee table before him, but they were all at least a week old, well past the date when they should have been handed in for recycling. The headlines were mainly concerned with the discovery of the wrecked starship *Darkwind*, and a few vague allegations of corruption within the Communications Guild. Stale news, not yet old enough to be interesting again through hindsight. Jamie Royal leant back in his luxurious chair and let his mind wander. Ever since he'd split up with his last partner his luck had gone from bad to worse. Madelaine Skye had been an excellent partner, but unfortunately she turned out to be somewhat overburdened with scruples. Partly her sister's fault. Dear Jessica. A nice-looking girl, much like Madelaine, but about as much use as a chocolate kettle. How a warrior like Madelaine had ended up with such a wet blanket for a sister was beyond him. Jamie smiled slightly, remembering. Jessica hadn't exactly been impressed with him, either.

Looking back, it was a wonder he and Madelaine had stayed together as long as they had. Much as he hated to admit it, Jamie missed her. If nothing else, she'd had enough sense to keep him away from people like this. Jamie smiled fondly. Sweet Madelaine, a good fighter and a better partner. If only things had been different . . . Jamie shook his head firmly. What was past was past, and should be forgotten.

Bored, he looked about him. The receptionist was buffing her nails with great thoroughness and intense concentration, but Jamie wasn't fooled. He'd spotted the throwing knife strapped to her shapely calf. He sighed regretfully, and then shifted uneasily in his recliner chair. There was such a thing as too much comfort. Get used to living in luxury and all too soon you started getting soft; and in Jamie's business growing soft could get you killed. Jamie Royal had enemies. He also had debts, which was why he'd come to Leon Vertue's body bank.

"Mr. Royal? Dr. Vertue will see you now."

"Very kind of him," murmured Jamie. The receptionist gestured languidly at the door to her left, and then went back to working on her nails. She didn't look up as Jamie walked past her desk, and he sighed resignedly. You can't win them all.

The door led into a long narrow corridor, brightly lit by a dozen lightspheres set into the ceiling at regular intervals. Jamie tore his eyes away from the lights and swallowed dryly. He'd known Vertue was rich, but such a conspicuous use of electricity impressed the hell out of him. Jamie could have lived in extreme comfort for over a year on what it must have cost Vertue just to have the lightspheres installed. He pulled himself together and hurried down the corridor. It wouldn't do to keep Vertue waiting. He was said to be touchy about such things.

The corridor turned a sharp corner halfway along, and finally ended in a single great door of polished steel. Jamie looked for a door handle, but there wasn't one. He waited patiently before the steel door, and studied himself in the bright, shining mirror. He looked more confident than he felt, but that wasn't saying much. He pulled his jacket straight, and adjusted his cloak so that it hung in a more flattering manner. The old grey cloak was showing its age, but it still kept out most of the cold and the snow, and that was all Jamie had ever asked of a cloak. He scowled at his reflection, trying hard to look tough and intimidating, but his mirror image remained stubbornly unimpressive. Jamie Royal was tall, thin, and despite being only in his mid-twenties, well on his way to being prematurely bald. His chin was weak, his stance was awkward, and if he had any muscles he kept them well hidden. It would have been easy to dismiss him as harmless, if it hadn't been for his eyes. Jamie's eyes were dark and intense and very much alive. They could express everything from camaraderie to staunch support to heartfelt sympathy without meaning any of them. They were a con man's eyes, and Jamie was very proud of them.

He shifted uncomfortably from foot to foot before the great steel door, his hands moving restlessly at his sides. He felt naked without his sword and dagger, but he'd had to leave them at reception. Vertue was possibly the most universally despised man in Mistport, and he didn't take chances. In certain quarters the reward for delivering his head, preferably unattached to the body, continued to rise. Jamie looked up at the security camera overhead, and smiled ingratiatingly. There was a faintly threatening hiss of compressed air, and the door swung slowly open. Jamie drew himself up to his full height and walked into Dr. Vertue's chamber as though he owned the place.

The walls of the vast room were lined with shining crystal. The glow from a single overhead sphere reflected brightly from the walls, filling the chamber with a sharp silver light. Jamie came to a sudden halt as the door slammed shut behind him. Dozens of bulky steel units took up most of the floor, and though Jamie had never seen them before, he knew exactly what they were: reclamation tanks. The means whereby a body could be broken down into its respective parts . . .

Each of the units was covered with a thick haze of frost, and Jamie shuddered as he looked about him. Cold as Mistport's streets were, this place was colder. The presence of death hung heavily on the freezing air, like the final echoes of a desperate scream. Jamie pulled his cloak tightly about him, and walked reluctantly forward to meet the two men who stood waiting for him beside the nearest reclamation tank.

The overly tall, stooped man on the left was Dr. Leon Vertue. Wrapped in thick furs of grubby white, he had the appearance and bearing of a hungry wolf. His long white hair hung in thick greasy strands, accentuating his gaunt features. His hands were large and powerful, but immaculately manicured. Surgeon's hands. Jamie recognised him immediately, though they'd never met before. Most people had heard of Dr. Vertue, but no one associated with him by

choice. Vertue was the owner-manager of Mistport's main
body bank. They were all illegal, of course, but a man who
needs an organ transplant to save his life isn't going to be
too fussy about where the replacement organ comes from.
And there were always men and women from the back
streets and alleyways who would never be missed. . . .

The man standing beside Vertue was a stranger to Jamie,
but he recognised the type. The man looked hard, vicious,
and competent, and he wore his long jet-black hair pulled
back in a mercenary's scalplock. The sharply defined lines
in his face showed him to be in his early forties at least,
but there was nothing soft or tired about the corded muscles
that stirred restlessly as the mercenary moved lightly from
one foot to the other. He wore a plain black thermal suit
and a black fur half-cloak. There was a sword on his left
hip, and a gun on his right. His face and forehead bore the
ritual scars of the Hawke Clan, which meant that he was
one of the Empire's finest professional fighting men. It also
meant he was very expensive. Jamie wondered how many
men the mercenary had killed in his long career, and then
quickly decided that he didn't want to know. Even standing
perfectly still and relaxed, there was something . . . dangerous about the man. Jamie looked away and wished fiercely
that he was somewhere else. Anywhere else.

He glanced uneasily through the glass top of the reclamation tank before him. Curling blue mists seethed and
roiled continuously in the unit, as though struggling to
escape. Jamie wondered briefly if the tank contained a
body, and if so, whose. He told himself firmly that it was
none of his business, and looked back at Dr. Vertue and his
mercenary. Jamie coughed politely to show he was waiting for them to open the conversation, and Vertue smiled
lazily at him. The doctor's pale eyes and long white hair
gave him an anemic, washed-out look, but Jamie wasn't
fooled. Vertue's smile showed him for the predator he
was.

"Dear Jamie," said Vertue silkily. "So nice of you to
come and see me at such short notice. Not that you had
any choice in the matter, of course."

"Of course," said Jamie. "Now what the hell do you want?"

The mercenary stiffened slightly, but Jamie carefully kept his eyes fixed on Vertue. He couldn't afford to sound cowed, or they'd walk all over him. He knew, and they knew, he was going to end up doing whatever Vertue wanted, but if he acted like a servant he'd get treated like one. His only chance of getting out of this with his hide intact was to act as though he still had an ace or two hidden up his sleeve. Though given his present situation, he'd have settled for a jack or a ten.

"I want you to do me a favour, Jamie," said Vertue, still smiling. "And in return, I'll do you a favour. What could be more simple?"

"What indeed?" said Jamie easily. "Suppose you get a little more specific, and I'll tell you whether or not I'm interested."

"Would you like me to break one of his arms?" asked the mercenary. His voice was low, calm, pleasant; he might have been asking the time or making polite conversation.

"Maybe later," said Dr. Vertue. "You have to make allowances for Jamie, my dear Blackjack. He has hidden qualities."

"I don't have to make allowances for anyone," said Blackjack. "But you're the boss."

Jamie felt a few beads of sweat appear on his forehead, despite the cold. He had no doubt the mercenary had meant what he said.

"Forgive me for seeing you in this intemperate climate," said Vertue, "but I have a job here that really can't wait much longer. You understand how it is; I wouldn't want the merchandise to spoil. . . ."

"Anyone I know?" asked Jamie flippantly.

"I believe so," said Dr. Vertue. "Her name was Skye. Madelaine Skye."

Jamie fought to keep his face impassive. *No . . . Oh no, not Madelaine . . .* They'd been partners for almost three years. They'd never been lovers, but they could have been. Madelaine Skye, a good woman to have at your back in a fight, or at your side in a bar. They'd worked together on a hundred different jobs, on both sides of the law. He'd always admired her guts, and her expertise. The best damned partner he'd ever had. Jamie Royal had many acquaintances but few friends. And now he had one less.

You bastards . . .

His hands curled into fists, and then he glanced at Blackjack and saw immediately that the mercenary was just waiting for him to try and start something. Jamie fought down his anger, feeling it burn cold and fierce in his gut. There'd be time for revenge later.

"Who killed her?" he asked quietly.

"Who do you think?" said Dr. Vertue.

Jamie carefully avoided looking at the smiling mercenary. "So Madelaine's dead," he said finally. "Am I supposed to be impressed by this?"

"I'll settle for intimidated," said Dr. Vertue. "Are you ready to discuss business now?"

Jamie Royal took a deep breath, and let it out slowly. The cold air seared his lungs, and the pain helped to calm him. Not for the first time he swore to give up dice altogether. His winnings never lasted long, and when he lost he ended up in situations like this. Jamie had worked with all sorts in his time, but Dr. Leon Vertue represented an all-time low. There were those who said he'd been a clonelegger before coming to Mistport, and Jamie could well believe it.

"I'm always ready to discuss business," said Jamie steadily. "What did you have in mind?"

"Nothing too difficult," purred Dr. Vertue. "You are familiar with the Blackthorn tavern?"

"Sure," said Jamie. "Cyder's place. The most stonyhearted fence in Mistport, but her prices are fair. More or less."

Vertue took a slim package from under his furs and handed it to Jamie. He hefted it once, and raised an eyebrow at its weight.

"Cyder is holding a package for me," said Vertue. "I want you to go to the Blackthorn tavern tomorrow evening, pick up that package, and give her yours in return. I'm entrusting you with a great deal of money, Jamie; be careful not to lose it on your way to the Blackthorn."

Jamie nodded, and slipped the package into an inner pocket. "This package I'm picking up; what's in it?"

"A memory crystal. Do handle it with care, Jamie; as far as I and my associates are concerned, that crystal's safety is far more important than your own. Should the crystal prove to be damaged in any way, I would be most upset with you. Bring the crystal to me and place it in my hand, and your service to me will be complete. In return, I will take care of your debts. All of them."

"That's it?" said Jamie, frowning. "You must be crazy, Vertue. There are any number of couriers who could handle this for you, for a tenth of what it'll cost you to pay off all my debts. Why bother with me?"

"I need someone who is both discreet and reliable," said Vertue amiably. "Not to mention desperate. As I'm sure you're aware, the theft of memory crystals carries the death penalty in Mistport. You will do this little task for me, won't you, Jamie?"

"What makes you so sure you can trust me?"

"Your word is said to be good," said Vertue, smiling faintly as though the idea amused him. "And you and Cyder know each other well. Too well for either of you to even think of trying a double-cross."

"But just supposing I should," said Jamie. "What could . . ."

Blackjack leaned forward suddenly, and one scarred hand shot out to wrap itself around Jamie's throat. The mercenary bent Jamie back over the reclamation tank, and then grabbed his belt and lifted him up and out over the unit. Dr. Vertue opened the tank's lid, and Blackjack started to lower Jamie towards the curling blue mists. He kicked and struggled, gasping and choking for air, but he couldn't break the mercenary's grip. Jamie looked down into the mists with bulging eyes. The blue mists swirled eagerly, hungrily, and beyond them he could see light glinting on the many saws and scalpels that stood ready to pare him down to his essential elements; so much skin, so much bone and cartilage, various organs, and of course the eyes. There was always a demand for eyes. Blackjack lowered him into the curling mists, and only the mercenary's choking hand kept Jamie from screaming.

"Enough," said Dr. Vertue, and Blackjack swung Jamie away from the tank and placed him carefully on his feet again. He let go, and Jamie sagged against the side of the unit, gasping for breath and not even trying to hide the unsteadiness in his legs. To be placed alive into the reclamation tank, to die inch by bloody inch as the scalpels and saws cut into you . . .

I'm sorry, Madelaine . . . I can't even avenge you. I'm too scared.

Jamie realised he was leaning on the reclamation tank to support himself. He quickly pulled his hand away and stood up straight. Vertue chuckled quietly. Blackjack didn't even smile.

"You won't betray me, Jamie," said Dr. Vertue. "Who else can afford to pay off all your debts? And besides, if you should even contemplate such a thing, I'll send Blackjack to fetch you. You have very lovely skin, my dear Jamie. I could get five thousand credits for two square feet of your skin. Go to the Blackthorn tavern tomorrow evening. Collect the package from Cyder. Pay for it. Hurry back here. Got it?"

"Got it," said Jamie. "Can I go now?"

"By all means," said Dr. Vertue.

Jamie Royal turned and walked unsteadily out of the freezing cold chamber. His hands were trembling and his legs shook, but he had enough self-respect left that he wouldn't allow himself to hurry. They could scare him, but they couldn't make him run. The door swung open before him, and he stepped out into the corridor. He waited until the door closed behind him, and then he leant back against the cold metal and wiped at his face with a shaking hand. Sweat was pouring down his face, as though he'd just stepped out of a furnace rather than an icebox. Vertue and Blackjack were probably watching him on the security camera, but he didn't care anymore. Vertue hadn't said what he wanted the memory crystal for, but then he hadn't had to. There was only one place willing to pay that badly for a Mistport memory crystal. Only one place that could regularly supply Vertue with the kind of high tech he needed to run his business and maintain his lifestyle. Only one place that would supply a mercenary like Blackjack for a bodyguard. The Empire. Dr. Leon Vertue was an Imperial agent. And now, so was Jamie Royal.

If I didn't have so many debts . . .

Jamie shook his head bitterly, and walked away down the corridor. Memories of Madelaine Skye pressed close around him, but he wouldn't look at them. He didn't dare. It was her own fault; she should have chosen her partners more wisely.

Leon Vertue watched the monitor thoughtfully until Jamie disappeared around the corner in the corridor.

"Can he be trusted?" said Blackjack quietly.

Vertue shrugged. "He's reliable enough, in his fashion, and you frightened him quite convincingly."

"And when he's finished his work for us?"

"We can't leave any witnesses," said Vertue, smiling gently. "And there's always room in my units for one more body. There's so much demand these days."

Blackjack looked at him calmly. "That's a hell of a bedside manner you've got there, Doctor. Now if you'll excuse me, the *Balefire* will be landing soon, and I have a few security guards to bribe first."

"There's no rush," said Vertue. "The *Balefire* will be placed under quarantine until Port Director Steel returns from his Council meeting. And that won't be for some time. Meanwhile, I have another job for you. I want you to kill someone."

"When and where?"

"Tonight, at the city boundary; Merchants Quarter. The . . . target we discussed earlier."

"Good," said Blackjack, smiling slightly. "I've been looking forward to that."

He turned and left without waiting for Vertue's reply, and the door opened before him and shut after him. Vertue scowled at the monitor screen as Blackjack strolled unconcernedly down the corridor. Leon Vertue had seen things and done things that would have sickened any normal man, but still he was scared of the black-clad mercenary. Vertue pouted angrily. He didn't like to be scared; it upset him. Vertue had many ways of dealing with those who upset him, all of them thoroughly unpleasant. He smiled reluctantly as his memories calmed him, but still his frown remained.

He looked back at the monitor, but Blackjack had already disappeared from sight. Vertue licked his dry lips, and felt a little of the tension drain out of him. Even though they currently worked for the same masters, Vertue had never felt comfortable in the mercenary's presence. Under the polite phrases and stoic calm, he'd seen a deep contempt burning in Blackjack's eyes, a contempt for everything and everyone who wasn't strong.

Vertue scowled thoughtfully. He wouldn't always need the mercenary . . . and there was always room in the reclamation tanks for one more body. He smiled suddenly, and laughed softly to himself. Leon Vertue turned his attention to the reclamation tank before him, and ran his hand caressingly over the moisture-beaded lid. He thumbed a control and the swirling blue mists parted briefly, allowing him a glimpse of the cold white face below. Frost covered her staring eyes. She was very pretty. So very pretty. And her flesh would be so cold and inviting and helpless to his touch. . . .

+

CHAPTER THREE

Decisions in Council

THE Council chamber was surprisingly wide and roomy, but its timbered ceiling was as low as in any other dwelling in Mistport. The howling spring gales made living in tall structures without high-tech support a risky business. Oil lamps and blazing torches lent the chamber a comforting golden glow, and a battered old heating unit murmured quietly to itself as it supplied a slow, steady warmth. Faded portraits of past Councillors lined the panelled walls, the familiar brooding faces staring down at the present Council with a stern watchfulness. A great circular table dominated the room. Almost thirty feet in diameter, and carved from a single huge block of ironwood, it had been commissioned by the original Mistport Council over ninety years ago. Port Director Gideon Steel ran his plump fingers caressingly over the polished wood of the tabletop, and tried not to yawn as the arguments around him droned on and on.

His chair creaked complainingly as his two hundred pounds of weight stirred restlessly. Steel was beginning to think the meeting would never end. He'd been here six hours already, to no damned purpose he could see. As far as he could tell, it was just business as usual, and they hardly needed him for that. Unless it concerned the starport itself, he was quite content to let the other Councillors go their own way and do what they wanted. Steel had no interest in politics or government, and was only a Councillor because his position as Port Director demanded it. Unfortunately, there was one item on the present agenda that did affect the starport: the installing at the starport of the one hundred and fifty disrupter cannon from the recently discovered wreck of the *Darkwind*.

Steel laced his pudgy fingers together across his vast stomach and glanced round the Council table, not bothering to hide his boredom. Gideon Steel was a short fat man with calm, thoughtful eyes and a disturbingly cynical smile. He had just turned forty and resented it. He had little tolerance for fools or people who wasted his time, which was why he avoided Council meetings as often as he could get away with it. He sighed quietly, and tried to concentrate on the matter at hand. Eileen Darkstrom was still speaking, her harsh staccato voice echoing sharply back from the low ceiling. Steel sometimes wondered if she made such long speeches on purpose, so that when she finally finished, everyone would be so grateful they'd vote for anything she proposed, just to stop her from starting up again. Steel grinned. He wouldn't put it past her. Darkstrom had only been a Councillor for five years, but she'd already got more done in that time than all the other Councillors put together. She was a great one for getting things done, was Eileen Darkstrom.

She was a short, stocky woman in her late thirties, with a thick bush of bright red hair that burned like glowing copper in the lamplight. Her skin was pale and freckled, but what would have been pleasant enough features were marred by her constant scowl. Darkstrom was a fighter, and didn't care who knew it. Her green eyes blazed fiercely as she hammered on the table with her fist, and Steel winced in sympathy for the table. As one of Mistport's leading blacksmiths, Darkstrom's muscular arm was enough to frighten anyone, let alone a table fast approaching its century.

She was finally getting around to the matter of the *Darkwind*'s disrupters, but Steel had given up trying to follow her tortuous argument. He looked away, and his gaze fell on the tall, brooding man sitting to Darkstrom's left. He looked up, and their eyes met for a moment. Steel kept his features carefully impassive. Count Stefan Bloodhawk nodded curtly, and then turned his attention back to Darkstrom, his long elegant fingers laced together to provide a platform for his sharply pointed chin to rest on. The Bloodhawk was known to be well into his forties, but his aristocratic features were clear and unlined, and he had the lean musculature of a man half his age. His shoulder-length jet-black hair had been pulled back and tied with a scarlet ribbon, showing off his prominent widow's peak. There were those who said he dyed his hair, but never to the man's face. The Bloodhawk's dark eyes were hooded and unrelenting, like those of the ancient bird from which his Clan took its name, and his great beak of a nose and high-boned features only added to the resemblance. Steel frowned slightly, and lowered his eyes. There were many things he hated about having to attend Council meetings, and having to talk politely with the Bloodhawk was right at the top of the list.

Count Stefan Bloodhawk was a paragon of virtue. Everybody said so, including him. He was head of a dozen uncontroversial charities, ostentatiously supported the right causes, and was Chief Commander of the city Watch. He was constantly bringing cases of injustice to the Council's attention, and then demanding to know what they intended to do about it. He belonged to the proper associations, moved in all the right circles, and practised a cold courtesy that was somehow more infuriating than any open insult could ever be. Steel was not alone in wondering just what such a paragon of virtue could have done to end up Outlawed on Mistworld. The Bloodhawk kept himself to himself, and offered no clues.

Steel glanced at him, and then at Eileen Darkstrom. She and the Bloodhawk had been friends for years, and were rumoured to be lovers, though what the hell they saw in each other was quite beyond Steel. In his opinion, the Bloodhawk wouldn't know an honest emotion if it ran up and bit him on the arse. But then, Steel was just a little biased when it came to Count Stefan Bloodhawk. Over the years, Steel had made a great deal of money from his position as Port Director. He regarded it as a legitimate perquisite. He was careful not to be too greedy, and made sure his little extra ventures never interfered with his work as starport Director. Reasonable enough behaviour, he would have thought. Unfortunately, the Bloodhawk thought differently. More than once he'd used his position in the Watch to try and trap Steel into situations where he could be impeached. So far he hadn't succeeded, but of late Steel had had to be more than usually careful to cover his tracks. If Steel hadn't known better, he would have sworn the Bloodhawk was out to get him. The sanctimonious creep.

Steel looked across the table at Donald Royal, sitting slumped in his Chairman's seat, half asleep as usual. His wispy white hair hung uncombed in long feathery strands, and his face held more wrinkles than Mistport had streets. He'd been a huge and muscular man in his day, but although his frame was just as large, the muscles had slowly drifted away over the years, until now little remained of the giant he had once been. No one doubted his right to sit at Council; he'd earned that right through blood and sacrifice. His past deeds as both warrior and politician were legendary. But these days his mind tended to wander, and since he slept through most meetings anyway, Steel wasn't alone in wondering why the man couldn't just retire gracefully with honour and doze by his own damned fire.

Steel looked up sharply as he realised Darkstrom had finally stopped talking, and quickly joined in the polite applause as she sat down. Experience had shown that if Darkstrom felt she hadn't had enough applause, she was quite capable of getting up and starting all over again. Not for the first time, Steel hadn't a clue as to what the hell she'd been talking about, but since she'd always been solidly pro-tech, he had no doubt that she'd finally ended up backing his position over the disrupter cannon.

There was a quiet scraping of wood on wood as Suzanne du Wolfe pushed back her chair and rose to her feet. Steel sighed quietly, and braced himself. Du Wolfe meant well, but as an esper herself it was only natural that she should support the esper cause. Steel just wished she'd be a little less open and a lot less long-winded about it. Du Wolfe glanced quickly round the table, tucking a curl of her long auburn hair behind her left ear. Tall, lithe, and elegant, she was barely into her twenties and already heartstoppingly lovely. At first glance she seemed too young and innocent to be a part of Mistport's ruling Council, but there was a harsh strength in her dark, even eyes, and the beauty of her face was marred by the old whiplash scar that lay redly across her broken right cheekbone. The scar gave her face an odd, twisted look, and pulled up the right side of her mouth into a constant bitter half-smile.

The Empire distrusted its espers, and so kept them under a harsh and brutal discipline. Which was why so many of them ended up on Mistworld.

"Disrupters," said Suzanne du Wolfe quietly, her hands resting lightly on the tabletop as she leaned forward. "No one doubts their worth as weapons, but we all know their limitations. Cannon have a faster recharge time than handguns, but it still takes their energy crystals a good minute and more to recharge between each shot. With all respect, Councillor Darkstrom, there's nothing these disrupters can do that the esper shield can't do just as well, and much more efficiently."

She stopped, and raised her left hand. She frowned slightly, and a pale blue flame sprang into being, licking lazily around her hand without harming it. Du Wolfe smiled slowly, and the flame blazed up into a stream of bright, burning fire, leaping and flaring like a glowing fountain. The other Councillors leant back in their chairs, flinching from the searing heat. And then the flame was gone, with nothing left to show it had ever been there, save for the unnatural warmth that still permeated the Council chamber. Suzanne du Wolfe was a Pyro.

"The psionic shield has kept Mistworld safe from the Empire for almost two centuries. Working together, espers can hex a ship's tech and mindwipe its crew in less time than it takes a computer to bring its guns to bear. And espers don't have to stop to recharge. Disrupters are all very well in their way, but an esper will always be far more dangerous than any man-made weapon."

Suzanne du Wolfe sat down again, and looked around to see if anyone dared disagree.

"You may well be right," said Darkstrom, "but in the end espers are only human, and humans can make mistakes. Disrupter cannon just do as the fire computers tell them, and technology doesn't grow tired or irritable or make mistakes under pressure. A computer simply carries out its orders. No one here doubts that the psionic shield has proved itself to be an invaluable defence; I merely suggest that the time has come to augment that shield with a high-tech system of high-class weaponry. You've never seen what disrupter cannon can do to a starship, Councillor du Wolfe. I have."

"We're all familiar with your history as a starship Captain," said Suzanne du Wolfe sweetly. "But that was a long time ago. No doubt the Empire has improved their force shields since then. If we try to match their technology with ours, we're always going to be at a disadvantage. They have vast sources of high tech to draw on, while ours are already running out. Our only hope is the psionic shield; the Empire will never come up with a defence against espers."

"I'm not suggesting the psionic shield should be disbanded," said Darkstrom with noticeably heavy patience. "The shield will still be there, but as a backup provision, in case the tech system should somehow fail. This would free your fellow espers from the need to spend long arduous hours on shield duty, and enable them to take on other tasks where their skills are more needed. At any given time, there are two hundred espers sitting in a trance at the command centre, waiting on the off chance that the Empire might decide to launch an attack. Meanwhile, Mistport is falling apart around us because we don't have the technology or the espers to keep it running smoothly."

"Right," growled Steel. "We can always use more espers. The psionic shield has always had one major drawback; it takes a minimum of two hundred espers working together to raise an effective shield. To fight off an attack by the entire Fleet, we'd need five times that number. What happens if for any reason we couldn't raise that many?"

"There are over two thousand espers in Mistport alone," said du Wolfe sharply. "And another fifteen hundred scattered among the outlying farms."

"There are now," said Darkstrom. "But only half of them are experienced enough for shield duty. And can we be sure there'll always be that many? Esp doesn't always breed true."

"Right," said Steel. "Finding the wreck of the *Darkwind* has been a stroke of immense good fortune, and we'd be fools not to make the most of it. In case you've all forgotten, it's getting harder all the time for smugglers to break through the Empire blockade. We're running out of high tech, and it's getting damn near impossible to maintain what technology we have. Even the best-tended machinery will break down in time, and we're nowhere near being able to build our own high tech. The *Darkwind* has provided enough systems and spares to maintain us for a few more years, but the disrupter cannon are the main jewels in the treasure chest. For the first time, we have a chance to make Mistworld completely safe from Imperial attack.

"Now with respect, fellow Councillors, I must insist on a decision. I've been away from the command centre too long as it is. The technicians are standing by, ready to install the disrupters. I must insist on an answer."

"For once it seems we are in agreement, Director." The Bloodhawk's quiet voice was cold but impartial. "I see no point in further discussion. Since the disrupters are intended to work with the esper shield, rather than replace it, I see no reason why they shouldn't be installed. The future of the psionic shield can be discussed at a later date. Now, since we all have other duties compelling our attention, I call for a vote. I vote Aye."

"I vote Nay," said Suzanne du Wolfe quickly.

"Aye," said Eileen Darkstrom.

"Aye," said Gideon Steel.

Everyone looked to Donald Royal, who sat up a little straighter in his chair, blinking vaguely.

"We are voting on the installation of disrupter cannon at the command centre," said Count Stefan Bloodhawk.

"I know," snapped Donald. "I'm not senile yet, Blood-hawk. Now we've got cannon, it's only sensible we make use of them. I vote Aye."

"Well," said Steel, rising ponderously to his feet. "If there's no further business . . ."

"Sit down, Gideon," said Donald Royal, smiling slightly. "Your precious command centre can manage without you for a little while longer yet."

Steel sank wearily back into his chair, which complained loudly on receiving his weight again. "All right, Donald," he said patiently. "What is it this time? If it's about the sewers again, we can't afford the time or the technology or the engineers. I know we need sewers—I had to walk through the same streets to get here—but for the time being we'll just have to go on managing without them."

"Mind you, the smell is getting worse," said Darkstrom.

"How can you tell?" asked du Wolfe.

"It takes longer to scrape off my boots."

"Desperate though our need for sewers is," said Donald Royal heavily, "we have something more important to discuss. Hob hounds have appeared at the city boundaries. The beasts are at our gate once again."

For a moment, nobody said anything. Steel frowned, and found himself reaching automatically for the gun on his hip.

"Have there been any actual sightings?" asked Eileen Darkstrom.

"Several," said Donald grimly. "And three deaths, all in the Merchants Quarter. One of the victims was a little girl. She was only five years old."

Steel shook his head disgustedly. The winter had barely begun, and already the cold was worse than at any time since Mistport records began. As the temperatures fell lower and lower, and game became increasingly scarce, it was only to be expected that the Hob hounds would leave their bleak mountain passes and open tundras, and come sweeping down to raid the outlying farms and settlements, and then the city. The hounds were always hungry.

"What's being done?" asked the Bloodhawk.

"I'm sending Investigator Topaz and a company of the Watch into the Merchants Quarter to check conditions," said Donald Royal slowly. "They'll make a start first thing tomorrow. It's not much of a response, but with the weather as it is, I daren't send any men out at night. Still, if there are any answers to be found, I daresay Investigator Topaz will find them."

That she will, thought Steel grimly. He'd had dealings with Topaz himself, and wasn't in any hurry to repeat the experience. The last time the Bloodhawk had tried to nail Steel, he'd sent Topaz to look for evidence. If it hadn't been for some extremely fast footwork on Steel's part, she'd have found it. Still, it had to be said that the Investigator was a good choice when it came to hunting down Hob hounds. Even the hounds had enough sense to be scared of Topaz.

"What about the outlying farms?" he asked suddenly. "Any news from them on the hounds?"

"Communications are still out because of the blizzards," said du Wolfe, just a little smugly. "The Espers Guild are keeping essential news passing, but so far there've only been a few vague references to the hounds. A few people have gone missing in the storms, but we've had no killings reported."

"That's odd," said Darkstrom slowly. "The hounds don't usually bypass the farms. And surely there should have been some reports of approaching hounds before this."

"Yes," said Donald Royal. "There should have been. It's as though the damn animals just appeared out of nowhere." He stopped short, and glanced worriedly at Suzanne du Wolfe. "You said the blizzards had hit the farms; how will that affect our food supplies here in the city?"

Du Wolfe shrugged. "Shouldn't affect us much. Bloodhawk, that's more your department, isn't it?"

"There'll be some shortages," said the Bloodhawk calmly, "But nothing to worry about. Most of our supplies come from underground hydroponics these days. We're in no danger of going hungry. Not in the short term, anyway."

"I don't see what else we can do at this time," said Darkstrom, getting to her feet. "I move we adjourn until the

Investigator returns with more up-to-date information."

"Seconded," said Steel quickly.

Donald Royal shrugged, and sank back into his chair, the fire already fading from his eyes as the tiredness returned. Steel got to his feet as du Wolfe and the Bloodhawk pushed back their chairs, and as quickly as that, the meeting was over. Steel made polite goodbyes to his fellow Councillors, and then hesitated as he saw Donald Royal had made no move to rise from his seat. The others paid no attention, but Steel could tell something was wrong. Royal was usually a stickler for courtesy. Steel waited till the others had left, and then moved back to pull up a chair and sit down facing the old Chairman.

"Donald," he said quietly. "It's me, Gideon."

"I'm glad you stayed," said Donald slowly, his voice firm and unwavering though his eyes remained weary. "I need to talk to you, Gideon. Private business, not Council."

"Of course," said Steel. "I'll help if I can. You know that."

"It's about my grandson," said Donald Royal.

"Jamie," said Steel ruefully. "I might have guessed. What's he been up to this time?"

"What do you think?" said Donald. "Gambling, of course. He owes money. I've had to help him out on occasion before, but those were always small loans, and he always repaid them. From what I've heard, this time his debts are a great deal larger, and he owes them to some rather unpleasant people. So far, he hasn't dared come to see me, but no doubt he will eventually. You're his friend, Gideon; see if you can talk some sense into him. He can't go on like this. He can't afford it, and neither can I."

"If I can find him, I'll do what I can," Steel promised. "But you know Jamie; he only hears what he wants to."

"Yes," said Donald Royal quietly, bitterly. "I know."

Steel shifted uncomfortably in his chair. He knew it couldn't be easy for a living legend like Donald Royal to have a grandson like Jamie, but the lad had been in tight spots before, and always got out of them in the end.

If nothing else, Jamie Royal was a survivor.

"I'll get in touch with you as soon as I hear anything," Steel said finally, and Donald nodded slowly, his old eyes vague and far away. Steel got up, and crossed quietly to the door. He looked back once, but Royal was still sitting in his chair, lost in his yesterdays. Steel left, closing the door quietly behind him.

He hurried down the bare wooden stairs to the lobby. It had been more than six hours since dinner, and he was starving. He could have eaten a horse and gnawed on the hooves. He tempted himself with thoughts of sweetbreads and fresh cream pastries, and took the stairs as quickly as his bulk would allow. He paused in the lobby to tap his personal code into a monitor console, on the off chance there was a message waiting for him, and the screen immediately cleared to show him the duty esper at the starport command centre.

"Director, I've been trying to contact you for hours."

"Sorry," said Steel. "The Council meeting dragged on longer than any of us expected. But we've got the go-ahead for the disrupters; you can tell the technicians to start installation immediately."

"Director, we've had a refugee ship arrive from Tannim; the *Balefire*. A medium-size ship, around five million tons. She had to crash-land on the main pad, but she came through it well enough. I've placed her under strict quarantine, and put the centre on Yellow Alert. The *Balefire*'s Captain says that Tannim's . . . gone. I really think you should get back here as soon as possible."

Steel shook his head sickly. "So, the rumours were true. Tannim has been Outlawed. The whole damned planet."

"Yes, Director. According to the *Balefire*'s Captain, the Imperial Fleet just dropped out of hyperspace, took up orbit around Tannim, and then scorched the planet lifeless. There's no telling how many millions died. There was no warning given. None at all."

"There never is," said Steel. "Dear God, a whole planet . . . Follow standard procedures, duty esper. I'll be with you as soon as I can. Any problems with the *Balefire*?"

"I'm not sure, Director. I've had the port espers scanning the ship, and apparently they've been getting some rather . . . unusual readings."

Steel frowned. "How do you mean, unusual?"

The duty esper shrugged unhappily. "It's not easy to explain, sir. I think you'd better come and take a look for yourself."

"If I must, I must," said Steel. "Maintain Yellow Alert, and contact the city Watch, just in case anyone tries to break quarantine. Any other problems can wait till I get there."

He blanked the monitor, and thought wistfully about sweetbreads and pastries. The esper scan was probably just a false alarm, but he didn't feel like risking it. In his own way, Director Steel took his duties seriously.

CHAPTER FOUR

Killer in the Mists

THE sun had just begun its slow crawl up the sky as Investigator Topaz and Sergeant Michael Gunn led their company of Watchmen through the Merchants Quarter. The early morning light filtered unevenly past the thick curling mists, and the sun was little more than a pale red circle, glimpsed dimly through the fog. The night's bitter cold was falling reluctantly away, and the icicles hanging from roofs and gutters and windowsills had all developed their own persistent drip of icy water.

The winding, narrow streets were still mostly deserted, but already the first few beggars and street traders had begun to appear from dark back alleys and sheltered lean-tos. And here and there, lying half-buried in the snow, were the stiff unmoving bodies of those who'd been unable to find shelter from the cold. All too many of them were children, left to wander alone in the bitter night, bereft of family or shelter or hope. The Watch passed the bodies by, paying the pathetic heaps of rags no real attention; it was too common a sight to be worth a second glance. One of Mistworld's first lessons was the futility of mourning over things that could not be changed, or even eased. The Outlaw planet was a harsh world, and cared little for the life it reluctantly sustained.

A lone horse moved slowly out of the mists towards the Watch, its rider huddled inside a thick black cloak. Horse and rider moved with an eerie silence over the snow-covered cobbles, forming slowly out of the fog like some shadowy phantom. Investigator Topaz kept a wary eye on them as they passed slowly by and disappeared back into the mists. The cloaked and hooded rider had paid the Watch no attention, but in this kind of area it was wise to trust nothing and nobody.

Topaz strode on through the thick snow, one hand resting lightly on the butt of the holstered gun at her side. Her eyes flickered at every alleyway and side street she passed, but nobody challenged her, and the shadows remained just shadows. It seemed the threat of the Hob hounds had been enough to keep the human vermin off the streets, for a time at least. Topaz frowned. The city boundary wasn't far now, and Topaz hadn't much experience of Hob hounds. She knew what everybody knew, that they were quick and they were deadly and there was no defence against them except to attack first, but that was all she knew. She had a strong feeling that might not be enough.

She glanced at her husband, walking quietly beside her. Sergeant Michael Gunn was an inch or so taller than her five foot six, but his broad shoulders and muscular frame made him seem shorter. He was in his mid-thirties, but as yet his face and body had made no concessions to either his hard life or the passing of time. His long brown hair was pulled back in a scalplock, the sign of the mercenary. Gunn had been a Sergeant of the city Watch for over five years, but he liked to keep his options open. His dark laughing eyes were fixed on the street ahead, and his stride was loose and easy, almost as though he was looking forward to his encounter with the Hob hounds. Topaz smiled slightly. Maybe he was; Michael Gunn needed excitement the way most men needed food and drink.

The boundary wall loomed out of the thickening mists before them, a huge twenty-foot barrier of stone and mortar that marked the outer limit of the Merchants Quarter, and the edge of the city. The stonework was scarred and pitted from the unrelenting weather, but the four-feet-thick wall was still strong enough to keep out most of Mistworld's predators. Unfortunately, a twenty-foot leap was nothing to a Hob hound. Topaz glared thoughtfully about her as Gunn spread out the Watchmen in a defensive pattern.

They moved silently and cautiously into the surrounding warren of side streets and alleyways, checking the snow for recent tracks. Gunn came back to join Topaz, and took his gun from his holster to check the energy charge. It was almost full. He put the disrupter away, and looked gloomily about him.

"Hob hounds in the city . . . If you ask me, the Council's gone daft. Everyone knows the hounds don't get this far south until midwinter at the earliest. Do you think this could be some kind of drill?"

Topaz shrugged. "Could be, I suppose. But then, you never can tell what the damned hounds are going to do from one year to the next."

Gunn grunted an acknowledgement, and glanced dubiously at the boundary wall. There could be half a hundred hounds gathered on the other side of that wall, and he'd never know it until they came scrabbling over the top. *They should have built some eye-slits into the damned thing*, he thought. Gunn sniffed disgustedly, and looked back at his men. The Watchmen had trampled the surrounding snow into slush, and half of them were so far away they were little more than shadows moving in the mists. The fog muffled most sounds, and even the slow, gusting wind had been reduced to a dull, faraway keening. At least it had finally stopped snowing. Gunn sniffed heavily and wiped his nose on the back of his glove. Ever since he'd first come to Mistworld six years ago, he'd had one damned cold after another. He was beginning to forget what it was like to have a sense of smell. He stamped his feet hard against the packed snow, trying to drive out some of the cold that was already gnawing at his bones. He should have brought his cloak. He glanced at Topaz, standing quietly beside him, and smiled fondly. She never seemed to feel the cold, or if she did, she refused to give in to it. There were those who mistook her poise and elegance for coldness, but Gunn knew better. Topaz prided herself on her control; that was what made her such a deadly fighter. Not for the first time, Gunn looked admiringly at his wife and wondered what he'd done right to deserve her.

Investigator Topaz was a medium-height, slim, handsome woman in her late twenties, who wore her sword and her gun with a casual competence that was both disturbing and intimidating. Her close-cropped dark hair gave her classical features a calm, aesthetic air. Her face was always composed, and her stance was relaxed but unyielding. Most people considered her a cold fish, but Michael Gunn had always admired her poise. Topaz had her fires and her needs, but she shared them only with him. Perhaps because he was the only man who'd ever earned her trust.

The fog seemed to be growing thicker, and the sun was lost to sight. Lanterns glowed bravely on the surrounding walls, their light the only landmarks in the endless sea of grey. The mists pressed close about Topaz, leaving a sheen of moisture on her hair and cloak. The Investigator frowned thoughtfully. The Hob hounds preferred a heavy fog to do their hunting in. She thought about drawing her gun, but immediately decided against it. To do so this early might be misinterpreted by her men as a sign of weakness, and Topaz had sworn never to be weak again. She tried not to think about her past with the Empire, but her memories were always with her. Memories of the things she'd done, the things the Empire had made her do; all the many deaths . . . Topaz closed her eyes a moment, forcing back the past by concentrating on her assignment. There was always work, to bury the memories. Topaz had a lot she needed to forget, but sometimes it seemed to her that even on Mistworld there was no escape from the Empire; the spectre at the feast, the wolf at the gate. Topaz opened her eyes and glared coldly at the mists around her. She was free, and she would stay free, even from her own memories. Her hand closed tightly around the pommel of her sword, and her heavy Investigator's cloak of navy blue settled about her shoulders like the weight of past sins.

"Chasing Hob hounds," growled Michael Gunn. "We should be tracking down last night's burglar, not wasting our time with this nonsense."

"We have our orders."

Gunn muttered something under his breath, and Topaz smiled slightly. "What's the matter, my husband? Pride hurt?"

"Something like that. I would have sworn an oath our security could keep out anyone but a Poltergeist, but that flaming roof runner just walked right in like our defences weren't even there. And it's more than that; it's knowing that someone else was in our house, our home, invading our privacy. . . ."

"He didn't get the crystal. You came back in time to stop him."

"There is that. Though if I hadn't had to go to the toilet, maybe the sensor on the bedroom door would have caught him." Gunn shook his head unhappily. "At least the crystal is safely at the command centre now, and out of our hands. Anything that happens to it from now on is their responsibility."

"Exactly," said Topaz calmly. "The Hob hounds are our responsibility."

"All right, all right." Gunn leaned against the boundary wall, the harsh uneven stone pressing uncomfortably into his back. His broad, stocky body was full of a nervous energy that gave him an edgy, restless look even when standing still. His right hand rested on his gunbelt, not far from his disrupter, while his dark, darting eyes probed the shadows of the nearby alleys. The rest of the Watch were methodically searching the alleyways and side streets for traces of the hounds, poking their swords and pikes into the darker doorways and openings. So far all they'd found had been half-a-dozen cats and one rather startled drunk.

Topaz rested her hand on her holstered gun, but knew that if the hounds were here, they'd have to be fought with cold steel in the end. Out of the whole company, only she and Gunn had disrupters. Energy guns were rare on Mistworld. Still, a reliance on energy weapons just made you soft in the long run, and Mistworld had its own ways of dealing with the weak. Gunn shivered suddenly, and Topaz frowned.

"You're cold," she said brusquely. "I told you to wear your heavy cloak."

"I don't like cloaks. They get in the way when you're fighting."

"They keep you warm when it's cold. Here." She took off her own cloak and draped it round her husband's shoulders, ignoring his protests. "Don't argue with me, Michael. I don't feel the cold like you. I've been trained to survive much worse extremes of temperature than this."

"You and your Investigator's training," muttered Gunn, pulling the cloak about him nonetheless and fiddling with the clasp. "Even a Hadenman couldn't do half the things you claim."

"Wear the cloak," said Topaz firmly, but her eyes were full of fondness. Topaz had spent many years as an Investigator, a paid murderer in the service of the Empire. She'd been very successful in her work, until she met the mercenary called Michael Gunn. He'd taught her to feel human again. Not long after, they'd both been Outlawed, and they had come, as so many before them, to Mistworld, the rebel planet. The only surviving rebel planet. Now Topaz and Gunn were both Sergeants in the city Watch, guardians of law and order, a fact that never failed to tickle Gunn's sense of irony.

Topaz still kept the title of Investigator. Even she wasn't sure why.

"You ever seen a Hob hound, close up?" asked Gunn.

Topaz shook her head. "You have, haven't you?"

"Yeah. I led the raid up at Hardcastle's Rock, this time last year. The place was crawling with the ugly beasts. The hounds had killed every man, woman, and child in the town, far more than they could ever have hoped to eat. They killed just for the joy of it. Most of what's written about the hounds is rubbish. The largest one I ever saw was barely ten feet long, and they're not poisonous. They don't need to be. They run on all fours, they're covered in fur, and the head is long and wolfish, but that's all they have in common with a hound. They're always hungry, and they move so fast they seem like a blur. Their fur is white and their hearts are dark. They delight in slaughter and the torturing of prey."

"They should feel right at home in Mistport," said Topaz, and Gunn cracked up. He loved Topaz's dry sense of humour, mostly because it was so rare.

Topaz suddenly became very still, and Gunn froze in place beside her. The Investigator's face had formed into harsh, unyielding lines, and her eyes were hunter's eyes.

"What is it?" asked Gunn quietly.

"There's something out there," said Topaz, her voice little more than a murmur. "Something moving, deep in the mists."

"Here in the Quarter with us?" Gunn looked casually about him, but all he could see were the shifting shadows of the nearby Watchmen. "Is it a hound?"

"I don't think so. It feels more like a man. At about four o'clock, I'd say."

Gunn glanced in the indicated direction. All he could see was the curling mists, but suddenly his skin was crawling beneath his scalplock as all his old mercenary's instincts kicked in. The feeling of being watched and studied was all at once so overpowering he wondered how he could have missed it for so long. Assuming, of course, that his clash with the burglar hadn't suddenly turned him paranoid. Gunn whistled quietly, and three Watchmen appeared out of the mists before him.

"Anything to report?" he asked casually, but his hands moved surreptitiously in the mercenary's hand signals he and Topaz had carefully taught their men. His voice was routine, but his hands said, *We're being watched. One man. Four o'clock. Find him.*

"Haven't seen anything, Sergeant," said the most senior of the Watchmen, nodding slightly.

"Okay," said Gunn. "Keep looking."

The Watchmen faded back into the fog, and were gone. Topaz looked at Gunn.

"Do you think they'll find him?"

"I doubt it," Gunn admitted. "Whoever's out there has to be bloody good to have got this close without either of us catching on earlier. But who the hell would be that interested in us?"

"Empire agents?"

Gunn shook his head slowly. "There'll always be some Empire spies in Mistport, but we were never important enough to justify any of them coming after us here."

Topaz looked at Gunn thoughtfully. "So why is there somebody out there watching us?"

"Hounds! Ware the hounds!"

Topaz and Gunn drew their disrupters at the Watchman's shout and moved quickly to stand back to back. Watchmen boiled out of their hiding places and peered quickly about them, swords and pikes at the ready. Somewhere out in the fog a man screamed shrilly, and the sound was cut suddenly short. And out of the curling mists the Hob hounds came howling.

Their white fur blended into the fog, so that it was hard to tell where the one ended and the other began. Only their bright emerald eyes showed clearly against the mists, together with the steaming scarlet maws that gaped wide to show long, vicious teeth. The hounds moved through the fog like wild, demonic ghosts, and their cry was full of an endless hunger and an endless hate. They leapt among the Watchmen, rending and tearing, and blood flew on the freezing air. Men and hounds rolled together on the hard-packed snow, sword and fang searching for a dropped guard or a bared throat. One Watchman thrust his pike deep into a hound's side, spiking it to a sturdy wooden door. The hound screamed and struggled, refusing to die until the Watchman cut its throat with his dagger. Two hounds pulled down a Watchman and tore him to pieces almost before he had time to scream. Gunn took careful aim with his disrupter, and the searing energy beam shot out to burn clean through a lunging hound. It fell silently to the snow and lay still, its fur burning fiercely. Gunn slipped the disrupter back into its holster and drew his sword. The gun was useless until its energy crystal had recharged, and that would take at least two minutes. A lot could happen in two minutes. Gunn hefted his sword eagerly, and headed for the nearest hound.

The snow and slush were stained with crimson and littered with the dead and the dying, and still the Hob hounds leapt and tore among the milling Watchmen. Steel flashed in the lantern light, and the air reverberated to the savage howling of the hounds. Gunn and Topaz moved with deadly skill through the thick of the fray, guarding each other's back. Topaz shot a hound as it leapt for her throat, and then threw herself to one side as the burning body crashed past her to slam against the boundary wall. Another hound came flying out of the mists towards her, and Topaz knew there was no time to draw her sword. She opened her mouth and sang a single, piercing note. The tightly focused beam of esper-backed sound smashed the hound into the snow. It quivered once and then lay still, blood seeping from its ears and muzzle.

Topaz holstered her gun and drew her sword. She looked quickly about her, and her heart missed a beat as she realised Michael Gunn had become separated from her in the fighting. She relaxed a little as she saw her navy blue cloak moving among the purple-cloaked Watchmen, and forced herself to concentrate on the matter at hand. Gunn had been a mercenary for over ten years; he could look after himself. Her sword sheared clean through a hound's rib cage, the keen-edged New Damascus steel barely jarring on the splintering bones. The hound collapsed and scrabbled helplessly on the bloody snow. Topaz killed it quickly, and then a heavy weight slammed into her from behind, and she and the attacking hound fell together in a clawing, struggling heap. Topaz swore viciously as a flailing paw raked across her thigh. She pushed the pain to the back of her mind, and thrust her sword deep into the hound's guts even as its jaws reached for her face. The hound howled with rage and pain, and then fell limply across her, soaking her furs with its steaming blood.

Topaz pulled herself out from under the dead weight, and staggered to her feet. Her wounded leg ached fiercely. She looked down and saw her left thigh was slick with blood, only some of it the hound's. She shrugged, and looked away. The muscle was still intact, and the leg still held her weight. That was all that mattered. She looked down at the dead hound, and shivered in spite of herself. Nine foot long, if it was an inch. The eyes were already glazing over, but its paws still twitched, as though searching for the enemy that had killed it.

Topaz hefted her sword and looked about her, but the fight was over. The Watchmen were finishing off the last few wounded hounds with their pikes, and the air no longer reverberated with the howling of the hounds. The only sounds now were the ragged breathing and occasional moans of pain from the surviving Watchmen. Topaz did a quick head count, and found that although they'd been facing a full dozen Hob hounds, she'd lost only nine Watchmen from her company of twenty-five. Topaz grinned harshly. The Hob hounds were certainly impressive, but muscles and claws and fangs were no match for handguns and cold steel. She looked round for Michael Gunn, to share her triumph with him, but he was nowhere to be seen. A sudden chill wrapped itself around Topaz's heart.

"Michael? Michael?"

There was no reply. Topaz gestured quickly to the Watchmen, and they spread out through the surrounding back streets and alleyways, calling their Sergeant's name. It didn't take long to find him. Topaz saw the answer in the Watchman's face as he came to tell her. She followed him into a narrow alleyway, and stared silently at the unmoving body of her husband. Michael Gunn lay face down in the blood-soaked snow, his sword still in his hand. A dead hound lay only a few feet away. Topaz knelt beside her husband, her face as cold and composed as ever. She reached out a hand to take his shoulder and turn him over, and then stopped when she saw the ragged hole burned through the navy blue cloak. A cold and deadly rage surged through her as she realised the Hob hound hadn't killed her husband. Michael Gunn had been shot in the back with an energy gun.

There's someone out in the mists, watching us. . . .

Topaz placed her hand gently on Michael Gunn's shoulder, and squeezed it once. "Rest easy, my husband. I swear upon my heart and upon my honour that I will avenge you. I promise you blood and terror, Michael; blood and terror to our enemies."

She paused a moment, almost expecting him to repeat the mercenary's curse after her, but the only sound in the alleyway was the distant moaning of the wind. Topaz patted Gunn's shoulder once more, as though to apologise for leaving him, and then she rose slowly to her feet and walked out of the alley to rejoin the silently waiting Watchmen.

"The Sergeant is dead," she said quietly. "Carry him back to his home. I will notify the Council that the Hob hounds have been dealt with."

Her voice was calm and perfectly composed, and if she cried any tears, they stayed locked inside her. Topaz was an Investigator.

CHAPTER FIVE

Balefire

STEEL sighed, and put down his cup. They'd forgotten the sugar again. Eleven years he'd been Director of Mistworld's only starport, and they still couldn't remember to put sugar in his coffee. It wasn't even real coffee. He leant back in his specially reinforced chair, and stared sourly about him. Computer banks and monitor screens lay spread out to every side of him, piled one on top the other as often as not. Less than half of them still worked at any given time. The heavy wooden desk before him was overflowing with reports and schedules and inventories, but for the moment he couldn't work up the energy to deal with them. Steel felt tired and sluggish and irritable, and the *Balefire* worried at his nerves like a nagging toothache.

All around his soundproofed glass cubicle the starport control tower worked on with its usual air of grim urgency. There was always more to be done than there was time to do it in, and everybody knew it. The technology broke down faster than it could be repaired, work piled up as deadlines were constantly shortened, and every year the damned winter blizzards arrived out of nowhere and buried the landing pads under seven feet of snow. The command centre carried on as best it could, and prayed for better days.

Gideon Steel sat slumped in his chair and gnawed thoughtfully at the last piece of sweetbread. He reached for the console keyboard built into his desk, and tapped in a code. The command monitor screen lit up, and after a moment the swirling colours slowly formed into a clear image. Looming out of the curling mists like a great steel mountain, the

Balefire lay brooding on the main landing pad; the last ship out of Tannim before the Imperial Fleet scorched the planet lifeless. Steel's chair creaked in complaint as his two hundred pounds stirred uneasily. As Port Director, Steel was personally responsible for every ship that landed at the port, and the *Balefire* was a mystery. Steel disliked mysteries. He scowled at the screen, and scratched absently at his bald patch, as if to stir his thoughts into action. As the only surviving planet to break free of Empire rule, Mistworld was the end of the line for those the Empire Outlawed; you either made your way to Mistport or your scalp hung from a bounty hunter's belt. Normally, when the Iron Empress Outlawed a whole planet there were thousands of refugees caught offworld. Strange that no other ships had come calling. . . .

The screen flickered, and the picture broke up into a mass of swirling colours. Steel cursed wearily, and heaved himself up out of his chair. He moved quickly over to the command monitor, and slammed a meaty fist down onto the top of the set. The screen flickered again, and then cleared reluctantly to show the *Balefire*. Steel shook his head slowly, and returned to his chair. The sooner the first assignment of spare parts arrived from the *Darkwind*, the better. The command centre's systems were becoming increasingly jury-rigged and improvised, and therefore, not surprisingly, increasingly unreliable. The whole damn place was falling to pieces around him, and there was nothing he could do about it. Steel picked up the latest smuggler manifests from his desk and leafed disgustedly through the flimsy papers. Typical. He needed memory crystals and solar energy converters, and what had the smugglers brought him? Lightspheres, heating units, and flush toilets. Steel threw the manifests down, and squeezed his eyes shut a moment. He had no right to complain. The smugglers risked their lives every time they braved the Empire blockade; it was only to be expected they'd concentrate on goods they knew they could get a good price for. And anyway, as the smugglers so often pointed out, beggars can't be choosers.

Steel opened his eyes and looked out of his glass cubicle at the surrounding command centre. Technicians and espers moved purposefully back and forth from level to level, tending the machinery and keeping alive the complex beast that the starport had become. Thick swirling fog pressed close against the vast steelglass windows of the control tower, isolating it from the rest of the landing field. Only the espers and the monitor screens kept Mistport functioning, and there were never enough of either. To Steel's left lay the navigation systems, and to his right, the communications net. Directly before him, where the main computer banks had once been, there were now a row of camp beds. Lying on those beds were fifty men and women with blank faces and empty eyes. Each one of them had an intravenous drip strapped to his arm, feeding them nutrients. Steel flinched at the sight of them, but didn't look away. They were his responsibility, like every other part of Mistport. In a sense, they were his children; a fact that never ceased to torment him. When the computers had first started to break down, he had sought out and gathered together the only kind of people who could replace a computer: lightning calculators and idiot savants, all of them with just enough esp to link up with a telepath. Take enough of these people and put them together with a handful of espers, and you ended up with a rough equivalent of a computer. A thinking machine. It was a poor substitute at best, and every now and again one of the units would have to be replaced. The weaker minds tended to burn out.

"Director."

Steel looked back at his command monitor. The *Balefire*'s image had disappeared from the screen, and in its place was the worried face of the duty esper. He was barely into his twenties, but already his face showed deep-etched lines of care and worry. *We're starting them too young,* thought Steel. *And asking too much of them. How long before we're reduced to breaking in children, as long as they've got the esp we need?* He sighed, and shook his head wearily.

"Yes, lad. What is it?"

"The Captain of the *Balefire* has given us access to his flight computers, Director. Apparently, just before his ship dropped into hyperspace, his onboard cameras were able to catch the last few moments of Tannim's Outlawing. I thought you might want to see the recording."

"Of course. Run it."

Steel keyed his command monitor into the main system, and watched impassively as the screen showed him the death of a planet.

Hundreds of Empire ships surrounded Tannim, pouring down destruction. Refugee ships trying to flee the planet were blown out of space almost before they left the atmosphere. The searing disrupter beams showed stark and bright against the dark of space, and the planet writhed beneath them like an insect transfixed on a pin. The oceans boiled, and volcanoes and earthquakes ripped apart the land. The ice poles melted, and the air was churned into an endless maelstrom of storms and hurricanes. And still the Imperial Fleet grew larger as more and more ships dropped out of hyperspace and into orbit, and still the disrupter beams stabbed down, scorching the planet lifeless.

How many millions dead, how many millions . . .

The monitor screen went blank, and Steel sat for a long while in silence, staring at nothing. It was one thing to know that a planet's entire population had been destroyed; it was quite another to watch it happening. And yet he couldn't let it affect his judgement. He daren't. He had to be true to his duty; the protection of Mistport. He reached out and slowly tapped a code into his console. The command monitor lit up again.

"Duty esper."

"Yes, Director?"

"Have you any more information on those strange readings your people picked up from the *Balefire*?"

"Nothing definite, sir. Our sensors detected a concentration of energy levels which suggests that most of the ship's passengers are being carried in cryogenic units, but even so, our espers are still picking up some very unusual life signs. There's something strange aboard the *Balefire*, Director. Something cold and powerful and . . . alien."

"Alien? You mean an alien life form?"

"I don't know, Director. None of us have ever come across anything like this before. Whatever it is the *Balefire*'s carrying, it's well shielded. It could be anywhere aboard the ship."

"Do you think this creature's dangerous?"

"I couldn't say, Director. But it is disturbing."

Steel pursed his lips thoughtfully and tapped them with an index finger. "Get me the *Balefire*'s Captain."

"Yes, Director."

There was a pause as the screen went blank, and then a slow, grim voice issued from the monitor's speakers.

"This is Captain Starlight, of the *Balefire*."

"Welcome to Mistport, Captain," said Steel.

"Never mind the damned amenities; my hull's breached in a dozen places, my ship's systems are falling apart, and my cargo hold's full of refugees. How long before I can unload and get a repair crew in here?"

"I'm sorry, Captain. Until the *Balefire*'s been fully inspected and cleared, no one will be allowed to leave your ship for any reason. My security people are armed and have been given orders to shoot on sight."

"What?"

"Mistport's already suffered one Empire plague ship, Captain. We don't take chances anymore."

There was a long silence.

"How are your crew, Captain?" asked Steel politely. "What condition are they in?"

"Pretty bad. Most of them are dead, back on Tannim. I had to raise ship while I had the chance; I couldn't wait for them. . . . The few I have with me are exhausted. They've each had to do a dozen men's work. They need medical attention, Director. I take it you will at least allow a doctor to come on board?"

"I'm sorry," said Steel.

"You can't be serious, damn you! My crew needs a doctor. They could die!"

"Then they die."

The words seemed to echo endlessly on the silence.

"If just one of my men dies needlessly . . ."

"Save your threats, Captain. I've heard them all before."

"Aye. I'm sure you have."

"My espers did a thorough scan on your ship, Captain. They picked up some . . . interesting readings."

"Is that it? Is that the reason you're keeping us cooped up in this death ship? Just because a few bloody freaks have a bad feeling about us? I'll have your head for this!"

"I doubt it," said Steel calmly. "But I may have to take yours. We'll talk again later, Captain."

He broke the connection without waiting for an answer. Everyone on Mistworld understood the concept of the Trojan horse. For those with short memories, Mistport's cemeteries were full of reminders. There was a sudden blast of noise behind him, and Steel winced as he turned quickly round to find Jamie Royal leaning nonchalantly against the open cubicle door. The young esper grinned at Steel, and trimmed an immaculate fingernail with a wicked-looking dirk.

"Gideon, how are you doing?"

"Close the door!" Steel roared. "Can't hear myself think with all that noise!"

Jamie nodded casually, put away his knife, and pushed the door shut with his elbow. The uproar of voices and machinery was cut off instantly. Steel leant back in his chair and hid a smile behind his hand. He liked Jamie, though he often wondered why. The man drank too much, lived beyond his means, and would come to a bad end. If an outraged husband didn't kill him first.

"Hello, Jamie. What are you doing here?"

"I've been helping install your new cannon."

Steel raised an eyebrow. "Since when did you develop a taste for honest work?"

Jamie smiled sheepishly. "My creditors were becoming insistent."

"I'm surpised they could find you."

"So was I. I must be slipping."

Steel had to laugh. "So, Jamie, how did you come to be involved with our disrupters? What you know about high tech could probably be engraved on your thumbnail without undue difficulty."

"I've been acting as an interface between the technicians and your living computer." The young esper shuddered suddenly. "You can't imagine what that's like, Gideon. Those poor bastards have just enough mind left to realise what's been done to them. Neither man nor machine, but something caught horribly between the two. Inside, they're screaming all the time."

"You think I like using that monstrosity? I don't have any choice, Jamie. We've less than half the computers we used to have, and those still on-line are all linked into vital areas of port machinery. We need those people, Jamie; the port can't function without them."

"That doesn't make it right."

"No. It doesn't."

Jamie smiled suddenly. "Hark at me, preaching to you. What is the world coming to?"

"I sometimes wonder," growled Steel. "What do you think of the new defence systems?"

"They're all right, if you like that sort of thing."

"You might try and sound a little more impressed, Jamie. Those cannon are strong enough to punch through an Imperial cruiser's shields."

Jamie laughed, and seated himself elegantly on the edge of Steel's desk, one leg idly swinging. "Still putting your faith in technology rather than people, Gideon? The psionic shield has kept Mistworld safe for almost two hundred years, and no damned machinery is ever going to replace us. We're better and faster than any gun you ever saw."

Steel groaned theatrically. "Not you as well, Jamie. I've already spent hours arguing this out with the damned Council." He broke off suddenly, and looked grimly at the young esper. "I had time for a little chat with your grandfather. He's worried about you."

"He's always worried about me."

"Usually with good reason. Are you in trouble again, Jamie?"

"No more than usual."

"Jamie . . ."

"Don't worry, Gideon. I know what I'm doing. I owe a few people money, that's all. I'm taking care of it."

Steel knew better than to push for an answer once Jamie's face took on that bland, innocent look. In his own way, Jamie had his pride. He got himself into messes, so he had to get himself out. If it had been anyone else, Steel would have called it a matter of honour. . . .

"So, what can I do for you, Jamie?"

"It seems I need your permission to leave the centre, and right at this moment a rather delightful blonde is waiting impatiently for me to join her."

"Is she married?"

"How would I know?"

"I thought you were still seeing Madelaine Skye; or has she been arrested for tech-running again?"

Jamie's face froze suddenly. "I couldn't say. I won't be seeing her again."

"But I thought you and she . . ."

"Not anymore."

Steel decided not to ask; he didn't think he really wanted to know. His life was complicated enough without getting himself involved in the never-ending intrigues of Jamie Royal's love life. "All right," he said finally, smiling in spite of himself. "I'll fix it so you can leave early. We can manage without you, I suppose."

Jamie grinned, snapped off a salute, and left the cubicle, carefully shutting the door behind him. Steel watched him walk jauntily away, and shook his head ruefully. Jamie would never change. Steel turned his attention back to his command monitor, and for a long time he sat quietly, studying the mist-shrouded hulk of the starship *Balefire*. After a while he leant forward and tapped a code into his console.

"Yes, Director?"

"Call Investigator Topaz of the city Watch and tell her . . . tell her she's needed."

Steel signed off without waiting for his order to be acknowledged, and sank back in his chair, his fat hands

clasped loosely across his ample stomach. It had been almost
three years since he'd seen Topaz; he'd hoped the gap would
be a great deal longer. Out of all the people the Bloodhawk
had sent after him, only Topaz had come close to actually
proving anything against him. But with a strange refugee
ship on the main landing pad, and the disrupter cannon
still being installed . . . Steel smiled sourly. Whatever else
you could say about her, Topaz was very good at finding
answers.

Steel's hand strayed to his bald patch again, and he pulled
it back. *I worry too much,* he thought irritably. *Getting soft.*
He picked up his cup of unsugared coffee and sipped at it.
The coffee had gone cold.

Topaz moved slowly about her living room, picking things
up and putting them down again. A log stirred in the open
fire, and the flames jumped higher for a moment before the
wood settled again. The crackling flames were very loud
on the quiet. A single lamp shed a warm, comfortable
glow across the room, but the shadows were still very
dark. Topaz moved slowly among her possessions as though
searching for a lifeline, but they gave her no comfort. She
looked at her padded armchair beside the fire, but didn't sit
down. She was too restless to settle yet. The room seemed
too big and empty with just her in it. She and Michael Gunn
had lived together as man and wife for almost seven years,
and in all those years they'd never been separated from
each other for more than a few days at a time, and then
only rarely. She looked at his chair, on the other side of
the fireplace, and realised with something like shock that
he'd never sit in it again. She looked away, but everywhere
she looked reminded her of Michael.

And Michael Gunn was dead.

It hurts . . .

She'd made the arrangements for his funeral. Everything had been taken care of. Michael had wanted to be
cremated; he didn't believe in graves or cemeteries, and
he had a quiet horror of the bodysnatchers. No flowers,
by request. Michael always said that flowers were for the

living. So Topaz had accompanied her husband's body to the crematorium and watched impassively as his coffin was consigned to the flames. A small choir sang something tasteful in the background. Afterwards, the manager gave her an urn full of ashes he said were Michael's, and Topaz took it home with her. It didn't weigh much. She put the urn in a cupboard under the stairs and left it there.

Died in the morning, cremated in the afternoon. Ashes to ashes, dust to dust.

It hurts . . . like somebody hit me.

She wandered slowly, listlessly, through the living room, her mind far away as she searched for some kind of reason for Michael's death. He had his share of enemies, all mercenaries did, but few of them had the money or the resources to reach him on Mistworld. And assassins with energy guns were very expensive. Lord Raven had sworn vengeance over the affair of Shadrach's Burning. *Gunn and Topaz running sword in hand through the blazing courtyard while a hundred warriors in jet and silver murdered each other in a mindless frenzy. Behind and above them, the ancient castle blazed against the moonless night.* But the old Lord had been mad and dying even then, and his son had shown no interest in feud and vendetta.

Tobias Skinner still carried a grudge from the time Topaz and Gunn had murdered his brother. *The crowd roared as the slavemaster died, and Topaz held up the severed head to show it to the crowd.* But Skinner no longer had the guts or the money for this kind of vengeance. Topaz shook her head slowly, and finally sank into her armchair. None of it made any sense. She'd already thought of a dozen old enemies, and dismissed them all. If any of them had arrived at Mistport, now or in the past, she'd have known. She still had her contacts.

She sat brooding in her chair, her muscles aching from the continuous strain of being unable to relax. Her wounded thigh still troubled her with a dull persistent ache. Her head was pounding and her hands shook. She folded her hands together in her lap and stared into the fire. The day was slowly wearing on, and tired as she was, she still hadn't gone to bed. She had tried, but found on entering the bedroom that she couldn't stand the thought of sleeping alone in the empty bed. She didn't feel like sleeping anyway. She leant her head back against the chair and stared unseeingly up at the ceiling. Thoughts moved sluggishly through her mind, drifting here and there, unable to rest. Memories, plans for revenge, theories of guilt and murder . . . none of them made any sense. The memories cut at her like so many knives, but she couldn't get away from them. Everywhere she looked brought back another memory. And anyway, she wouldn't give them up even if she could. They were all she had left of Michael now. Emotions roared within her like great consuming flames, but still her face remained calm and composed. She'd worn her mask a long time, and knew that without it she'd break down completely. And she didn't have time for that now. She'd do her mourning later, after she'd tracked down Michael's killer. She had no faith in the Watch finding the murderer. Mistport was full of murderers. And besides, the Watch dealt only in justice. Topaz wanted revenge.

She reached out to the table beside her chair and picked up a small wooden casket. She held it before her for a long moment, just looking at it, remembering, and then she snapped open the catch and raised the lid. Inside the casket was an ornately fashioned steel bracelet. Topaz took it out and hefted it in her hand, then slipped it round her left wrist and locked it firmly in place. It was a personal force shield. They were rare on Mistworld, even more so than energy guns. Topaz had brought it with her when she and Gunn had escaped from Darkmoon's Standing and headed straight for Mistworld. She hadn't worn it in Mistport; with Gunn and the Watch to guard her back, she'd never felt the need. Now he was gone, and she had a killer to find, alone. The bracelet weighed heavy on her wrist. Michael had been working on it for the past few months, trying out an idea he'd had. Michael loved to tinker.

Topaz stirred restlessly, needing to be going somewhere, doing something. . . . But as yet she had no clues or leads to follow. Her mind was still too shocked to work logically, and she knew it. Until the shock wore off she was in no condition to begin her search. She sighed quietly. In the meantime, she needed something to do, to occupy her mind and keep her from thinking. She knew she ought to be gathering up Michael's things and sorting through his . . . effects, to decide what she was keeping, and what would have to go. But she couldn't do that yet. That was too final, too much like saying goodbye forever.

The monitor screen on the far wall chimed discreetly, and Topaz jumped at the sudden noise. She waited a moment to be sure she had control of herself again, and then she got up from her chair and walked unhurriedly over to the monitor. She entered her code and the screen lit up to show her a familiar face: John Silver, the duty esper at Mistport command centre.

"Hello, John."

"Hello, Topaz. I heard about Michael. I'm so sorry."

"Thank you."

"Have the Watch come up with any leads?"

"Not yet."

Silver hesitated. "Topaz . . . are you all right?"

"I'm fine, John. What was it you wanted?"

"Port Director Steel asked me to call you. We have a problem with a refugee ship that landed here earlier today. Steel wants you to come and take a look at it."

Topaz smiled coldly. "He must really be in a panic if he asked for me."

"Topaz, if you don't want to do this, I quite understand. We can always find somebody else."

"No, I have no other commitments. I'm free to take the assignment."

"If you're sure . . ."

"I'm sure."

"Very well. The Director will meet you on the main landing pad in two hours' time. The ship is the *Balefire,* out of Tannim. I'll tell the Director you're on your way."

"Thank you, John. And thank you for your sympathy. You were always a good friend to Michael and to me."

"You're welcome, Topaz. If you need anything, you know you can always call me."

"Yes."

"Goodbye, Topaz."

"Goodbye, John."

The monitor screen cleared, and Topaz turned it off. She stared at the blank screen for a while, and then turned abruptly away. If nothing else, the *Balefire* would give her something to do until she found the lead that would put her on the trail of Michael's killer. She smiled slowly as a thought came to her. She'd find Michael's killer, but not as a Sergeant of the city Watch. The Watch were limited by rules and regulations. Topaz would hunt her prey as an Investigator. Her smile became cold and grim, and her eyes held a dark humour that had no mercy in it. She left the living room and went upstairs to her bedroom, to change her clothes. She still had her old Investigator's gown. She'd sworn never to wear it again, but that was a long time ago, when Michael was still alive.

Topaz was an Investigator, and Mistport was going to learn what that meant.

CHAPTER SIX

Partners in Crime

BLACKJACK waited patiently by the bare stone wall that marked the starport perimeter. The landing pads lay hidden in the fog. The sun was sliding quickly down the sky towards evening, and the mists were growing steadily thicker as the temperature fell. Blackjack glanced casually about him, but so far no one had challenged his right to be inside the perimeter wall. At first glance Mistport security seemed extremely lax, with nothing to prevent anyone from just walking out onto the landing field, but Blackjack knew better. His trained mercenary's eye had already identified the concealed proximity mines that lay between the pads and the perimeter. Mistworld as a whole might be lacking in high tech, but the starport had its fair share and more. Blackjack stared thoughtfully at the brightly glowing control tower, on the far side of the port. The glaring electric lights blazed through the mists with undiminished fury, the glowing windows like so many watchful accusing eyes.

Blackjack pulled his cloak about him, and tried not to think about the port sensors. They were supposed to have been taken care of, but the first rule of a mercenary was to trust no one, especially your allies. The second rule was not to worry about things beyond your control. Either he was safe or he wasn't, and he would deal with each situation as it arose. His gaze moved away from the tower and fell on the newly installed disrupter cannon, spread out in a semicircle on the eastern perimeter, their shining silver barrels aimed proudly up at the fog-shrouded skies.

The mercenary eyed the huge guns with respect. He'd seen what disrupter cannon could do, even in inexperienced hands. Enough cannon could destroy an entire planet, leaving nothing on its surface but vast oceans of slowly cooling ashes. Blackjack had never been to Tannim, but he had nevertheless shuddered when he heard the planet had been Outlawed. He turned to look at the vast, battered hull of the *Balefire*, standing alone on the main landing pad. The starship was a wreck, and the mercenary felt a quiet admiration for the Captain who had brought that ship down safely.

Blackjack glanced about him, but there wasn't much else to look at. The only other ships on the pads were the dozen or so assorted vessels belonging to the few smugglers still brave enough to crash the Empire blockade. A few dim figures moved quietly through the freezing mists, mostly security Watchmen and field technicians. The whole port had an air of desertion and desolation. Mistport had been designed to handle a hundred ships, everything from skimmers to starcruisers, but that was long ago, in the days of Empire. Mistport had won its freedom from the tyranny of Imperial rule, but only by paying a very heavy price. Technology was the lifeblood of a starport, and Mistport was running dangerously low. The landing pads hadn't been repaired or extended since the Empire first built them, almost three centuries ago. The high-impact crystal that could withstand the blast of a starship's engines and sustain its million tons of weight was now cracked and dull, worn slowly away by the unrelenting storms and cold.

Blackjack looked round sharply as two figures moved slowly out of the mists towards him. He let one hand rest on the butt of his gun, hidden from sight by his cloak, and then relaxed a little as one of the men lifted his hand in the prearranged recognition signal. A *moue* of distaste pulled at the mercenary's mouth. Paying bribes to traitors was hardly his idea of a day's work, but Vertue gave the orders and Blackjack had no choice but to obey them. For as long as the contract lasted. Afterwards . . . Blackjack smiled suddenly, though his eyes remained cold.

The two men followed a tortuous, invisible path through the hidden pressure fields and proximity mines. The location of the safe paths was a closely guarded secret, revealed only to those Watchmen responsible for starport security. Unfortunately for the starport, Watchmen were only human, and every man has his price. Or his breaking point. Blackjack didn't know why Vertue should want a map of the safe routes, and didn't much care. He had his orders.

The two security Watchmen finally came to a halt before him, and Blackjack bowed politely. The Watchmen nodded their heads briefly in return, and for a moment the three men stared silently at one another. Both security men were tall and lean, and at least partly anonymous in their thick purple cloaks and padded helmets. They both carried pikes, the heavy steel heads gleaming dully in the light from the control tower. Yet for all their similarities, Blackjack had no difficulty in telling them apart. The one with the scarred face was Sterling; the one with the golden eyes was Taylor.

Blackjack's hand tightened on his gun butt. He'd heard a lot about Taylor, none of it good. Word was that Taylor was a Hadenman, and one look at those madly glowing eyes was enough to convince Blackjack that he was indeed facing one of the rare and legendary augmented men of lost Haden. Taylor's face was pleasant enough, almost handsome in its way, but the glaring golden eyes gave his features a wild, inhuman look. Even standing still, he gave an impression of strength and speed, and a savagery barely held in check. Blackjack was tempted to draw his gun and shoot Taylor where he stood; the man was dangerous. But he had his orders. And besides, the mercenary had an uneasy feeling he might not be fast enough. . . .

The man at Taylor's side had to be Sterling, the ex-gladiator from Golgotha. Which was also fairly impressive; there were reputed to be even fewer survivors of the Golgotha Arenas than there were survivors from Haden. Blackjack decided that Vertue had known what he was doing after all, in sending a mercenary on a simple payoff job. These two Watchmen were both hard, experienced

fighters. Blackjack smiled slightly. When all was said and
done they were still amateurs, while he was a professional.

"You're Blackjack," said Taylor suddenly. His voice had
a harsh, rasping buzz, alien and subtly disturbing. It had no
place in a human throat. "I was expecting Vertue himself.
Where is he?"

"The doctor is busy," said Blackjack easily. "He sent me
in his place."

"Prove it."

Blackjack pulled off the thick leather glove on his left
hand and showed the two Watchmen the heavy gold ring
on his finger, carrying Vertue's seal. Taylor nodded, and
Blackjack pulled the glove back on. His hand had been
exposed to the evening air for only a few moments, but
already his fingers were numb.

"I was told to ask about the memory crystal," he said
evenly. "Has it been installed?"

"Not yet," said Sterling. His voice was light and pleasant, in stark contrast to the ugly scars that marred his
face. And yet bad as the scars were, they could easily
have been repaired by any competent surgeon. Blackjack
assumed Sterling wore them as a reminder of his past.
Or possibly as a kind of boast. *Look at my scars; all this
I endured, and still I survived.* Blackjack listened closely
as the ex-gladiator spoke, searching the pleasant, civilised
voice for clues to the man's character.

"The crystal hasn't been delivered yet," said Sterling.
"When it has, I'll lock it into the computer systems myself.
Once the computer's on-line, no one will bother to check
the crystal; they'll assume it's already been checked."

"You'll have the crystal sometime this evening," said
Blackjack. "I'll see to it."

"After this evening it'll be too late," said Sterling.

"I said I'll see to it," said Blackjack. "Now, have you got
the map?"

"Have you got the money?" asked the ex-gladiator, his
right hand moving casually to his belt.

Blackjack pushed back his cloak, careful to let both the
security men see the holstered disrupter on his hip. Hanging

from his belt, next to the gun, was a large leather pouch that clinked musically as Blackjack hefted it in one hand. "Fifty in gold, as agreed. Where is the map?"

Sterling took his hand away from his belt and pulled a folded wad of paper from inside his sleeve. He handed it to Blackjack, who gave him the leather pouch in return. Both men moved slowly and deliberately, careful to make no moves that might be misinterpreted. The transaction completed, they both stepped back a pace. Sterling opened the pouch, glanced inside, and then pulled the drawstrings shut again and nodded quickly to Taylor. The two Watchmen relaxed a little. Blackjack tucked the thick wad of paper into an inside pocket without even bothering to look at it.

Taylor raised an eyebrow. "Don't you want to check the plans?"

"If they're not right, and you've cheated me, I'll have to kill you both," said Blackjack calmly. "Do you think I ought to check them?"

Sterling smiled slowly, and the scars on his face flexed and writhed as though they were alive. "You're very free with your threats, mercenary. I spent seven years in the Arenas, and graduated undefeated. What makes you think you'd stand a chance against me?"

Blackjack's hand slammed forward in a straight-finger jab that sank deep into the ex-gladiator's gut, just below the sternum. Sterling's breath shot out in an agonised gasp, and he sank slowly to his knees, his face horribly contorted. Blackjack turned unhurriedly to face Taylor, who hadn't moved an inch.

"He talks too much," said Blackjack. "Even worse, he's out of condition. I'm not."

Taylor looked at him steadily with his disconcerting golden eyes. "Neither am I," he said quietly, in his harsh, rasping voice. "Don't push your luck, mercenary."

"Not unless I have to," said Blackjack. "Now pick up your friend and get him out of here. I don't think we should be seen talking together. I wouldn't want anyone to think I associated with the likes of you by choice."

Taylor smiled suddenly. "I'm going to remember you, mercenary."

He bent down and picked Sterling up with one hand. The ex-gladiator must have weighed all of two hundred and fifty pounds, but the Hadenman lifted him easily. There was a disquieting strength hidden somewhere in Taylor's wiry frame. Hadenman. An *augmented* man. He settled Sterling comfortably over his shoulder, nodded once to Blackjack, and then walked off into the mists. Blackjack took his hand away from his gun. He'd never fought a Hadenman before, and wasn't sure he wanted to.

Still, he thought calmly as he watched Taylor disappear into the mists, *it might be interesting someday to discover just how good a fighter an augmented man is. . . .*

The Blackthorn tavern had known better days. Grubby silks hung at the blue-tinted windows, and a small fire crackled dully in the large fireplace. Most of the tables and booths were occupied, but the customers ordered only the cheapest wines and made their ale last. The air was full of songs and laughter, but the gaiety had the forced, almost desperate sound of people determined to enjoy themselves while they still had the chance. Not for the first time in Mistport's short history money was in short supply. A slow-moving, cadaverous barman supplied drinks of dubious quality to the regular patrons scattered the length of the long wooden bar. The ancient oil lamps hanging from the overhead beams gave the smoky air a comfortable golden haze, like a fading photograph or a half-forgotten memory. The unpolished walls were stained with old wine and recent blood. The Blackthorn was a lively place on occasion. Sawdust on the floor hadn't been changed in weeks, but nobody complained. The Blackthorn had known better days.

Cyder sat in her private booth at the rear of the tavern, and shared wine with Jamie Royal. A tall and willowy platinum blonde who would admit to thirty years if pressed, Cyder was popularly regarded as the most stonyhearted fence in Mistport. She never argued a price and she never gave credit. She had few friends and her enemies were dead.

She toyed with a loop of her long silvery hair and smiled prettily at her companion. Jamie sipped cautiously at his wine, and glanced at the heavy brass-bound clock over the bar. He put down his goblet and gazed reproachfully at Cyder.

"You said he'd be here by now."

"Cat goes his own way," said Cyder calmly. "What do you want with a memory crystal, Jamie?"

"I've a buyer."

"I'd guessed that, my sweet. The last time you were here you were so desperate you even begged me for a loan."

Jamie winced at the memory. "You're right, I should have known better. There were . . . debts to be paid."

"You never could throw dice worth a damn, Jamie."

He laughed, and looked round the tavern. Two Wampyr had started a fight, and the bartender was taking bets.

"So, how's business, Cyder?"

"It's been better."

"Money's scarce all round."

"That it is. Where did you find a buyer for a memory crystal?"

"Does it matter?"

"I'm curious."

"Don't be." Jamie sipped at his wine, pulled a face, and put his goblet down, pushing it firmly to one side. Cyder didn't blame him. She wasn't wasting a good vintage on Jamie Royal.

"Are you sure this Cat can be trusted?" he asked, checking the time again.

"He's the best roof runner I've ever worked with," Cyder said mildly. "You can trust him as you trust me."

They shared a sardonic smile.

"Maybe he ran into some trouble," said Jamie.

"He'll manage," said Cyder. "He always does."

"Even against a Siren?"

Cyder looked at him sharply, her bright blue eyes suddenly cold and forbidding. "No one said anything to me about a Siren."

"They wouldn't. But I've been doing a little checking, on my own behalf." Jamie smiled grimly. "I don't go into anything blind. It wasn't difficult finding out the address you'd been given. Turns out that particular house is the home of Investigator Topaz. I take it you've heard of her?"

"Everybody's heard of her."

"Right. Do you still think he'll be here this evening?"

Cyder thought for a moment, and then smiled brilliantly, all the worry gone from her face. "He'll be here."

"And the Siren?"

"I don't think she'll bother him much."

"Cold bitch, aren't you?" said Jamie Royal. Cyder smiled sweetly.

"Harsh words, dear Jamie, from an Empire agent."

Jamie pushed back his chair and was quickly on his feet, a throwing knife poised in his hand. Cyder kept herself carefully relaxed. Anywhere else in the tavern the bartender would have shot Jamie dead the moment he drew a weapon on her, but here in her private booth there was no one to help her. Cyder wasn't particularly worried. It would take a lot more than Jamie Royal to worry her. She reached casually for her goblet, and even managed a small chuckle.

"Come on, Jamie. You're not the only one who can work things out. Who else would take care of all your debts in return for one memory crystal? Put the knife away; you're in Thieves Quarter, remember? I don't give a damn who anyone works for, as long as their money's good."

She sipped slowly at her wine, studying Jamie warily over the goblet's rim. He nodded abruptly, and his knife disappeared back into his sleeve. He pulled his threadbare cloak about him, and tried for some kind of dignity.

"We all do what we have to," he said flatly. "I'll be back in an hour for the crystal. Don't waste my time with a duplicate."

Cyder nodded, and Jamie left without saying goodbye. Cyder finished the wine in her goblet, her lips thinning away from the dregs. With fewer ships than ever touching

down at Mistport, good wine grew scarce, along with everything else. Cyder had run the Blackthorn tavern well since
she'd won it in a poker game, but unless things improved
soon, she'd probably lose it to her creditors. With so little
around worth stealing, she barely made enough from her
fencing to pay the bills as it was. Which was why Cyder
dealt with Empire agents. Hard times breed hard people.

She rose gracefully to her feet and swept out of her
private booth. The fight between the two Wampyr was
over and the loser was being dragged away. Cyder smiled
and nodded as she made her way through the crowded bar,
bestowing a cheerful word here and a merry wave there, her
long, silvery hair tossing from side to side. It was a long
way to her private stairway at the back of the tavern, but
somehow she kept on smiling. *Keep the customers happy,
love, keep the customers happy.*

Cat ran swiftly across the tiled and gabled roofs, jumping
casually from level to level over drops that would have
turned the stomach of any observer. More than once he
climbed easily up sheer walls where the untrained eye
would have sworn there were no foot- or handholds to be
had, and his white-clad figure became nothing more than
a dim blur in the curling mists as he drove himself unrelentingly on. He was late, and he knew it. After escaping
from the Siren, he'd followed his normal routine and found
himself a safe hole to hide in while the immediate hue and
cry blew over. He'd slept through the day and awakened
to find it already evening. Throwing off the Siren's attack
must have taken more out of him than he'd realised. He'd
checked the time by the Main Square clock, winced, and
then headed for the Blackthorn as fast as he could. Cyder
didn't like him to be late.

He ran nimbly across a slanting, snow-covered roof and
threw himself out into space across a dark, narrow alleyway. The ground was a long way down, but Cat didn't care.
Heights had never bothered him. He landed easily on the
steep tiled roof opposite, and padded carefully down to the
edge. He sank down on his haunches, glanced quickly about

him, and then slithered over the edge of the roof to hang by his heels from a precarious outcrop of guttering. The stout wooden shutters below him were closed and bolted. Cat hammered on them with his fist, waited impatiently, and then hammered again. There was a long pause. Cat had just drawn back his fist to try again when the shutters flew suddenly open, almost taking his head with them. Cat took a firm hold on the two solid steel hoops set specially into the stonework above the shutters, and swung lithely down and in through the window. Cyder helped him in, and then leaned out the window to look quickly around. The street below was deserted, and all the nearby windows were still securely shuttered. Cyder pulled her shutters closed and slammed the bolts home.

Inside, a blazing fire warmed the tiny, low-roofed room, and Cat darted over to stand before it, throwing aside his gloves to warm his numb hands at the dancing flames. The gloves' heating elements didn't work properly, which was why he'd been able to buy the thermal suit relatively cheaply. He grimaced as feeling slowly returned to his fingers, and then shook his head back and forth as the pain gradually died away. A hand tapped him on the shoulder, and Cat looked round to find Cyder glaring at him.

"You're late. Where's the crystal?"

Cat unlaced the leather pouch from his belt and Cyder snatched it from him, spilling the glowing memory crystal out onto her palm. She favoured Cat with a quick smile from her generous mouth before hurrying over to a nearby table to examine the crystal under a technician's loupe. Cat smiled fondly at Cyder as he pulled off his boots and then stripped off his thermal suit and draped it carefully over the back of a handy chair. He crouched naked in front of the open fire, savouring the heat on his bare skin. He grinned broadly as the cold seeped slowly out of his bones, and then he straightened up and indulged in a long, satisfying stretch. He turned away and put on the simple woollen tunic set out to warm before the fire. He looked at Cyder, still totally immersed in the crystal, and wondered, not for the first time, what he'd done right to find her.

Beautiful as an Arcturan firebat, and about as deadly, Cyder was the best fence he'd ever worked with. She knew her business, and she always got him a good price. Of course, she cheated him shamefully on occasion, but that was only to be expected. Cat didn't care. Cyder set up his targets, gave him a haven from the night's cold, and owned his heart, though he'd never tell her that. She might use it against her.

Cat could feel a faint vibration coming up through the thinly carpeted boards beneath his feet. He smiled slightly. It must be getting quite noisy down below. A room directly over a tavern wasn't the most peaceful of places, but for a deaf mute it raised no problems at all. There was a glazed pot simmering over the fire, and Cat's stomach rumbled as there came to him the smell of his favourite stew. Taking the ladle and bowl set out for him, he served himself a generous portion and carried it over to the nearby table where thick slices of fresh bread and a mug of steaming ale lay waiting.

Cyder put down her eyeglass as he sat down opposite her, and leaned across the table to kiss him thoroughly. "Well done, my darling; the crystal's everything my contact said it was. Your cut will keep you in spending money for some time to come. Did you have any trouble?"

Cat shrugged, and shook his head innocently. Cyder laughed.

"Someday I'll stop asking. You only lie anyway."

Cat grinned and tucked into his stew, shovelling it down as though afraid it might disappear at any moment. He chewed and swallowed with an almost frantic speed, pausing only to take great mouthfuls of the chewy, thick-crusted bread. Cat had gone hungry too often in the past to take any food for granted. In all the time Cyder had fenced for him he'd never once missed a meal, but old habits die hard. He caught Cyder watching him reproachfully, and slowed down a little.

He ate his second helping at an almost leasurely pace, and watched Cyder's lips carefully as they told him the day's news. Such pretty lips . . . Cat hadn't heard a voice or spoken a word since the Empire smuggled a mutated virus into Mistport when he was a child. Hundreds had died; he was one of the lucky ones. He could read lips and talk clumsily with his fingers, and had a gift for insulting mimicry, but he couldn't even hear an esper; his natural shields were too strong. Cat didn't mind. For him, silence was a way of life.

On the roofs it made no difference at all.

He leant back in his chair as Cyder carried on talking. His bowl was empty, and his belly was comfortably full. He sipped appreciatively at his mulled ale and watched happily as Cyder told him of her day and its happenings. Cat slept most of the day so as to be fresh for the night. He didn't like the day much anyway. The sun was too bright, and there were too many people about.

"There's a starship on the pads," said Cyder. "The *Balefire*, with refugees from Tannim. All no doubt carrying a few trinkets of great sentimental value they'll sell fast enough when they get a little hungry."

Cat grinned, mopped the last traces of stew from his bowl with a crust of bread, and popped it into his mouth. Only the rich could afford to buy passage as refugees, which meant good pickings for the likes of him. Cat smiled comfortably. Things were looking up.

✝

CHAPTER SEVEN

Bitter Vengeance

BLACKJACK stood at his ease in Leon Vertue's luxuriously equipped office, and listened calmly while Vertue shouted at him. The mercenary was tempted to look away and run his gaze over the fine paintings and tapestries that adorned the walls, but he didn't. That would have been rude. Instead, he stared politely at the doctor, his face calm and impassive, until Vertue finally ran out of insults and began to calm down a little. Blackjack had served many masters in his time as a mercenary, and gave each of them the respect and attention they deserved, but even masters like Vertue were entitled to politeness. The doctor finally fell silent and leaned back in his padded chair, breathing harshly. He ran his fingers through his thinning hair and glared at the reports set before him on his desk. Blackjack glanced at the visitor's chair, but didn't sit down. He hadn't been invited to. He stood at parade rest, staring straight ahead of him, and waited patiently for Vertue to get to the point. Vertue finally pushed the papers aside and transferred his gaze to the mercenary.

"Damn you, Blackjack, you've ruined everything. According to these reports, Investigator Topaz is already on our trail. It's only a matter of time before she finds someone who can lead her to us."

"None of our people will talk," said Blackjack. "They're too scared. I've seen to that."

"You don't know Topaz."

"I can still kill her."

"Not now you can't," snapped Vertue irritably. "If you'd killed her when you were supposed to, instead of hitting her damned husband by mistake, we'd have got away with it. As it is, we don't dare touch her."

Blackjack said nothing. He could have defended himself by pointing out he had no way of knowing Michael Gunn would be wearing his wife's distinctive cloak. He might have mentioned the appalling conditions, with the fog and the hounds. But he chose not to. He had no interest in excuses, whether from others or from himself.

Vertue rose from his chair and moved away from his desk to stare out the window. Outside the wide pane of steelglass the evening mists lay still and heavy, enveloping the city in a featureless grey haze. Vague silhouettes of surrounding buildings showed dimly through the haze. Street lights glowed amber and gold and crimson, islands of light in an ocean of uncertainty. *She's out there somewhere*, thought Vertue grimly. *She's out there, looking for me*. He remembered Topaz's cold, implacable face, and couldn't repress a shiver. Topaz was an Investigator, and knew nothing of pity or honour or mercy. Vertue turned away from the window to face the politely waiting mercenary, and fought to keep his face calm and his voice steady.

"We can't afford any more contact with the Investigator," he said quietly. "Any further attempts on her life, successful or not, would only draw attention to her. For the time being, you leave her strictly alone."

"That's what I have been doing," said Blackjack. "Did you bring me all the way here just to tell me that?"

"Hardly," said Vertue coldly. "I have another assignment for you. You remember Taylor and Sterling?"

"Of course. The two Watchmen who provided us with information on the starport's internal security. Is there some problem with them?"

Vertue smiled grimly. "It seems they feel they haven't been paid enough for their services. Either we come up with more money, or they'll feel it their duty to turn us in."

"Leave it to me," said Blackjack. "I'll handle it. Do you mind if I kill these two?"

"Not at all," said Leon Vertue. "But if you do, I want the bodies. Particularly the Hadenman."

Blackjack nodded courteously, waited a moment to see if there was anything more, and then turned and left. Vertue watched him go, and shook his head slowly as the door closed quietly after the mercenary. The man was too cool, too controlled . . . and far too dangerous. Vertue knew Blackjack was no threat to him for as long as their contract stood, but no contract lasts forever. Vertue nibbled at a fingernail, then snatched his hand away. He frowned, and reluctantly made a decision. He leant forward and tapped a memorized code into the comm unit built into his desk. The monitor on the wall opposite turned itself on, but the screen remained blank. After a moment, a cold distorted voice issued from the speakers.

"Yes, Vertue. What is it?"

"I've given the mercenary his orders. He'll take care of Taylor and Sterling for us. I've warned him to stay away from Topaz."

"Good. We're nearing a delicate stage in our plans, and Blackjack is becoming too conspicuous. As soon as he's dealt with Taylor and Sterling, I think it would be best if he was removed from the picture."

"You mean kill him?"

"Certainly not, you damned fool! Do you want the whole Mercenaries Guild on our backs? I mean pay him off, get him a berth on a smuggler's ship, and get him the hell off Mistworld as quickly as possible. Is that clear?"

"Yes, sir. I'll see to it. About the Investigator . . ."

"Forget her. Once Taylor and Sterling are dead, and Blackjack is safely offworld, there'll be no trail left for her to follow. Don't contact me again, Vertue. Your part in this is over. I'll call you in future, should it prove necessary."

The speakers fell silent. Vertue pulled a face at the blank screen and turned it off. He wasn't some underling or servant, to be spoken to in such a manner. And it was unthinkable that the mercenary should just pick up his money and walk away unscathed after all the trouble he'd caused. Especially since the body bank was so short of raw materials.

• • •

Investigator Topaz picked up Marcus Rhine by his shirt front and slammed him back against his office wall. The cheap plaster cracked under the impact. Rhine clawed feebly at Topaz's hands, his feet kicking a good six inches above the floor. Both his eyes were puffed nearly shut, but he could still see clearly enough to cringe when Topaz drew back her fist to hit him again.

"The name," said Topaz. "I want the name of the man who murdered my husband."

Rhine nodded agreement as best he could, and Topaz dropped him in a heap on the floor. She stepped back and seated herself gracefully on Rhine's desk. Papers that had once lain in neat piles on the highly polished desk were now scattered across the floor. Some of the papers were spotted with blood. Rhine's two bodyguards lay dead by the open door. For a man who made his living by threats, extortion, and violence, Rhine should have paid more attention to his defences. He should also have known better than to refuse to speak to Investigator Topaz. Rhine sat up painfully and leant back against the wall, gradually getting his breathing under control. He was a medium-height, rangy man with square, blocky hands and a great leonine head of tawny hair. He wore smart clothes in a sloppy manner, and though his face was painted in the latest fashion, his teeth were black and rotting. All in all, he looked very much like a rat with delusions of grandeur. His face bore the ritual scars of the Rhine Clan, but most of those scars were now hidden or distorted by blood and bruises.

"Talk to me," said Topaz, and Rhine flinched.

"You must be mad," he said thickly, blood trickling down his chin from his split lips. "When you attack one Rhine, you attack us all. My family will have your head for this."

"To hell with them and to hell with you," said Topaz calmly. "You've got a name, and I want it. You always know names, Marcus. And don't threaten me with Clan vengeance; you're not that important. You Rhines only exist because the Watch is usually too busy to waste time cleaning you out. You're just a cheap little bone-breaker, Marcus, and that's all you'll ever be. Now give me the name."

"Sterling," said Rhine sullenly. "He's a Watchman, part of starport security. Used to be a gladiator a few years back. He didn't point the gun at your husband, but the word is he might know who did. You'll find him at the Redlance."

He cowered against the wall as Topaz got to her feet, but she just overturned his desk with a casual flip of her hand and then walked past him to the door without a glance in his direction.

"You'd better be right about this, Marcus," she said quietly, and closed the door behind her. She walked unhurriedly through the wrecked reception area, ignoring the damage she'd caused. A buxom secretary sat slumped in a corner, groaning quietly as she felt cautiously at her broken nose. She'd made the mistake of drawing a knife on the Investigator. Topaz ignored her too, and made her way out onto the street.

She paused outside the door and breathed deeply, as though trying to rid herself of a foul smell. The freezing air burned in her lungs, but she barely noticed. Topaz had been trained to withstand far worse. Evening had fallen and the light was fading fast. It had just begun to snow again and the mists were growing thicker. The wind had dropped to a bare murmur and the fog lay heavily across the city. Topaz could barely make out the far side of the street she stood in. A typical winter's night in Mistport. Topaz settled her sword comfortably on her hip and drew her handgun to check the energy level. The crystal was barely half-charged, but it was enough. She holstered the gun and strode off down the street. She'd never visited the Redlance tavern before, but she knew of its reputation. All the Watch did. If it was for sale, you could buy it at the Redlance. Drugs, whores, children, secrets . . . everything had its price.

The snow on the ground had been trampled into slush by the crowds that still filled the narrow streets. Most of them were workmen hurrying to get home before the real cold began, but there were also hordes of beggars and street traders, trying for one last coin while the temperature permitted. The mists curled sluggishly as the bitter wind murmured among the stone-and-timbered buildings, and thick icicles hung unmelting from every gutter and window ledge. The passers-by were all huddled in thick furs and heavy cloaks, and Topaz drew more than one startled glance as she strode through the streets in her formal Investigator's uniform. Her thick navy blue cloak covered only a long robe of silvercloth, and her face and hands were bare. Topaz took no harm from the cold, and within her heart she was warmed by her own unrelenting fury. Michael was dead. Her husband, the only human being she'd ever cared for, was dead; murdered. And she would have a vengeance for that death.

The Redlance lay deep in the rotten heart of Thieves Quarter. There were those who saw the Quarter as a single sprawling slum, infested with all the worst kinds of villains, but in reality it was no worse than any other part of the city. It was just a little poorer than most, and a lot more obvious. The Watch Commanders kept saying they were going to clear out Thieves Quarter once and for all, but somehow there were always other, more important things for the Watch to do. And besides, when all was said and done, Mistworld was a planet full of criminals, for only the Outlawed ever came to Mistworld. As long as you didn't rock the boat too much, nobody cared. For those who got out of hand, the Watch enforced the law, and the law knew no mercy. But there are always those who think themselves above the law, and they need their own private places to do business. Places like the Redlance.

Topaz strode grimly on through squalid streets and filthy back alleys until finally she came to the Redlance tavern. It looked like any other tavern in any other street; a small, nondescript building with a single flickering oil lamp to mark the swinging sign above its door. The stonework was discoloured and pitted from long exposure to snow and fog, and the two small windows were both securely shuttered. Just another tavern . . . but the Redlance's door gave it away. Seven feet high and four feet wide, the huge slab of ironwood was studded with intricate patterns of gleaming steel. The Redlance's door was designed to keep people out, and it did so very efficiently. Topaz stood before the door a moment, and then struck it once with her fist. There was a barely perceptible hum as the minicamera over the door swivelled to look down at her.

"You know who I am," said Topaz. "Open the door."

There was a long pause, and then the door swung slowly open and Topaz entered the tavern. A deafening roar hit her like a fist as she stepped inside, and the stale air was thick with smoke and sweat. Topaz stood at the top of the narrow stairway leading down into the tavern, and looked out over the packed crowd in search of the man she'd come to see.

The constant noise broke against the bare stone walls, which threw it back again. Laughter, insults, and the cries of bravos nerving themselves to fight mixed one with the other in an unrelenting assault on the hearing. Men and women from all ranks and stations stood side by side, drinking too much and laughing too loudly. An average night for the Redlance. Topaz moved slowly down the stairway, keeping one hand on the butt of her gun under cover of her cloak. No one paid her any attention beyond a brief, sideways glance; in a place like the Redlance everyone was careful to mind their own business. Topaz stopped halfway down the stairs and frowned thoughtfully. There was no trace of Sterling. Topaz considered searching through the crowd for him, but immediately discarded the idea. She wasn't in the mood for a slow, polite line of enquiry. She made her way with careful grace down the remaining stone steps, worn down and polished by countless booted feet, and headed through the milling crowd to the bar at the rear of the tavern. Everyone made way for her without having to be asked. They knew who she was. A few men looked as though they might object to her presence, but one look at her cold determined face was enough to convince them not to press the point.

On reaching the bar, Topaz glanced unhurriedly about her until she spotted Pieter Gaunt, the owner of the Redlance. Gaunt was tall and muscular, with a shock of dark curls surrounding a bland, amiable face. His clothes tried hard to be fashionable, and almost made it. He was at least fifty, but looked thirty from a distance. He was known to have murdered seven men, three with his bare hands, and rumour put the count much higher. He made some of his money from drugs and prostitution, for old times' sake, but most of his income came from the acquiring and selling of information. Topaz's mouth twitched. Gaunt was about to undergo a new experience: the giving away of information for free. She loosened her sword in its scabbard and made her way through the crowd towards him. At the last moment, a large and extremely muscular bodyguard stepped forward to block her way. His right hand hovered over a sheathed short-sword, and his left hand held a spiked knuckle-duster.

"I'm here to see Gaunt," said Topaz, raising her voice to be heard over the din.

The bodyguard shook his head, and lifted the knuckle-duster to hold it in front of her face. He grinned suddenly, and slowly brought the spikes closer to her skin. Topaz kneed him in the groin, waited for him to bend forward, and then rabbit-punched him. The bodyguard collapsed on the floor and lay very still. A woman nearby screamed suddenly, but Topaz was already turning to face the second bodyguard. If anything, he was even bigger than the first, and he carried his sword like he knew how to use it. Topaz drew her disrupter and shot him through the chest. The vivid energy beam ripped through him in a split second, and rushed on to blast a wide crater in the wall behind him. The bodyguard fell dead to the floor, smoke rising gently from the charred wound in his chest. The Redlance was suddenly quiet, the only sound a low whisper that ran swiftly through the watching crowd.

Energy gun . . . energy gun . . .

Topaz looked at Gaunt, and smiled slowly. It wasn't a pleasant sight, but Gaunt didn't flinch. He stepped forward to join her, being careful to keep his hands away from his sides and not make any sudden movements. Close up, his bland and amiable features fooled no one. His eyes were dark and cunning, and a feeling of overt menace hung about him, like the scent of freshly spilled blood.

"That's two good men you've just killed," he said quietly, his voice pleasant and assured. "They'll be expensive to replace. I trust you had a good reason for killing them."

"I had to get your attention," said Topaz. "I'm looking for someone. You know where he is."

Gaunt shook his head. "I don't betray people to the Watch. It's bad for business."

"I don't want him for the Watch. I want him for myself."

Gaunt studied her thoughtfully, taking in her Investigator's robe and cloak. He shrugged. "Give me the name."

"Sterling. Starport security. Ex-gladiator."

"I know him. Wait here and I'll bring him to you."

Topaz nodded curtly, her eyes colder than the Mistport night. Gaunt turned and walked away, and the crowd silently made way for him. He finally disappeared through a door behind the bar, and Topaz was left alone with the packed, unmoving crowd. She swept her gaze across them, and they stared warily back, their eyes dark with barely suppressed hate and fear and suspicion. Someone stirred to Topaz's left, and she lifted her right hand slightly to bring her gun into clear view. The stirring subsided, and the long silence continued. Topaz had the feeling of being alone in a strange forest, surrounded by angry and dangerous animals. A slight smile touched her mouth at the aptness of the comparison, and then she thought of Sterling, and the smile vanished. The door behind the bar swung open and Gaunt came out, followed by Sterling. Topaz nodded calmly when she saw the scarred face, and switched the gun to her left hand. Sterling and Gaunt came out from behind the bar, and Topaz drew her sword.

"Sterling," she said harshly, her voice ringing on the quiet, "I have come for you."

Sterling stopped a good ten feet away and studied her warily. "So you're Topaz," he said finally. "I always thought you'd be taller."

Topaz just looked at him, and said nothing. Sterling glanced round the watching crowd, as though looking for sympathy or support, but whatever he found in their faces didn't seem to reassure him. He looked quickly at Pieter Gaunt.

"Are you going to let her do this? Just walk into your place and take one of your people away?"

"You're not one of mine," said Gaunt calmly. "If you don't want to go with her, that's up to you." He looked at the crowd. "Make some room."

The throng of patrons fell back at his quiet command, forming a wide circle around Topaz and Sterling. Gaunt stepped quickly back into the crowd as Topaz moved slowly forward. Sterling backed cautiously away. He drew a long, gleaming scimitar from the scabbard on his hip, and then drew a disrupter from a concealed shoulder holster. He slapped the inside of his left wrist against his hip, and a yard-wide square of glowing light appeared on his left arm: a force shield. Topaz smiled grimly and activated her own force shield. The two shields hummed quietly on the silence as the two combatants slowly circled each other. Topaz moved gracefully, confidently, running the simple rules of combat through her mind. *A gun takes at least two minutes to recharge between each shot. A force shield is only good for ten minutes' continuous use; after that, the crystal needs half an hour to recharge before it can be used again. A shield will stop a sword, but reflects a gun. A sword never needs recharging.*

Sterling cut at Topaz's throat with his scimitar, and she caught it easily on her shield. She swept her sword out in a long arc for his gut, and he brought his shield down just in time to block it. Their swords flashed crimson and gold in the lamplight as they circled each other, searching out strengths and weaknesses, looking always for the opening that would let them use their guns. Hit the shield at the wrong angle, and the energy beam would come right back at you. And if you found an opening and missed, the odds were you'd never get a second chance. Unfortunately, a moving target is very hard to hit when you have to watch out for a sword as well.

Topaz and Sterling cut and parried, thrust and recovered, their swords meeting and flying apart in a flurry of sparks.

The two shields slammed together again and again, static sparking between them where the two energy fields met. Sterling used all his old gladiator's tricks, plus a few new ones he'd picked up in Mistport, but to no avail. Topaz might not be his better with the sword, but she was strong and fast and tireless, driven by some inner demon, while he . . . had got soft. His breathing grew harsh and ragged, and sweat ran down his forehead to sting his eyes. His sword grew heavier with every blow, and his arms and back ached unmercifully. *I should have shot her from cover when I had the chance*, he thought bitterly. *Who would have thought the bitch would be this good a fighter?* And still they circled each other, swords probing and cutting and thrusting in a never-ending rhythm. Sterling glared at the face before him, cold and savage and pitiless, and a slow fear ate at his heart.

And finally he made a mistake, his first and his last. He leant too far forward in a lunge, and couldn't pull back in time. Topaz's sword flashed down to sink deep into his thigh, cutting clean through to the bone and flying out again in a flurry of blood. Sterling screamed and fell full-length on the floor as his leg collapsed beneath him. His shield flickered and went out. He lifted his gun for a last desperate shot, and Topaz leant quickly forward and slammed down her force shield. The razor-sharp edge of the energy field cut cleanly through his wrist, severing his hand and cauterizing the stump in the same moment. Sterling screamed again, and fainted. Topaz stepped back and looked about her to see if anyone cared to dispute her win. Nobody did. She turned back to Sterling, then quickly lifted her gun to cover Gaunt as he reached for the disrupter Sterling had dropped.

"Don't try it," said Topaz. "Don't even think about it."

"Of course," said Gaunt. "The spoils of war." He straightened up and stepped back into the crowd. Topaz sheathed her sword, and bent warily down to retrieve the gun. She shoved it into her belt, straightened up, and then glared coldly at the unconscious ex-gladiator.

"Wake him up," she said curtly to Gaunt.

Gaunt nodded to his bartender, who produced a bucket of soapy water from behind the bar. Gaunt took the bucket and emptied it over Sterling. He came to in a rush, coughing and spluttering. Topaz turned off her force shield and holstered her gun. Then, taking the front of Sterling's tunic in one hand, she hauled him to his feet and slammed him back against the bar. She pinned his legs with her body and then slowly increased the pressure of her arm, pushing his chest steadily back until Sterling thought his spine would break. He lifted his arms to try and stop her, and then nearly passed out again when he saw the blackened stump of his left arm. Topaz pushed her face close to his, and Sterling trembled at the cold implacable anger he saw there.

"Who killed my husband, Sterling? Tell me his name."

"I don't know his name," Sterling muttered, and then he gasped as Topaz increased the pressure on his chest. "My back! You're breaking my back!"

"Tell me his name. Tell me who murdered my husband."

"Taylor knows! Ask him! He was my partner, he knows all the names. I just followed his orders."

"And where do I find this Taylor?" asked Topaz. She smiled humourlessly as Sterling hesitated, and the muscles in her arm bunched and corded as she bent him back a little further. Sterling's face contorted in agony.

"Taylor's a Hadenman. Works for Mistport security, like me. He knows who killed your husband. Ask him!"

"And there's nothing more you can tell me?"

"Nothing! I swear it!"

"I think I believe you," said Topaz. "Which is unfortunate, for you."

Her arm muscles suddenly swelled, and Sterling screamed once as his spine snapped. Topaz drew her sword and cut his throat in one swift motion, stepping quickly back to avoid the jetting blood. Sterling fell limply to the floor and lay still.

"That's one for you, my husband," said Topaz quietly. She looked slowly around her, and the surrounding crowd fell back, unable to meet her burning gaze. Even Gaunt looked away. Topaz smiled briefly and made her way undisputed out of the Redlance tavern.

The silence held while she climbed the stairs and opened the door, but the moment the door closed behind her, the crowd returned to its original noisy and boisterous mood. The roar of sound returned, only slightly muted by what had been witnessed. Gaunt gestured to two of his men, and they dragged away Sterling's body and then returned for the two bodyguards. A serving wench set about cleaning up the blood with a bucket and mop. Blackjack emerged from the door behind the bar and made his way over to join Gaunt.

"Thanks for not telling her I was here."

"She didn't ask me," said Gaunt.

"If she had, would you have told her?"

Gaunt shrugged. "Right now, I don't think there's anyone in this city who could deny that woman anything."

Blackjack nodded slowly. "I think you may be right, Gaunt. You may well be right."

A dozen city Watchmen were waiting for Topaz when she left the Redlance tavern. She stopped outside the door, and glanced quickly about her. The Watchmen had fanned out to cut off all the exits. Topaz looked at the man in charge, and nodded resignedly.

"Hello, John. Looking for someone?"

"Port Director Steel still needs you," said John Silver, the starport duty esper. "In fact, he needs you urgently."

"That fat old thief can wait," said Topaz shortly.

"No, he can't; he's running out of time."

"Then get somebody else."

"It has to be you, Investigator."

Topaz scowled, and searched Silver's face for some sign of weakness. Instead, she saw only a weariness and a calm sense of duty that sat oddly on his youthful features. He wore a set of thick, superbly cut furs topped by the scarlet cloak of the esper, but they couldn't disguise his lean muscular frame. He wore a simple short-sword on his hip in a well-worn scabbard. Silver had been a pirate before coming to Mistworld, and Topaz knew that if it came to a fight she'd have to kill him to stop him. And she wasn't sure she could do that. Silver had brought both her and Gunn into the city Watch, and given them both a reason for living when they both needed one badly. He was the nearest thing Topaz had to a friend.

"How did you find me?" she asked finally, more for something to say than because she really cared.

"You left quite a trail," said Silver. "Including four wrecked taverns and more than sixty injured people. They're still trying to get one man down from a chandelier in the Green Man."

"I'm close, John," said Topaz urgently. "I'm so close to finding the man who killed Michael. I can't let you stop me. I daren't let the trail get cold."

"You're needed at the starport, Investigator. There's something strange aboard the *Balefire*. Steel thinks it could be a threat to the whole of Mistport, and you know he doesn't panic easily. You must come back with us, Topaz."

"Or?"

"There's a warrant for your arrest. You've upset several prominent people in the course of this evening, and they all want your head. As yet the warrant isn't signed. If you agree to help Steel, it won't be."

"You think I give a damn about your warrant?"

"Don't throw your life away for no good reason, Topaz. Michael wouldn't have wanted that."

"I swore him the oath of vengeance. The mercenary's oath."

"This job shouldn't take you long, Topaz. A few hours, at most. In the meantime, if you'll tell me your lead I'll have these men track it down for you."

Topaz looked around at the silent Watchmen. "And if I don't go back willingly, you'll have me dragged. Is that it?"

"Pretty much," said John Silver. "That's why I came with them. You just might be able to take out all these Watchmen, but you wouldn't kill me."

"Are you sure of that?"

"No. But then, where's the fun in being sure?"

He laughed cheerfully, and after a moment Topaz smiled in reply.

"I'm looking for a starport security man called Taylor," she said finally. "He's a Hadenman, and he knows who killed Michael."

"Shouldn't take us long to find him," said Silver confidently. "By the time you're finished with Steel, we'll have him waiting for you."

"I hope so," said Topaz, "Because if you let him slip through your fingers, John, I may kill you, friend or no."

She walked away into the swirling mists, and after a moment Silver and the Watch followed her back to the starport.

✛

CHAPTER EIGHT

Starlight

DIRECTOR Steel waited impatiently by the main landing pad, scowling at the night's cold and gnawing hungrily at a sweetmeat. The sun had been down a good hour and more, and the night chill was growing steadily worse. It was going to be a hard winter. Steel chewed slowly, savouring the rich flavour of the confection, and stamped his feet on the snow to keep them warm. He always felt the cold worst in his feet. The *Balefire* towered high above him, a mountain of gleaming steel beside which the slender control tower with its bright electric lights seemed nothing more than a garish toy. There was no wind, and the mists hung heavily across the landing field, muffling everything in a featureless grey blanket. And out of the mists came Investigator Topaz.

Her face was grim and brooding, and she came stalking out of the fog with a long, impatient stride that was all the more intimidating because it was entirely unselfconscious. Steel studied her thoughtfully as she approached him, and began to wonder if perhaps he'd made the wrong decision. He respected and he feared Topaz, but he hadn't a single clue as to what went on behind those cold, implacable eyes. From what he'd been hearing, she'd spent most of the day and evening blazing a bloody trail through the seamier side of Thieves Quarter, in search of the man who'd killed her husband. Steel admired her for it; he wouldn't have entered that part of Thieves Quarter without a disrupter in each hand and an army of Watchmen to back him up. And yet the Topaz he remembered from three years earlier had always been cold and unemotional, letting nothing get between her and her work, and it was that impartial Investigator's skill he needed now.

He frowned slightly as he watched her draw near. She was supposed to have been wounded fighting the Hob hounds, but you couldn't tell from looking at her. If she felt any trace of pain or weakness, it didn't show in her face or in her bearing. Part of her Investigator's training, Steel supposed. He looked again at her face, and smiled slightly. Topaz didn't look at all happy about being called away from her vengeance. Steel felt no regrets. He needed her help, her Investigator's cunning. He bowed politely to Topaz as she finally came to a halt before him, and she nodded curtly in return before turning away to stare up at the *Balefire*.

The massive starship brooded sullenly on its pad, the vast burnished hull glowing ruddy from the surrounding torches before disappearing into the mists. Jagged holes pockmarked the stem and stern, and one whole section lay broken open to the mercy of the bitter cold. A central vane had been stripped of its covering, the naked steel struts pitted and corroded like ancient bones. It was a wonder the *Balefire* had held together long enough to reach Mistworld. Steel scowled, and took another bite of sweetmeat. He distrusted wonders.

"How long before we can go aboard, Director?"

The dry, harsh voice startled him, and Steel had to swallow quickly to empty his mouth before answering.

"Depends on the Captain. He knows we're here."

"Why send for me, Steel? There must be others in the Watch with more experience than me."

"You're different," said Steel flatly. "You used to be an Investigator."

Topaz looked at him sharply. "What makes you so sure you need an Investigator?"

"My espers have scanned this ship a dozen times, and the results are never the same twice. There's something unusual aboard this ship, something . . . strange."

"Alien?"

"Possibly. Whatever it is, it's dangerous. That's the one thing my espers do agree on. It's dangerous, it's powerful, and it's hiding somewhere on the *Balefire*. I need you to help me find out what it is, and how best to deal with it. That is what an Investigator is for, isn't it?"

Topaz laughed suddenly, and Steel stirred uncomfortably at the bitter, unforgiving sound. "Shall I tell you what an Investigator is for, Steel? The Empire takes us when we're still children, and destroys what makes us human. We're not allowed emotions. They might weaken us. We're not allowed conscience or empathy or compassion. They might interfere with our training. The Empire shapes our bodies and moulds our minds, and when they've taught us all they know about killing and deception and the uncovering of hidden truths, they send us out among the stars, to the frontiers of the Empire. We investigate new alien cultures as they are discovered, and determine whether they pose any threat to the Empire. If they do, or if we think they might, we have to advise the Empire on how best to subjugate or destroy the aliens. Enslavement or genocide; there's not much difference in the end. They call us ambassadors, but really we're just highly skilled assassins. And that, Steel, is what an Investigator is for."

Steel shifted from foot to foot uncertainly, and searched for something to say. "Right now, all I care about is whatever's hiding in the *Balefire*. Are you going to help me or not?"

Topaz shrugged. "The sooner this is over with, the sooner I can get back to my own business. If there is an alien aboard this ship, I'll find it."

"Thanks."

Topaz looked at him suspiciously. "Why are you here in person, Steel? Afraid the refugees might try to smuggle some valuables past you?"

"I know my duty," said Steel coldly. "I carry it out."

"For a price."

Steel looked away, unable to meet Topaz's sardonic gaze. "I hear you had a little trouble delivering our memory crystal, Investigator."

"Bad news travels fast. A burglar tried to steal the crystal one night; apparently no one had told him I was a Siren."

Steel smiled slightly. "How very unfortunate for him. Has he been identified yet?"

"Not yet," said Topaz. "Somehow he got away from me."

Steel raised an eyebrow.

"The crystal was still locked securely within its casket," said Topaz evenly. "And it was still there when I delivered it to your security people. As you are no doubt happy to hear, Director."

"Of course, Investigator, of course."

Steel took another bite at his sweetmeat, pulled his cloak tightly about him, and glanced curiously at Topaz's choice of outfit. He'd noticed immediately that she was wearing her old Investigator's uniform again, but thought it best not to comment on it if she chose not to. As he watched, Topaz turned slightly away to look at the *Balefire*'s main airlock, and Steel saw a charred hole in the back of the thick navy blue cloak. He realised he was looking at the hole left by the energy beam that had killed the Investigator's husband. Steel shivered suddenly, not entirely from the cold. How could she bear to wear the damned thing? He shrugged slightly, and looked away. The moon shone palely through the mists, and a light snow was falling. Steel wolfed down the last of the sweetmeat and wiped his greasy fingers on his furs. He quickly pulled his glove back on and beat his hands together to drive out the cold. If Topaz thought her presence was going to be enough to stop him collecting his usual tithe from whatever loot the refugees had brought with them, she could damn well think again. He'd just have to be a little more careful, that was all.

Captain Starlight sat in his command chair, staring out over the smoke-blackened bridge. His flight computers were silent, their lights dimming as the power levels fell. The main viewscreen was dead, and only static whispered from the speakers. Empty seats that should have held crew members stared accusingly back at him. When he slept, which wasn't often, Starlight heard his dead crew calling to him. Another light snapped out as the ship's main computers continued shutting down any system that wasn't essential to the ship's integrity. Starlight couldn't bring himself to care. He'd seen the damage reports; the *Balefire* wasn't going anywhere without a major refit. Darkness gathered on the bridge, and accusing shadows waited at the corners of his eyes.

Starlight stirred slowly in his chair, tiredness dragging at his limbs like chains. Two thirds of his crew lay dead on Tannim, burned to ashes and less than ashes by the Empire hellships. His ship was a wreck, and he was an Outlaw. Starlight grinned mirthlessly. Poetic justice? Hardly. He'd broken his share of laws and regulations—what starship Captain hadn't?—but he'd done nothing to deserve this.

And my poor crew . . .

He remembered their voices, screaming from the comm units as the *Balefire* fought her way through the outer atmosphere, her shields shuddering under constant fire from the Empire's ships. He would have waited for his crew if there'd been time, but there was no time, no warning, and he hadn't dared wait. It had been close enough as it was. Ten of his remaining crew were dead. Twice as many more were injured. And his passengers . . . his passengers. They'd known the risks when they came to him, when the Outlawing of Tannim was only the barest rumour. They'd known what might happen if things went wrong. They'd known all the risks and accepted them, but neither they nor he could possibly have predicted what had happened; the terrible thing he'd had to do to save his ship. . . .

Captain Starlight stared around his empty bridge. His surviving crew were sleeping in their quarters, or trying to. There was nothing left for them to do now. Nothing left for anyone to do. Starlight rose slowly to his feet, weariness surging through him in a slow, familiar tide. The Port Director was waiting to see him, and Starlight had put it off long enough. He had his duties to perform, while he was still Captain.

They might have taken everything else from him, but he still had that.

• • •

Steel glanced surreptitiously at Topaz as she stared grimly into the surrounding fog. He wondered what she was seeing deep in her own thoughts. If there was anything in her of grief or sorrow for the husband she'd lost, she showed none of it to the watching world. Even her revenge had been a cold and determined affair.

A sudden hum of straining machinery brought Steel's attention back to the *Balefire*, as the main airlock slowly irised open, metal grating on metal amid an outrush of stinking air. Steel scowled, and tried to breathe only through his mouth. He stepped forward and peered warily into the open airlock. The great ribbed-steel chamber was fully a hundred feet across, and dimly lit by a single glowing lightsphere set over the door inside the airlock. The ceiling and the far wall were lost in shadows. The foul smell slowly cleared as Mistport's freezing air entered the chamber, and Steel stepped cautiously in through the open door, followed by Topaz. He'd never liked iris doors. He was always afraid they were going to suddenly contract and close before he could get out of the way. He moved slowly forward, and a dim figure stirred in the shadows at the rear of the chamber. Steel stopped where he was, and frowned uncertainly.

"Captain Starlight?"

The figure moved slowly forward into the light. A tall, grey-haired man with hooded eyes, his cloak hung about him like a dirty shroud. His silver uniform was torn and bloodstained. His face was drawn and haggard, and his deep sunk eyes were full of a weary bitterness.

"I'm Starlight."

Steel nodded briskly as Starlight finally came to a halt before him. "Port Director Gideon Steel, at your service, Captain. This is Investigator Topaz."

Starlight glared at Steel, obviously struggling for control. "My passengers are all refugees from Tannim. Their planet is dead; they have nowhere else to go. Will they be safe here?"

Steel shrugged. "As safe as anywhere. Mistworld is a poor world, and a harsh one. Your passengers will have to fend for themselves, or starve. And we have to check them out first."

"Of course." Starlight smiled wearily. "We might all be Empire spies."

"Yes," said Topaz. "You might."

Starlight looked at her, and Steel coughed discreetly.

"How many refugees have you brought us, Captain?"

"There were fifteen thousand. Most are dead now."

"What happened?" asked Topaz.

"I killed them," said Captain Starlight.

The *Balefire* was full of sound as Starlight led Steel and Topaz through an endless maze of steel corridors. There were constant creaks and groans as metals contracted and expanded under Mistport's varying cold, the brief furtive sounds like so many unseen mice. From time to time a sudden sputtering noise would make Steel jump, as one or another piece of machinery would give up the ghost and cease to function. Starlight and Topaz paid no attention to anything they heard, their faces equally cold and distant. Steel muttered under his breath and did his best to keep up with them. Though he was damned if he could see what all the hurrying was for; the cargo bay would still be there when they got there.

The overhead lights flickered uncertainly, and faded one by one as the ship's computers slowly fell apart, their memory crystals gradually wiping clean as the power levels dropped. The air was breathable, but thick with the unpleasant fumes of burning insulation and spilt coolant, suggesting that the circulating pumps were already breaking down. The heating elements were out, and Mistport's cold was already permeating the ship. The *Balefire* was dying.

"Why you?" said Starlight suddenly, looking curiously at Topaz. His voice echoed on the still air. "Why an Investigator?"

"That was my idea, actually," said Steel quickly. "My espers discovered something rather unusual aboard your ship."

"Yes, I remember," said Starlight. "But there are no aliens aboard the *Balefire*."

"My espers quite definitely detected something. . . ."

"I don't give a sweet damn what your espers detected! I know my own ship. There's me, my crew, and the refugees. Nobody else."

"No aliens among the refugees?" asked Topaz.

"None."

"You won't mind if I inspect the ship for myself."

"Do I have a choice?"

"No."

They walked a while in silence.

"You said you killed most of the refugees," Steel said carefully. "What happened, Captain?"

"You'll see," said Starlight. "We're almost there."

He led the way through a narrow tunnel and out onto an equally narrow walkway, and there they stopped. All around them there was nothing but darkness. Light from the tunnel didn't extend beyond the walkway. Steel glanced uncertainly about him. Although he couldn't see more than a yard in any direction, he was nonetheless disturbed by the faint echo that accompanied even the smallest sound. And then huge lights flared overhead as Starlight fumbled at a wall control, and Steel shrank back against the wall as the main cargo bay sprang into being before him. The bay was a single vast chamber of ribbed steel a hundred thousand yards square. Golden light shimmered on the walls and reflected back from the thousands of suspended animation units that filled the cargo bay. The surviving refugees from Tannim slept soundly, undisturbed. Stacked one upon the other from wall to wall and from floor to ceiling, the sleep cylinders lay waiting like so many crystal coffins.

"Tannim was already under attack when I raised ship," said Starlight, moving slowly along the narrow walkway, which now showed itself to be set high up on the cargo bay wall. Steel and Topaz followed close behind him. Within the nearest cylinders, they could just make out a few of the refugees, floating like shadows in ice. "The Imperial Fleet was dropping out of hyperspace by the hundreds. Refugee ships were being blasted out of the sky all around me. The *Balefire* was under attack, and my shields were giving out. I needed more power, so I took it from the sleep cylinder support systems. I had no choice."

Steel frowned thoughtfully. Even with the extra power, the *Balefire* shouldn't have survived long enough to drop into hyperspace. He shrugged; maybe she just got lucky. It happened. And then the significance of what Starlight had said came home to him, and he looked at the Captain of the *Balefire* with growing horror.

"How much power did you take from the cylinders, Captain? How much?"

Starlight leaned out over the walkway's reinforced barrier, and tried for a life support readout on the nearest sleep cylinder. None of the lights came on. Starlight dropped his hand, and turned back to face Steel and Topaz.

"The ship needed the power. I couldn't return it until the *Balefire* was safely into hyper. By then, it was too late."

"How many?" asked Topaz. "How many of your refugees survived the power loss?"

"Two hundred and ten," said Captain Starlight softly, bitterly. "Out of fifteen thousand, two hundred and ten."

CHAPTER NINE

Darkstrom and the Bloodhawk

THE wreck of the *Darkwind* lay half-buried in the snow fifteen miles due north of Mistport, in the shadow of the Deathshead Mountains. Between the city and the mountains lay a huge raised plateau covered with hundreds of feet of accumulated snow and ice. The curving mountain range chanelled the roaring winds so that they swept across the plateau in a single broad front, bludgeoning the snow utterly smooth and level, and wiping it clean of all forms of life. Even the Hob hounds avoided the plateau. The snows stretched unbroken and undisturbed for over twenty miles in every direction, and the temperature never rose above freezing, even in what passed for Mistworld's summer. It was a bleak and desolate place, and it kept its secrets to itself. It had no name; it needed none. Everyone knew of the plateau and its dangers. There were stories of the few brave souls who'd tried to cross it, both alone and in teams, but in all of Mistport's short history, no one had ever succeeded. You either took the long route around the plateau, or you didn't make it.

Things might have stayed that way for some time, if it hadn't been for Arne Saknussen's attempt to cross the plateau. He and his team had only been out on the snow five days when they made their discovery. Like many great discoveries, it happened entirely by accident. The wind had been blowing constantly for the last three days, and the snow was like a solid wall. The compasses were useless so close to the mountains, and Saknussen's party crept along at a snail's pace for fear of losing their direction.

And then the wind turned into a blizzard, and Saknussen called a halt. His men set thermite charges to clear out a hollow in which they could shelter from the storm, but in the panic of the moment they miscalculated the strength of the charges. The blast killed ten men and injured as many more, but when the wind finally died down, Saknussen and the other survivors found themselves looking down into a hollow half a mile deep, at the bottom of which lay the wreck of the *Darkwind*.

That part of the plateau looked very different now. The sides of the hollow had been carefully sculptured and reinforced to provide easy access to the wreck. A series of windbreaks had been set up to protect the small town of fortified shelters that had grown up around the site. And down in the hollow more than half the *Darkwind*'s length had been painstakingly cleared of snow. The long stretch of burnished hull showed stark and alien against the packed snow, like the hide of some immense metallic snake. Great derricks and cranes stood bunched together before the only opening in the hull, ready to winch out the various pieces of technology as they were brought to the airlock. Seen from the distance the derricks and cranes looked like nothing so much as awkward matchstick men, bending and straightening endlessly against the blinding white of the snow.

Eileen Darkstrom clambered awkwardly down from the power sledge that had carried her across the plateau, and stretched her aching muscles. The glare from the snow was painfully bright despite her dark glasses, and the bitter wind cut at her like a knife. She pulled her cloak tightly about her thick furs, and stamped her boots experimentally on the packed snow. It seemed firm enough, but she didn't like knowing there was nothing under her feet but hundreds of feet of snow. Darkstrom decided firmly that she wasn't going to think about it, and moved forward to the rim of the crater to look down at the wreck of the *Darkwind*. Her gaze drifted hungrily along the length of the gleaming steel. Councillor Darkstrom had been Mistport's leading black-smith for almost twelve years, but she'd never forgotten her time as a starship Captain. And then she smiled wistfully as she realised her main concern now was how quickly the ship could be gutted for its technology. How are the mighty fallen.

She looked away, and glanced around as she waited for the Bloodhawk's sledge to catch up with her. All across the wide plateau the mists were so thin as to be nearly transparent. The midday sun shone brightly overhead, and no clouds moved in the clear blue sky. The Deathshead Mountains loomed up to her left and right; great blue-black crags topped with snow. They were supposed to be volcanic, and occasionally rumbled menacingly to prove it. Hot sulphur springs bubbled up out of their cracked sides, raising the temperature of the mountain slopes just enough to make them habitable. But so far, there were only a few human settlements on the slopes; the Hob hounds saw to that.

Darkstrom looked back into the crater, and scowled. Earlier this year she'd pulled every string she could think of to try and get herself assigned to the plateau. The machinery coming out of the *Darkwind* made it a technician's dream, and she'd been determined to be a part of the project. But the Council wouldn't let her go. They said she was too valuable where she was, in Mistport. Now, finally, she was right where she'd wanted to be, and she couldn't stay. The only reason she was out on this Godforsaken plateau was to find out why communications were out between the farms and settlements and the city.

The coughing roar of a sledge engine caught her attention, and she looked round to watch the Bloodhawk's sledge glide quickly over the snow towards her. The low, squat machine slid to a halt beside her and then shuddered into silence as the Bloodhawk shut off the engine. He climbed gracefully down from the sledge and stretched elegantly. Even after several hours spent hunched over the sledge's controls, Count Stefan Bloodhawk still looked every inch an aristocrat and a gentleman. His furs were of the finest quality, and his cloak hung in a becoming manner. His slim frame and gracious bearing were more suited to a debating chamber than this desolate plateau. But the Bloodhawk had always shown a strong sense of duty and let nothing stand in his way, least of all his own preferences. Which was perhaps one of the reasons why Darkstrom loved him so very much. He came over to join her, and they hugged each other awkwardly through their furs. He put an arm round her shoulders, and looked down into the crater. The cranes and the derricks were still hard at work, the roar of their engines little more than a distant murmur.

"Stefan," said Darkstrom finally, "what are we doing here? Grief knows I can use a rest from the sledge, but we can't afford too many stops if we're to reach Hardcastle's Rock before nightfall."

"The Rock can wait a while," said the Bloodhawk calmly. "I've been talking to Councillor du Wolfe on the comm unit. It seems some of the technology leaving the *Darkwind* hasn't been arriving in Mistport. Since we had to pass the site on our way to Hardcastle's Rock, I said we'd stop and take a look at what's been happening here. It shouldn't take long. And besides, I know how much you've wanted to have a good look round the *Darkwind*."

Eileen Darkstrom shook her head ruefully, a slow smile tugging at her mouth. Sometimes she thought he knew her better than she knew herself. Saknussen's crater was actually some way off their route, but she hadn't been able to resist at least taking a quick look at the *Darkwind*. Once the Bloodhawk had realised where she was leading him, he must have contacted Mistport and looked for some excuse that would let them stop at the site a while. Bless the man.

"All right, Stefan," she said gruffly. "I suppose we can spare the time for a brief visit. What kind of tech has been going missing?"

The Bloodhawk shrugged, and led the way along the rim of the crater towards the nearest set of steps leading down to the *Darkwind*. "It's hard to say, exactly. Most of the technology seems innocuous enough in itself; it's only when you put the various pieces together and see what they have in common that the losses become rather . . .

disturbing. They're all the kind of thing that would be very useful to a clonelegger or a body bank."

Darkstrom swore viciously. She'd take an oath there were no cloneleggers on Mistworld, but there were several illegal body banks. The Council and the city Watch spent a lot of their time trying to find the evidence that would close the evil places down. She ran the various names through her mind, trying to pick out those with enough money or influence to stage something like this. "Vertue," she said finally. "Leon Vertue; it has to be."

"He's a possibility, certainly," said the Bloodhawk. "But there are others. Let's take this one step at a time. First, we'll check with the on-site security, and see exactly what technology has gone missing. Then we'll check which personnel had access to that technology. And then . . ."

"We play it by ear."

"Exactly, my dear. We ask questions, poke into corners, and generally make ourselves obnoxious. I can be rather good at that, when I put my mind to it."

"Indeed you can," said Darkstrom solemnly.

The Bloodhawk smiled. "So can you," he said generously.

They laughed together, and started down the wide snow steps cut into the side of the crater.

Inside the *Darkwind* it was comfortably warm. Darkstrom pushed back her hood and pulled off her dark glasses, glad to be out of the cutting wind and away from the endless glare of the snow. She looked curiously about her as the Bloodhawk stepped out of the airlock to join her. It had been twelve years and more since she had last set foot in a starship, but the gleaming steel corridor brought memories flooding back. It was almost like coming home again. The walls were smooth and featureless, unrelieved by any ornament or decoration. The Empire didn't want its crews distracted from their duties. The overhead lightspheres glowed brightly, probably powered by a site generator, but the gentle, almost inaudible hum was just as she remembered. The first time you joined a ship the never-ending hum from the lights drove you crazy, but after a week or so you just didn't hear it anymore.

Darkstrom walked slowly down the wide, spacious corridor, the Bloodhawk at her side. He said nothing, recognising that she was caught up in old memories, but stayed close at hand in case she needed him. Without looking round, Darkstrom reached out and took his hand in hers. She felt in need of some support. She'd forgotten how much she missed being Captain of her own ship. No, she corrected herself, that wasn't quite true. She hadn't just forgotten; she'd forced herself to forget. It was the only way to stay sane. She walked a little more quickly, as though trying to leave her memories behind her.

Captain Darkstrom of the *Daemon*. Five years of unblemished service. Not one unsuccessful mission on her record. One of the best Captains in the Fleet, and headed for higher things. And then one of her cousins was Outlawed for keeping the wrong sort of company, and Eileen Darkstrom was politely reminded that regulations clearly stated no relative of an Outlaw could be allowed to command a starship. They told her she would have to resign her commission, or face being cashiered.

At first, she couldn't believe they meant it. Surely the regulation couldn't apply to someone like her, with her record. When she finally realised they did mean it, despite all she'd done for the Empire, Darkstrom took her ship and her crew out into the stars, and turned pirate. She did well enough for a year or two, but took little pleasure in it. She had no taste for the endless blood and destruction. Eventually she made one raid too many, and the Empire was waiting for her. The *Daemon* went down, and she had to run for her life in a battered ship's pinnace. Some time later, having fled from ship to ship and planet to planet, she ended up on Mistworld and started a new life, first as a blacksmith and then also as a Councillor. Sometimes she wondered which of the two positions was the most important. Darkstrom shook her head suddenly. Things hadn't been all bad since she came to Mistworld. She had her freedom, something she'd never known in the Empire, and more importantly, she'd met and fallen in love with Count Stefan Bloodhawk. She squeezed his hand gently, and smiled as he squeezed it back.

The corridors slowly filled with people as Darkstrom and the Bloodhawk made their way deeper into the ship. Technicians had broken into the corridor walls and were checking through the systems to see what was worth salvaging. Darkstrom was impressed by how well the *Darkwind* had stood up to its crash-landing. According to the reports she'd seen, the stern was cracked open and the lower decks were nothing more than a mass of crumpled metal, but here amidships everything seemed more or less intact. Presumably the packed snow had absorbed some of the impact. Certainly the technicians seemed busy enough. Darkstrom moved casually among them, asking questions about the work, the technology; getting the feel of things. Most of the technicians relaxed a little once they realised she talked their language, and the Bloodhawk was careful to keep well in the background. He could be rather intimidating in situations like this, and he knew it.

On the whole, the men seemed happy enough with the way things were going. There were the usual complaints about living conditions, but nothing serious. They understood the realities of life out here on the plateau. Slowly, carefully, Darkstrom began to drop a few questions about the missing technology. Most of the men didn't know what she meant, or claimed not to, but there were enough grim faces and sudden silences for her to be sure that some of them knew more than they were telling. Darkstrom took a few of these to one side and pressed them for details, using all her charm and her Councillor's influence. And finally somebody whispered a name. Joshua Crane.

"There's nothing definite on him," Darkstrom said thoughtfully to the Bloodhawk, as the two of them made their way deeper into the heart of the ship. "But he's our best bet. He's been in the right place at the right time just a little too often. From the sound of it, this operation's fairly small-scale; it could be just a one-man job at this end."

"It's the man at the other end I want," said the Bloodhawk. "The man who gives the orders. I detest tech runners. When bloodsuckers like Vertue start hoarding machinery for themselves, it brings the whole of Mistport that much closer to collapse."

"Just remember we want this Joshua Crane alive," said Darkstrom, and smiled as the Bloodhawk reluctantly took his hand away from his sword hilt. "A dead technician might stop the looting for now, but without the name of his master, it'll only start up again later. I hope it does turn out to be Leon Vertue. I think I'd enjoy watching him hang. There's hardly a family in Mistport that hasn't lost someone to his damned bodysnatchers."

"He'll get what's coming to him," said the Bloodhawk.

Darkstrom smiled in spite of herself. The Bloodhawk was always so sure of himself.

The overhead lights grew fewer and far between as the two of them headed down to the main Engineering Bays. Few of the between-deck elevators were working, and Darkstrom had to rely on her old memories of the ladders and walkways. She was surprised at how much of the ship's layout she still remembered after all the years, but even so, she had to stop every now and again to make sure she was on the right track. The *Darkwind* was the same class and type of ship as her *Daemon*, but she'd rarely had occasion to visit her own Engineering Bays in person. It was on one of her brief stops to get her bearings that she first got the feeling she was being watched. A few corridors and several sharp turns later, she was sure of it. She glanced at the Bloodhawk to see if he'd noticed it too, and almost smiled as she saw his hand was near his sword hilt again. He met her eyes and nodded slightly. They stopped at the next intersection and looked casually about them, as though checking their route.

"He's behind us," said the Bloodhawk quietly, his lips barely moving. "About seven o'clock."

"Got him," said Darkstrom softly. "Do you think he's got a gun?"

"No. If he had, he'd have used it by now. I think it would be best if we split up. I'll go back the way we came, as though I'm heading back to the main section. Then, when he goes after you, I'll circle round and take him from behind."

"Sounds fine to me."

"You don't mind being used as bait?"

"Stefan, I can take care of myself in a fight. I wear a sword, and I know how to use it. You really must stop worrying about me. Now, on your way. And remember, we want him alive."

"I'll remember."

He turned and walked unhurriedly back down the corridor, while Darkstrom strode off towards Engineering. The hairs on the back of her neck prickled uncomfortably, and she was hard pressed to keep her hand away from her sword. She could feel the unseen watcher's presence. He was very close now. She was tempted to stop and look around, but she didn't. Her instincts told her he was there, and they'd never played her false before. She kept her hand away from the sword on her hip, and tried hard to look unconcerned. And yet despite all her instincts and anticipation, the arm that snaked suddenly round her throat caught her completely by surprise. She started to struggle, and then stopped as her attacker held up a vicious barbed dirk before her eyes.

"Shout out and I'll kill you," rasped a quiet voice beside her ear. "Who are you?"

"I'm Councillor Darkstrom."

"You picked the wrong place to go looking for trouble, Councillor," said the quiet voice. "And you really shouldn't have sent your friend away."

"He'll be back."

"Not in time."

"Are you Joshua Crane?"

There was a slight pause. "You just said the wrong thing, Councillor. Anything else, and I might have let you go, but now you know my name. . . ."

"I'm not the only one who knows."

"Then I'll just have to take care of your friend as well. It's too late now for the Council to send anybody else. The last consignment's already gone, and I'll be following it as soon as I've taken care of this last bit of business. There's a lot of money waiting for me in Mistport, and neither you nor anyone else is going to stop me."

"You can't kill a Councillor and get away with it." Darkstrom kept her voice calm and even, trying hard to sound confident. Crane just laughed.

"You'd be surprised what you can get away with, Councillor. You really shouldn't have let your friend go. Now I don't have to hurry this. I can have a little . . . fun, first. Fun for me, that is. I don't think you're going to enjoy it much, Councillor."

The dirk gleamed dully in the dim light as Crane turned it slowly back and forth. The barbed steel edge moved gradually closer to Darkstrom's face, and she tried to pull her head away. Crane tightened his stranglehold, and she couldn't move at all. The point of the dirk bit into her face, just above the right cheekbone, and a thin stream of blood rilled down her face. Crane slowly pulled the dirk down, lengthening the cut he'd made. Even above the pain, Darkstrom could feel the faint tug of her flesh parting under the keen edge, and the fresh blood that dribbled down her face. She groaned once, and then slammed her elbow back into Crane's ribs. Twelve years as a blacksmith had given Darkstrom a good set of muscles, and Crane grunted loudly as the sudden blow drove the air from his lungs. The dirk stopped moving, and Darkstrom back-elbowed him again, putting all her strength into it. Crane's stranglehold loosened. She stamped down hard on his left instep, and felt a bone crack under her boot. The dirk fell away from her face as Crane moaned with pain, and she threw herself forward, out of his reach. She hit the floor rolling and was quickly back on her feet, reaching for her sword. And then she stopped, and watched grimly as Crane fell heavily to the floor, clutching with desperate hands at the great crimson wound in his neck. Blood streamed through his fingers as he lay twitching on the floor, and then his hands fell away from his neck, and he lay still. After a moment, he stopped breathing. The Bloodhawk stepped out of the shadows, stared briefly at the unmoving body, and nodded, satisfied. He set about cleaning his sword with a piece of cloth. Darkstrom shook her head angrily.

"Dammit, Stefan, we wanted him alive!"

"I couldn't risk it. He might have killed you."

"I could have handled him."

"Perhaps. But he had steel in his hand and you didn't, and I didn't like the odds. There's blood on your face. Use this."

Darkstrom scowled at him, and then took the cloth he was holding out to her. She knew a peace offering when she saw one. She pressed the cloth to her face and dabbed gingerly at the narrow cut. It wasn't a bad cut, as cuts go.

"Are you all right, my dear?"

"I'm fine, Stefan. It's only a scratch."

"I was worried about you."

"Yes. I know. Let's get out of here. We can send some men back to clean up this mess."

"Did Crane mention any names to you; like Leon Vertue?"

"No. Just that there was money waiting for him in Mistport."

The Bloodhawk frowned thoughtfully. "Without a name, I don't think we can justify turning back. Our mission to restore communications with the city is too important."

"You're right, unfortunately. But it would have been nice to finally nail Leon Vertue."

"Yes," said the Bloodhawk, as he guided her back down the dimly lit steel corridor. "But don't worry, my dear; I promise you, he'll get what's coming to him."

CHAPTER TEN

Mary

NIGHT lay heavily over Mistport, and the full moon shone dimly through the thick mists that curled across the landing pads. Jamie Royal huddled inside his threadbare grey cloak and peered about him from the safety of the perimeter shadows. The landing field was deserted, and even the marker torches were burning low. He pulled a map from inside his cloak and studied it carefully by the light of a pencil torch. The small spot of light danced across the unsteady map as his hands shook violently from the freezing cold. Jamie swore under his breath, and fought to keep his hands still. The night was cold, and getting colder. Every breath seared his lungs, and he couldn't stop his teeth from chattering. He put the cold out of his mind as best he could, and concentrated on the map. The sooner he was finished with this, the quicker he could get out of the killing cold. Only a fool or a madman would linger out in the open during Mistport's night. Only the foolish, the mad . . . and the desperate. Jamie scowled, and studied his map.

The starport perimeter was dotted with pressure fields and proximity mines, but the safe paths through them seemed straightforward enough. Jamie put away his torch, and then carefully refolded the map and tucked it into his pocket. He'd already spent most of the evening memorizing the safe routes, but he liked to be sure. He glowered into the swirling mists and swore to himself that this was the last job he'd do for Leon Vertue, threats or no threats. He'd thought his job was over once he'd delivered that damned crystal to the Hadenman, but Vertue had insisted on this one last service. Blackjack had stood silently beside the doctor, smiling coldly, waiting for Jamie to try and refuse. Jamie wouldn't give him the satisfaction.

But I'll get you for this, thought Jamie fiercely. *I'll make you both pay for what you've done to me, and to Madelaine. My sweet Madelaine . . .*

He smiled sourly, and shook his head. He was going to have enough trouble getting out of this with his skin intact as it was, without hatching wild schemes to get back at Vertue and Blackjack. Revenge would have to wait for another time, assuming he ever came up with a plan worth a damn. Jamie glanced about him, listening carefully. No shadows moved in the mists, and no sounds disturbed the silence. According to his information, the Watch patrolled the perimeter at half-hour intervals. Plenty of time to sneak through the port defences and hide himself in the mists. Assuming nothing went wrong. He took a deep breath, and moved cautiously forward out onto the landing field.

The proximity mines were easy enough to spot, now that he knew what he was looking for, but the pressure fields were undetectable to the naked eye. The first you knew about tripping one was when the Watchmen came charging out of nowhere to grab you. Jamie gritted his teeth and plunged on into the mists. Either the map was right, or it wasn't, and if it wasn't, it was too late to worry about it now. The smugglers' ships loomed out of the fog to either side of him, long silver needles glowing ruddy from the flickering marker torches. The other pads were bare and empty, and Jamie felt horribly exposed and vulnerable as he padded silently through the mists. His imagination filled the endless grey haze with watching eyes and armed guards, and he could feel his heart hammering wildly in his chest. He stumbled to a halt as a huge dark shape formed suddenly out of the mists, and then he relaxed a little as he recognised the hull of the *Balefire*. He was in the right place. He padded quickly over to the reception area compound, and hid himself in the shadows of the outer wall.

He crouched on his haunches in the comforting gloom, and waited impatiently for his breathing to slow and his heartbeat to return to normal. *I'd make a lousy spy,* he thought ruefully. He shook his head and turned his attention to the straggling line of refugees emerging from the *Balefire*'s main airlock. They moved slowly, listlessly, across the landing pad, dressed in silks and fineries totally unsuitable for the bitter cold of a Mistport night, but none of them seemed to notice, or even care. Their faces were blank and their eyes were empty, and none of them looked back at the ship they were leaving. Lost and alone, hoping against hope, they came to Mistport as so many had before. Because there was nowhere else.

Jamie hugged himself fiercely inside his cloak, and straightening up, he stamped his feet hard to try and drive out the cold. He'd lost all feeling in his feet and hands despite his boots and gloves, and frost was forming in his hair and crackling on his face. Vertue or no Vertue, he couldn't stand this cold for long. If he couldn't find the refugee he was looking for quickly, he'd have to leave and take his chances with the damned mercenary. He snapped alert as he heard footsteps nearby. He glanced quickly round, and winced as he saw John Silver standing in the doorway of the reception compound. What the hell was the duty esper doing here? Jamie shrank back against the wall, trusting to the shadows to hide him. His mental shield was as tight as he could make it, and as far as Silver's esp was concerned, he should be invisible.

Silver moved away from the door, hesitated, and then walked slowly towards Jamie. The duty esper was frowning, but his attention seemed fixed wholly on the refugees. Jamie reached down and carefully eased the dirk out of his boot. The slender knife seemed heavy in his hand. He didn't want to kill Silver, but he couldn't afford to be caught. They hanged traitors in Mistport. Silver drew steadily nearer. Jamie pulled back his arm for the killing thrust, and waited for the duty esper to come in range. And then someone called from inside the compound, and Silver stopped and looked back. Jamie froze in position, hardly daring to breath. Silver turned and walked back into the compound. Jamie relaxed, letting his breath out in a great sigh of relief. He put away his knife, shaking all over with the relief from tension. The sooner this job was over, the better; it wasn't doing his nerves any good at all.

He raised his esp and cautiously probed inside the reception compound, careful to keep his own mind shielded. It seemed he'd arrived just in time; the first few refugees were just being processed. Jamie frowned. There were two other espers apart from Silver, and they seemed to be scanning the new arrivals very thoroughly, as though searching for something. He couldn't tell exactly what they were up to without dropping his shields and alerting the other espers to his presence, but he could guess. They were looking for the same refugee he'd been sent to find. Jamie grinned. Unfortunately for them, he was there to make sure they never got the chance to find her. He chose his moment carefully, and then delicately mindprobed the refugees in the compound. There were only four, and Jamie quickly dismissed them. Vertue had said she wouldn't be in the first few, and it looked like he was right. Jamie turned his esp on the refugees trudging slowly out of the mists, and probed them one by one as they approached the reception area. It was a long and wearying task, but Jamie stuck to it. He soon lost count of the refugees as they passed, but he didn't really give a damn. It was starting to look like he was wasting his time, and in a way he rather hoped he was. Treachery paid well enough, but his heart wasn't in it. He sighed quietly. There were still debts to be paid. . . .

And then a tall blond woman emerged silently from out of the mists. She wore the long, gaudy robes of Tannim's patrician class, now torn and grimy and spotted with dried blood. She couldn't have been more than twenty, but pain and sorrow had etched deep lines in her face. She was still good-looking, but she'd never be pretty again. She walked slowly and gracefully through the mists, staring straight ahead with a fixed, disquieting smile. Jamie reached out to her with his mind, and a single word answered him. *Mary.* Jamie smiled almost regretfully, and darted out of the shadows to intercept her.

"Hello, Mary. I'm Shadow, your contact."

She smiled at him, and Jamie shivered. Her eyes were cold and dark and very empty.

"Hello, Shadow. Mary has been programmed."

Jamie glanced quickly around to make sure no one had noticed them. Then, taking Mary's arm, he led her off into the swirling mists. He shot quick glances at her as he carefully retraced his path to the perimeter wall. She came with him unresistingly, not saying a word. Jamie was just as happy for her to stay that way. Her voice had been cold and unfeeling and somehow inhuman. What the hell had those Empire bastards done to her? And what did she mean, she'd been programmed? Jamie tried another mindprobe, but she had excellent shields, either her own or implanted by Empire mindtechs. Jamie shrugged, and hurried her on through the thickening fog. Vertue's contacts were supposed to have fixed it so that the control tower's sensors wouldn't pick them up, but Jamie didn't feel inclined to risk it any longer than he had to. He was beginning to get a very bad feeling about this whole operation. He glanced quickly at Mary. She was still smiling.

They reached the perimeter wall without being challenged, and Mary allowed Jamie to help her over the low stone wall. He quickly joined her in the narrow street, and then glared hurriedly about him. The mists were growing steadily thicker, and a light snow had begun to fall. Jamie shivered inside his thin cloak, and looked dubiously at Mary's flimsy robes. The night was cold, and getting colder. He was supposed to take her straight to Vertue's place, but the odds were she'd freeze to death on the way. Particularly if he had to waste time dodging the city Watch. Dressed as she was, Mary stuck out like a nun in a brothel. He had to get her some warm clothes, someplace where they wouldn't ask awkward questions. . . . Jamie smiled suddenly. The Blackthorn. Cyder was already connected with Vertue in some way via the energy crystal, so she wouldn't talk out of turn. And the tavern wasn't far off. Jamie took Mary's arm and hurried her along the dimly lit street. Cyder would be bound to have some clothes Mary could borrow. She might also have a few ideas as to what the hell was going on.

• • •

The Blackthorn was moderately busy when Jamie peered cautiously in through the open door. Most of the tables were full, and the bar was lined from one end to the other. The air was thick with smoke and the unrelenting chatter of people determined to have a good time while their money lasted. Jamie took a firm hold on Mary's arm and led her into the tavern. He wasn't sure how the crowd would affect her in her present state. For the moment she was looking straight ahead, ignoring everything and everybody, and Jamie tried to relax a little. He made his way to the bar, looking around for Cyder, but she was nowhere to be seen. A bravo in greasy furs reached out a hand to grab at Mary. She didn't react, but the bravo froze in place as he found Jamie's knife hovering before his left eyeball. The bravo swallowed dryly.

"Uh . . . no offence meant."

"None taken," said Jamie courteously, and pulled Mary on towards the bar. The bravo turned back to his jeering companions and did his best to pretend nothing had happened.

Jamie found an open place at the long wooden bar, and quickly filled it with Mary and himself. He waited impatiently for the tall, cadaverous barman to get to them, and glanced warily round the packed tables. He hadn't thought the tavern would be so full at this hour of the night. Mary's arrival in Mistport was supposed to be a secret, and here he was bringing her into a crowd of people who'd sell her out in a minute if they thought they could make half a credit on the deal. Jamie scowled. He couldn't take her to Vertue dressed as she was. She'd never make it. And anyway, Jamie felt badly in need of some advice. Things were getting out of hand. He looked round as the bartender finally approached, and tried for a relaxed and confident smile. It didn't feel at all convincing.

"I'm looking for Cyder."

"She's out on business, Mr. Royal."

"I've got to see her; it's urgent."

"I'm sorry, Mr. Royal, but she's not here. If you'd like to wait, she should be back any time now."

"Okay. Thanks."

Jamie took Mary's arm again and led her over to one of the private booths at the rear of the tavern. He sat down on one of the chairs, and then had to get up again and make Mary sit down. She stayed where he put her, still smiling gently to herself. Jamie collapsed onto his chair, and stretched out his legs. It felt good to be back in the warm again. He flexed his numb fingers, trying to work some feeling back into them, and wondered what the hell he was going to do. He couldn't afford to wait long, but on the other hand, he couldn't leave with Mary dressed as she was. He growled disgustedly, and silently damned Vertue to hell and back. It was all his fault, whichever way you looked at it. Jamie studied Mary thoughtfully. As far as he could tell, she hadn't moved an inch since he'd sat her in her chair. Her face was still calm and cold, and her eyes were far away. It was as though she was . . . waiting for something. Jamie scowled at her. She was still smiling. He looked away. The smile was starting to get on his nerves.

"Well, Jamie Royal, I didn't expect to find you here."

Jamie looked up sharply, his hand dropping to the knife in his boot, and then he relaxed slightly. "I might say the same about you, Suzanne. What is one of Mistport's leading Councillors doing in a dive like this?"

Suzanne du Wolfe shrugged, and pulled up a chair next to Jamie. "Passing through. Who's your friend?"

"Just someone I'm minding; a business deal. Look, Suzanne, I need a favour. I've got to take her somewhere in a hurry, and she can't go out in the night dressed like this. Have you got a spare cloak or something you could lend her? I was going to ask Cyder, but she isn't here."

Suzanne frowned. "Are you in trouble again, Jamie?"

"Aren't I always? These days, everything I touch turns to dross."

"Jamie . . . I heard about you splitting up with Madelaine. I'm sorry."

"Thanks." Jamie hesitated, and then looked steadily at Suzanne. "Suze, I'm in trouble. Real trouble. I need your help."

She smiled cynically, and leaned back in her chair. "All right. How much do you want to borrow this time?"

"No, Suze, it's not money I need. Or at least, not just money. It's your influence I need, your protection."

"Jamie, there's not a lot I can do for you. As a Councillor, I might be able to turn a blind eye to a few things, but . . ."

"You're not just a Councillor," said Jamie slowly. "You're also a Wolfe."

Suzanne's face hardened suddenly. "Du Wolfe, Jamie. I'm only a Wolfe by marriage, and Jonathan's been dead almost three years now."

"I know," said Jamie. "I helped hunt down the man who killed him, remember?"

"Yes. I remember."

"I'm asking you as a friend, Suze. Once you're made part of a Clan, you're always a part of it. They'll help, if you ask them. And they're the only ones who can give me the kind of protection I need."

"Come on, Jamie. Who could you possibly have upset that you'd need that much protection?"

"Leon Vertue," said Jamie quietly. "He's an Empire agent. He owns all my debts, and he had Madelaine killed."

"Oh, Jamie, no . . ."

"I've been working for Vertue these past few days; a mercenary called Blackjack made it clear that I didn't have any choice in the matter. Vertue's planning something, Suze, something big. I want out, but if I try to run he'll send that damned mercenary after me. I've got to have protection, or I'm a dead man."

"Jamie . . ."

"Please, Suze. I don't know what's going on, but it's got a real nasty feel to it."

"All right," said Suzanne du Wolfe. "I'll talk to the Clan, and see what they say. In the meantime, you'd better stick close to me. They won't dare attack you while I'm around. Now, what are we going to do about your lady friend here?"

Jamie Royal and Suzanne du Wolfe both looked at Mary, and then froze in their seats. Mary was smiling at them, and her eyes were darker than the night. Her time of waiting was over.

Cat hung by his heels from the roof's gutter and pounded angrily on the closed shutters with his fist, but they remained firmly shut. Cat scowled, and pulled himself back up onto the roof. Cyder should have been back by now. He crouched motionless on the snow-covered slates, lost in thought. The wind whirled the falling snow around him, and he shivered even inside his thermal suit. Finally he shrugged, and padded along the edge of the roof to the drainpipe. He swung easily over the edge and slid down the drainpipe to his emergency entrance: a narrow window that opened onto the hallway of the Blackthorn's upper floor. The shutter was always left unbolted and slightly ajar, as nobody but Cat was wiry and limber enough to clamber through it. Even so, he had a hard time of it when he tried, and Cat wondered if he was putting on weight. That was what eating regular meals did for you.

He wriggled free of the window frame, and dropped silently to the floor. He looked quickly about him, but there was no one there. The lamps burned brightly in their holders, but still there was a strange coldness to the air. He started down the hall, and then paused as a door swung open to his right. All of Cat's warning instincts suddenly kicked in, and he faded quickly back into the shadows of an alcove. The moment he'd done it he felt ridiculous. There was nothing threatening about a door swinging open. It probably hadn't been shut properly. But still he didn't move from the shadows of the alcove. Cat trusted his instincts. He studied the open door carefully. No light spilled out into the landing, and Cat realised that the room beyond the door was completely dark.

Nobody came out, and after a moment the door slammed shut. Cat waited, watching curiously, and then the door opened and slammed shut again. Cat felt his hackles rise as he watched the door open and shut time and again. There was a controlled, deliberate violence to the slamming door that disturbed him deeply. He chose his moment carefully, and then darted out of his alcove and on down the hallway while the door remained shut. The door flew open as he passed, and Cat flattened himself against the wall on the far side of the door. There was a pause before the door slammed shut again, but he didn't try to see what was waiting in the darkness beyond the door. He didn't want to know.

He padded softly down the corridor, scowling as he began to be seriously worried. The slamming door had to be making a hell of a noise, but nobody had come to investigate it. He headed for the stairs at the end of the hall, and then hesitated as he realised there was another door between him and the stairs. It was shut, and it seemed just an ordinary door. Cat approached it warily, but it remained closed. He studied the door thoughtfully, and then glanced at the stairs. More and more he was getting the feeling that something bad had happened in the Blackthorn. His instincts were telling him to get the hell out of the hallway, but the closed door intrigued him. He glanced back, and saw that the other door was still opening and shutting, opening and shutting. He looked back at the closed door by the stairs, and worried his lower lip between his teeth. Finally he took off one of his gloves, tucked it into his belt, and placed his bare palm flat against the wood of the door. If there was anyone moving about inside the room, he should be able to pick up the vibrations. But no sooner had he put his hand to the door than he snatched it away again. The door was shuddering. Cat licked his dry lips nervously, and forced himself to try again. Gradually he realised that what he could feel was the continuous thudding of somebody beating against the inside of the door with their fists. Cat backed away, and then hurried over to the stairs that led down to the bar.

What the hell had happened in the Blackthorn? And where was Cyder?

Cat hesitated at the foot of the stairs, facing the heavy wooden door that led into the bar. He never went into the bar when it was open for business; it wasn't safe. If the Watch ever found out he made his home at the Blackthorn, they'd never leave him or Cyder in peace again. And besides, after the two doors on the upper floor, he wasn't sure he wanted to see what was behind this door. But he had to find some answers. Cat braced himself, and pushed the door open.

Furniture lay scattered across the tavern floor like kindling. Deep gouges stretched across the walls like claw marks. All the mirrors were cracked and shattered, and broken glass was everywhere. Cat stood unmoving in the doorway, frozen in place by horror and disbelief. He looked slowly about him, trying to take it all in. The long wooden bar was cracked from end to end. Tables and chairs lay overturned, as through a strong wind had blown through the tavern. Wine and ale lay pooled on the floor like spilt blood. All the windows were broken, and the lamps and lanterns had blown out. The only light came from the smouldering fires that burned sluggishly here and there among the wreckage. And all around, moving in strange ways, were shadows that had once been men and women. Some sat listlessly, with their backs propped against walls or overturned tables. Their mouths gaped open, and their eyes saw nothing. Others lay on their backs, staring unseeingly at the ceiling, their heels drumming against the floor. Still more lay huddled under improvised shelters, their eyes tightly shut, their mouths stretched wide by raw, rasping screams that Cat couldn't hear. A few men and women lay dead among the wreckage, though no wounds showed.

Cat moved slowly forward. He glanced behind the bar, and winced. The bartender had died screaming, his hands pressed to his ears. Cat glimpsed a movement out of the corner of his eye and spun round, poised to run or fight as necessary. Cyder stood just inside the main door, surveying the scene in shocked amazement. Cat quickly made his way across the room to join her, stepping carefully round the various bodies. He took Cyder in his arms, and for a moment she clung to him, her face buried in his shoulder. Then she straightened up, and pushed him away. She looked around her wrecked tavern, and though her face was cold and hard, her shoulders were slumped in defeat.

"I'm finished," she said quietly. "There's no way I can raise enough money to put right this kind of damage. What the hell happened while I was gone? It looks like a bomb went off in here. A bomb, or a Poltergeist. Damn. Damn! Cat, you watch over the place while I go for a doctor. Maybe some of these poor souls can tell us what happened."

Cat nodded unhappily, not liking the idea of being left in the Blackthorn on his own, but by the time he looked round, Cyder was already gone. Cat shrugged, looked uneasily about him, and sat down by the open door to wait.

In a fire-blackened booth at the rear of the tavern, Jamie Royal and Suzanne du Wolfe lay sprawled across the table, quite dead.

Typhoid Mary had come to Mistport.

CHAPTER ELEVEN

Two Warriors

DONALD Royal's house stood near the inner boundary of Merchants Quarter, not far from the starport. When he and his wife had first moved in, their new home had been part of one of Mistport's most desirable areas, but that was many years ago. Now the house was old and crumbling and somewhat in need of repair, and so was the surrounding area. The great households had become lodging houses and tenements, and the old Playhouse was now a covered market. The well-off and the socially ambitious had long ago moved on to other, more reputable areas, but Donald had never moved. His wife had always loved their house, and since her death there was nowhere else he wanted to be. Besides, it was his house, and he wasn't going to leave it just to fit in with the vagaries of fashion.

Donald Royal had always been a very stubborn man.

He sat in his chair, in his study, and glowered unseeingly at his low-burning fire. Jamie had been dead nearly three days now, and the Watch were still no nearer finding out who killed him. They couldn't even agree on the manner of his death. His body had been badly burned, but the coroner's report had simply said heart failure. Donald shook his head slowly. He'd always said Jamie would die young, but he'd never really believed it. He hadn't wanted to believe it. Jamie had been his only living relation, the last of the Royal line. Donald had had such plans for Jamie, such hopes. . . . All gone now. One of the comforts of growing old was watching your children and grandchildren grow up, and helping guide them past the traps and pitfalls, and all the mistakes you made. There was a real satisfaction in knowing you'd done your best for them and they were the better because of it. And now it was all over. He'd outlived both his children and his only grandchild, and for what? To walk alone through an empty house, and spend the evenings sitting by the fire to keep the cold from his bones.

Donald Royal sank back in his padded armchair and let his eyes drift over the accumulated possessions of his life. Every painting and ornament, every piece of tech and stick of furniture, held its own special memory. Young Jack Random had sat in that chair opposite, when he first came to Mistworld to gather warriors for a rebellion on Lyonesse. That was more than twenty years ago, but Donald could still hear the fiery conviction in Random's voice as he spoke on the need for men everywhere to make a stand against the tyrannies of Empire. Donald had tried to explain that it wasn't as simple as that, but Random wouldn't listen. He'd gathered his little army, held them together with grand rhetoric and promises of loot and glory, and led them back to Lyonesse to face the waiting Empire. Some time later, Donald heard that the rebellion had been put down. Random's army had been cut to ribbons and the survivors hanged for treason, but Random himself had escaped, vowing revenge. Since then, Jack Random had led many rebellions on many worlds, but still the Empire stood. He hadn't yet learned what Donald Royal had learned long ago; that it would take more than force of arms to overthrow the Empire. The people still believed in the Empire, even while it betrayed and murdered them, and until they could be given something else to believe in, the Empire would continue its bloody rule.

Donald stirred uncomfortably in his chair as other memories came back to him. Lord Durandal had stood beneath that portrait as he expounded his mad scheme to enter the Darkvoid in search of the legendary Wolfling World. If he found it, he never returned to tell of it. And that ornate china vase had been given to Donald by Count Ironhand of the Marches, to commemorate the time they stood together with a single company of Watchmen and fought back over a hundred Hob hounds. Donald couldn't stand the ugly little vase, but he kept it so as not to upset the Count. Donald had always liked Ironhand. He frowned suddenly, as he remembered Count Ironhand had been dead for over fifteen years. Drowned, saving a child who'd fallen in the River Autumn. Brave and chivalrous, Ironhand, even to the end. They were all dead now; all the old heroes and warriors who'd held Mistport together and made it strong. Dead and gone down the many years, with only him to remember them and the glorious deeds they'd done.

And who'll remember me, when I'm gone? he thought slowly. *Who'll remember Donald Royal, except as a footnote in some dusty history book.*

And now Jamie was dead.

Donald shook his head slowly, a cold harsh anger building within him. He was old and he was tired, and he hadn't drawn a sword in anger in more than twelve years, but he was damned if he'd let his kinsman's death go unavenged. He levered himself up out of his chair and paced up and down before the fire, thinking furiously. Where to start, that was the problem. There was a time, not that long ago, when he could have just summoned a company of the Watch and demanded access to the investigation, but these days he had little real power. He'd lost interest in politics when his last opponent died, and since then he'd let things slip. He only stayed on with the Council out of a sense of duty. Besides, the Watch weren't getting anywhere. Going about it all wrong, as usual. Instead of concentrating on what happened to Jamie at the Blackthorn, they should have been asking what brought him there in the first place. There was also the question of what he was doing sharing a private booth with Councillor du Wolfe. They didn't have a damn thing in common. All right, they might have been lovers, but Donald would have sworn du Wolfe had better taste than that.

Donald scowled thoughtfully as he paced up and down, slowly grinding his right fist into his left palm. He'd have to go back further, try and discover what Jamie had been up to prior to his death. And that wasn't going to be

easy. Jamie never kept books or records on his various
dealings, for fear they'd be used against him in a court
of law. But who else would know? Donald stopped suddenly as the answer came to him. Jamie might not have
trusted anything to paper, but his old partner might have.
It hadn't been that long since they split up. And even if she
hadn't kept any records, the chances were she might know
something about why Jamie had gone to the Blackthorn on
that particular night.

Yes, all he had to do was find Jamie's old partner,
Madelaine Skye.

Donald stalked out of his study and hurried down the
gloomy hallway to an old, familiar cupboard. He fumbled with the key in his eagerness, but finally hauled the
door open. Inside the cupboard lay all his old swords and
daggers, still lovingly oiled and cared for and wrapped in
specially treated rags to protect the metal. He chose his
favourite sword and carefully unwrapped it. The length
and heavy weight of it felt good in his hand, as though it
belonged there. He smiled, remembering, and then slipped
the sword into its scabbard and buckled the belt around
his waist. He unwrapped a knife, and slipped it into the
top of his boot. He hefted his old throwing axe in his
hand, but reluctantly decided against it. He hadn't practised in so long, his eye was bound to be out. He put
the axe back, and instead gathered up a few useful odds
and ends and distributed them about his person. Just in
case.

He closed the cupboard door and locked it. The sword
at his hip seemed heavier than he remembered, but then,
he wasn't as young as he used to be. He grinned at the
understatement. Luckily, he'd always relied on skill as
much as muscle. He pulled on a pair of thick leather gloves
and wrapped his heaviest cloak about him. If he remembered correctly, Jamie had said Madelaine Skye had an
office in the old Bluegelt building in Guilds Quarter. About
an hour's walk, if he hurried. Donald Royal smiled. It
felt good to be doing something again, after all the many
years.

• • •

Guilds Quarter wasn't quite as impressive as Tech Quarter, but it was certainly just as prosperous. The squat stone-and-timber buildings had a smug, self-satisfied air of solidity and respectability. The streets were well-lit and reasonably clean, and beggars were firmly discouraged from loitering. Powerful men lived in Guilds Quarter, men on the way up. Or on the way down. It was that sort of place.

But Guilds Quarter, like every other Quarter, had its good areas and its bad areas. Madelaine Skye's office was in one of the worst sections, a shambling clutter of streets so close to the inner boundary that it was only just a part of the Quarter. The Bluegelt building was the tallest in its street, with three floors in all, but the brickwork was old and pitted, the façade was decidedly shabby, and the whole place exuded a distinct air of genteel poverty. Donald could remember when the Bluegelt had been one of the major merchant houses, but of late it had obviously come down in the world. He stood in the street outside, staring glumly at the dark, empty windows, and trying to get his breath back. When he was younger he could have made the walk easily, but at his age nothing came easily anymore. He moved wearily over to the great front door and leaned against it for a moment while he waited for his second wind. The lantern over the door shed a dirty yellow glow that illuminated very little outside its pool of light. Donald didn't care. There was little enough in this street worth looking at.

His breathing finally evened out, and he stepped away from the door and pulled his cloak tightly about him. The evening was fast turning into night, and he had to get inside soon, before the real cold began. He tried the door handle, and it turned easily in his hand. The door wasn't locked. Donald shook his head unhappily. The Bluegelt must really be on its way out to have such lousy security. He let himself into the building, and pushed the door shut behind him.

The long, narrow hallway stretched out before him, half hidden in shadows. A single oil lamp burned above the main door, its dim blue light flickering unsteadily as the oil ran low. Donald moved slowly forward into the hall, peering warily about him. The hall itself was clean, but bare. There was no furniture, no fittings, no portraits or tapestries on the panelled walls. The wooden floor had neither rugs nor carpet, and from the look of it hadn't seen a trace of wax or polish in years. The rats has deserted the sinking ship, and taken everything with them that wasn't nailed down. Doors led off the hallway to either side, but Donald didn't bother to check them. Nobody here would give a damn who he was or what he was doing, as long as he didn't disturb them. He glowered at the stairs at the end of the hall. He could clearly remember Jamie saying that Madelaine's office was on the top floor. Typical. Donald hated stairs. Even when he was feeling at his best, a long flight of stairs could still remind him how frail he'd become.

Three flights of stairs and several long rests later, Donald Royal stumbled to a halt before the second door along the narrow hallway on the top floor. The flaking paint on the door said MADELAINE SKYE: CONFIDENTIAL ENQUIRIES. Donald smiled slightly. He'd never met Skye before, but that sign told him a lot about her. A euphemism like that could mean anything you wanted it to. Basically, all it really meant was that Skye was for hire, if the money was right. He knocked politely on the door, and waited impatiently. There was no reply. Donald tried the door, but it was locked. He smiled wryly; at least somebody in this building understood the need for good security. He put his ear against the wood of the door and listened carefully. There wasn't a sound from inside the office. He straightened up and looked quickly about him, and then knelt before the door to study its lock. The only light came from a single lantern at the far end of the hallway, but it was enough for Donald's needs. He took a thin twist of wire from inside his left glove and inserted it carefully into the door lock. He jiggled the wire a moment, getting the feel of the tumblers, applied a little expert pressure, and the door was no longer locked. Donald removed the wire and slipped it back into his glove. Nice to know he hadn't

lost his touch. He pushed the door open and walked into
Madelaine Skye's office.

He shut the door behind him, and waited for his eyes
to grow accustomed to the gloom. The only light came
from a street lamp set just outside the window. Donald
shook his head grimly at the lack of shutters. The glass
in the window wasn't even steelglass. The security in this
building was apalling. He moved slowly forward into the
gloom as his eyes adjusted. It wasn't much of an office, as
offices go, but it had the bare essentials. There was a desk,
with a few papers on it. A fairly comfortable chair behind
the desk, and another, rather plain chair for visitors. Two
lamps he couldn't risk lighting. There was a battered old
couch, pushed up against the right-hand wall. A few neatly
folded blankets and a pillow lay piled at one end, suggesting
that the couch sometimes doubled as a bed. A large potted
plant stood alone on the windowsill. It had no flowers, and
its leaves were drooping.

Donald moved slowly round the office, trying to get
the feel of the place. It was cheap, but adequate. The
furnishings were rather functional, but there was nothing
wrong with that. Donald didn't much care for frills and
fancies, and distrusted those who did. And yet . . . the over-
all impression he got was one of desertion, as though Skye
had walked out some time ago and not come back. Donald
ran a finger across the desktop, and frowned at the trail he'd
left in the dust. He moved behind the desk, dusted the seat
of the chair with his handkerchief, and sat down. It was
even more comfortable than it looked. Donald stretched his
tired legs and looked about him. It was all very interesting,
but so far he'd seen nothing that would explain why Jamie
died. It had to have been some case he was working on. He
couldn't have been killed over his debts; everyone knew
Jamie always paid up eventually. Donald frowned thoughtfully. Maybe it was something he or Skye had stumbled on
by accident.

He took out his pencil torch, switched it on, and leafed
through the papers lying on the desk. Just memos and
reminders, mostly trivial stuff, and none of it current. The

paper should have been handed in for recycling long ago. No wonder there was a paper shortage. He looked speculatively at the two desk drawers. He tried them, and they were both locked. Donald did his trick with the wire again, and then pawed carefully through the contents of the two drawers. Again it was mostly everyday stuff, but finally he came up with a tan folder. It had been pushed to the back of the right-hand drawer, and left unlabelled. The folder contained three sheets of paper, each covered with notes written in a sprawling longhand. The writing was so bad he couldn't read half of it, but it seemed to be a report on the Hob hounds' movements around the outlying farms. Donald's frown deepened as he read on. As far as he could make out, the report seemed to suggest that the only reason the hounds were avoiding the outer farms and settlements was because they were being herded away. . . .

Donald stared blankly at the page in his hand. If this report was right, and Jamie and Skye had gone looking for more information, that might explain everything. Only the Empire had the interest and the resources to mount an operation like this, and they wouldn't have taken kindly to being investigated. Donald slipped the paper back into its file, and then frowned suddenly. If the Empire had wanted Jamie dead, one of their agents would have killed him simply and neatly, and then disposed of the body. They didn't leave traces, when it could be avoided. They certainly wouldn't have destroyed a whole tavern full of people just to kill one man. Donald scowled. Whoever killed Jamie, it almost certainly wasn't the Empire, which meant he was right back where he started. He sat back in his chair and hummed tunelessly, trying to make sense of it all. The folder and its contents were important, he could feel it, but he couldn't see how it linked in with Jamie's death.

"And just what do you think you're doing?"

Donald's heart jumped at the unexpected voice. He looked up, startled, to find a tall silhouette filling the open doorway. He sat up straight in his chair, and let one hand drift back to his sword hilt.

"I wouldn't," said the voice, and Donald moved his hand away again. He just had time to realise it was a woman's voice, and then he winced as the room was suddenly full of light, throwing back the gloom. His eyes quickly adjusted to the brightness, and he studied the newcomer warily. She stood just inside the doorway, holding up a storm lantern in her left hand. She was tall for a woman, easily five foot nine or ten. She had a tousled head of reddish-brown hair, falling in great waves to her shoulders. Her face was a little too broad to be pretty, but her strong bone structure gave her a harsh, sensual look that was somehow much more impressive. She wore thick mismatched furs under a battered but serviceable cloak. There was a sword on her hip, and her right hand held a throwing knife.

"I asked you a question," she said calmly. Her voice was deep, smoky, assured. "What are you doing here?"

"My name is Donald Royal. I'm looking for Madelaine Skye; I have some business to discuss with her."

The woman looked at him sharply, and then put away her knife with a quick, practiced motion. She moved over to the desk, put the lantern down, and studied Donald carefully.

"I'm Madelaine Skye. What do you want with me?"

The office seemed warmer and more comfortable with both its lamps lit. Donald Royal sat in the visitor's chair, which was just as uncomfortable as it looked, and studied Skye curiously while she talked. Having finally met her, it was easy to understand why Jamie had stayed with her for so long. Normally, Jamie's attitude to women had always been love them and leave them, and given the kind of women he usually went around with, it was hardly surprising. But Jamie and Madelaine Skye had been partners for almost three years, and this was undoubtably due to Skye. She was a dynamic yet very feminine woman, with enough energy in her to run a small generator. Donald had no doubt she'd made Jamie an excellent partner. He just wondered what the hell she ever saw in Jamie in the first place. He suddenly realised Skye was talking about the case she was working on at present, and he listened more carefully.

Information about the outlying farms and settlements was always hard to come by, Skye said, but of late it seemed to have dried up to the bare minimum. This had to be partly due to the recent storms, but even the esper network was having problems getting answers. Skye had been approached by Councillor Darkstrom, on a purely unofficial basis, and asked to look into the situation. She and the Bloodhawk were going out to Hardcastle's Rock to lead the official investigation, but Darkstrom had wanted her own, separate enquiries made at this end. Apparently she didn't trust some members of the Council.

Darkstrom hadn't said anything more than that, and for the money she was offering, Skye hadn't felt inclined to press her. So she started digging, and straight away she began hearing strange tales about the Hob hounds. From what Skye had been able to gather, it seemed the hounds were somehow being steered away from the farms and settlements. Communications had been all but sabotaged to keep a lid on this, but still the word had got out, in certain quarters at least. The men involved in the herding had gone to great pains to stay anonymous, but there was no doubt as to who and what they were. Empire agents. Why the Empire should want to protect the outlying settlements wasn't clear as yet.

Donald frowned, and leant forward. "But what has all this got to do with Jamie's death? Where's the connection?"

Skye shrugged. "Beats me. Jamie and I had already broken up before I took on this case. I'm not sure what he'd been up to lately; I've been . . . out of touch for a while. But it seems Jamie had been paying visits to a certain well-known doctor, Leon Vertue."

"The body bank doctor?"

"You got it. And everyone knows Dr. Vertue has solid links with the Empire."

"Maybe we should have a quiet word with him," said Donald slowly.

"We could try, but I doubt he'd see us."

"He'll see me. I'm a Councillor."

Skye laughed. "You think he'll give a damn, with his connections?"

Donald scowled, and nodded reluctantly. "All right, we'll have to approach this by a more devious route. We need someone who'll talk to us about Vertue's setup; someone who might know what Jamie was doing for the doctor."

"I know just the man, an old drinking companion of mine. A shifty little bugger called Donovan Shrike. He still owes me a few favours. But even so, the kind of information we're looking for is going to cost money. Lots of it."

"I have money," said Donald shortly. "Where will we find this informant?"

"At the Redlance."

Donald grinned suddenly. "Is that rat hole still there? I thought the Watch cleaned it up years ago."

"It's under new management these days, but by all accounts it hasn't changed much. Except for the worse."

"Very well. Let's get going."

Skye raised an unplucked eyebrow. "You want to go now? This evening?"

"Of course. The longer we leave it, the more likely it is the trail will get cold. Let's go."

"Wait just a minute. What makes you so sure I'm going to work with you? All right, you're Jamie's grandfather, and I know your reputation. I suppose everyone in Mistport does. They teach it in the schools these days. But that was a long time ago. I can't run a case and look after you at the same time."

"I can look after myself." Donald stood up, unlaced his purse from his belt, and threw it down on the desk. It landed heavily with a solid-sounding thud. "There's a hundred and fifty, in gold. As a retainer. You're working for me now. Is that acceptable?"

"Gold is always acceptable. And I was . . . fond of Jamie. All right, you've got yourself a deal. Just try not to get in my way too much."

"I'll try," said Donald. "Now can we please get a move on? I don't want to be caught out on the street when night falls."

Skye sighed, and got to her feet. She picked up the purse and laced it to her belt, then smiled suddenly at Donald. "I always wondered where Jamie got his stubbornness from."

Donald Royal hadn't been inside the Redlance for over twenty years, and was astonished to find the place hadn't changed at all. It was just as ratty and disgusting as he remembered. The air was thick with the smell of sweat and urine and assorted drugs, and the unrelenting clamour hurt his ears. It was a wonder to him that anyone in the packed crowd could hear anything in such a bedlam. He made his way slowly down the stone stairway into the tavern, followed closely by the cloaked and hooded figure of Madelaine Skye. For reasons best known to herself, she had insisted on pulling her hood all the way forward so that it hid her face. Donald had decided not to ask. He didn't think he really wanted to know.

No one paid him any attention as he made his way through the crowd to the bar. Donald felt just a little annoyed about that. On the one hand, the last thing he wanted was to draw attention to himself, but then again there was a time, not that long ago surely, when his entrance into a place like the Redlance would have stopped everyone dead in their tracks. He smiled sourly as he forced his way through the press of bodies. It was only to be expected, after all; half the people here hadn't even been born when he was busy making himself a legend. He stopped as Skye suddenly tugged at his arm and pointed out Pieter Gaunt, the new manager of the Redlance. Donald headed towards him, and was somewhat mollified when Gaunt recognised him immediately.

"Well, Councillor, this is a pleasant surprise," said Gaunt cheerfully, shaking Donald's hand just a little too firmly. "What brings the famous Donald Royal to the Redlance? Looking for a little something to warm your old bones, perhaps?"

Donald stared coldly at Gaunt. He didn't like the man's condescending tone in the least. "I'm looking for Donovan Shrike. Is he here?"

"He might be. Depends on what you want with him."

Donald looked steadily at Pieter Gaunt, and something in the old man's eyes took the mockery out of Gaunt's face. For a moment, something of the old Royal legend lived again, and Gaunt felt a sudden chill shudder through him. He remembered the things he'd heard about Donald Royal in his heyday, and somehow they didn't seem so unlikely anymore. The dark grey eyes locked unrelentingly onto his, and Gaunt swallowed dryly. *This man is dangerous*, he thought suddenly, and fought down an urgent need to call for his bodyguards. A cold sweat beaded his forehead.

"I want to see Shrike," said Donald Royal. "Point him out to me."

Gaunt started to nod agreement, and then the old man's hold over him was broken as one of his bodyguards stepped forward to stand between him and Royal. Gaunt tore his gaze away, and leant back against the bar as the tension drained slowly out of him. He looked again at Donald Royal, and saw only an old man in a shabby cloak, but still he shivered as he remembered the dark grey eyes that had held him so easily. *That man is still dangerous. . . .*

The bodyguard stabbed Donald in the chest with a stubby finger. "When you speak to Mr. Gaunt, you speak politely. Got it?"

Donald looked at him warily, taking in the man's great size and musculature. Madelaine was nowhere in sight. "This is a private conversation," he said politely. "I don't see any need for you to get involved."

"Tough. You looking for trouble?"

"No," said Donald, "I'm not looking for trouble."

"Good. Because you're leaving; right now."

"I haven't finished my business yet."

"Yes you have. I say so. Want to make something of it?"

"I really don't want any trouble. Just let me finish my business, and then I'll leave."

The bodyguard smiled, and flexed his muscles. "I guess your hearing must be going. You don't seem to be getting the message. You leave when I tell you to. Mr. Gaunt has better things to do than stand around listening to scruffy old men who think they can throw their weight about. Now, do you want to walk out, or would you rather go out on the end of my boot?"

"Do you know who I am?"

"No. Don't care much either. You should have walked while you had the chance. Now I'm going to have to teach you some manners, the hard way. I think I'll start with your fingers."

He grinned unpleasantly, and reached out a hand to take Donald by the arm. Donald's fist whipped out from under his cloak and slammed into the bodyguard's gut, just above the groin. The bodyguard let out his breath in a brief, sobbing grunt. His face screwed up in agony, and then he collapsed on the floor. Donald slipped the heavy steel knuckle-duster off his hand, and put it back in his pocket. There was a sudden scuffling sound behind him, and he spun round sword in hand just in time to see Skye stab another bodyguard through the heart. Donald nodded his thanks, and turned back to face Pieter Gaunt. The manager of the Redlance looked at his two fallen bodyguards and shook his head sadly. He'd fully regained his composure, and if his face seemed a little pale, that was probably just a trick of the light.

"I don't seem to be having much luck with my bodyguards lately," he said evenly. "It would appear you haven't lost your touch over the years, Councillor."

Donald smiled. "I'm as good as I ever was, only nastier."

"So I see. Who's your anonymous friend?"

"Just a friend who prefers to remain anonymous. Where's Donovan Shrike?"

"He's in one of the private booths, third from the left." Gaunt gestured at the row of enclosed wooden cubicles at the far right of the tavern.

Donald nodded politely. "Thank you. Please see that we're not disturbed." Sword still in hand, he moved away without waiting for Gaunt's answer. Skye moved quickly in beside him, and Donald noted approvingly that she hadn't sheathed her sword either. The heavy blade was a

comforting weight in his hand as he approached the row
of cubicles. The crowd parted before him and Skye and
closed again after them, without ever once pausing in its
various conversations. Drawn swords were apparently fairly
commonplace in the Redlance. Donald stopped before the
booth Gaunt had pointed out to him, and knocked on the
closed door. There was no answer. Donald pushed the door
open, and then came to a halt. A short, scrawny man lay
slumped forward across the booth's table. His throat had
been cut. Blood dripped steadily from the table's edge into a
widening pool on the floor. Donald moved quickly forward
into the cubicle, and pulled Skye in after him. He slammed
the door shut, and then searched the booth for clues while
Skye examined the body.

"I take it that is Shrike?" he said tightly.

"Yes," said Skye. "He hasn't been dead long."

"Somebody didn't want him to talk to us. Gaunt?"

"I doubt it. Not his style."

Donald gave up on his search, and looked thoughtfully
at the dead man. "At least now we know we're on the right
trail. . . ."

"There is that, I suppose," said Skye. "Damn! He could
have saved us a lot of time. Now what do we do?"

Donald frowned. "No one will talk to us after this. They'll
be afraid to. But we've still got one name left, someone we
know Jamie was working with."

"Leon Vertue."

"Right. It's too late in the evening to go after him now,
even assuming we could get past his security. And anyway,
I want to do a little background work on him first. Maybe
I can find some leverage to use against him. Give me your
code number and I'll call you sometime tomorrow."

"No, I'll contact you. My office doesn't have a comm
unit. Give me your private code, and I'll be in touch."

Donald shrugged. "If that's the way you want it." He
looked at Shrike's lifeless body, and then looked away.
Despite all the many deaths he'd seen down the years, it
never got any easier. Sudden, violent death still sickened
him, in his soul if not his stomach. In a way, he was

glad. It meant he was still human. He'd seen too many killing machines in his time. They usually ended up killing themselves when they ran out of enemies. He turned and left the cubicle, and Skye followed him, carefully shutting the door behind her. They made their way back through the crowd and up the stairway, and out into the night.

From the shadows of his private cubicle, next door to Shrike's, the mercenary called Blackjack watched them go. As soon as he'd seen Donald Royal enter the Redlance, Blackjack had known Shrike would have to be silenced. He knew too much, even if he didn't realise it himself. Blackjack looked thoughtfully at the hooded figure with Royal. It had been a woman's voice in the cubicle, but he hadn't recognised it. He'd better find out who she was. But first, it might be a good idea to run a check on Councillor Royal. He might be nothing more than an old man living on his legend, but he seemed to be doing all right so far. Maybe Vertue was right to be worried about him after all. Still, if worst came to worst, Councillor Royal could always have a little accident. It shouldn't be too difficult to arrange. Perhaps a fall; everyone knew old men had trouble with stairs.

Blackjack left the booth and strode confidently out into the tavern, to follow Donald Royal and his companion. It wouldn't do for anything to go wrong at this stage; not when Vertue's plans were finally nearing completion.

CHAPTER TWELVE

Gallowtree Gate

CYDER stood alone in the wrecked bar of the Blackthorn tavern. The city Watch had been and gone, and the dead and the mindburned had been taken away. That had been three days ago, yet despite all Cyder's efforts, the bar remained a wreck. The windows were cracked and starred. Deep gouges had been made in the panelled walls; they looked like claw marks, but no one knew what had made them. The great brass clock over the bar had stopped a few minutes after two. Its interior was intact and undamaged, but still the hands remained fixed in position. The tables and the chairs were gone; Cyder didn't have the money to replace broken furniture.

There were no customers; people were afraid to enter the Blackthorn. Cyder didn't blame them. She hadn't had a good night's sleep since the devastation, and often woke trembling from nightmares she preferred not to remember. Cat had altered his sleeping habits to spend the nights with her, and she found some comfort in his arms, but even he couldn't protect her from the dreams. It wouldn't be so bad if she'd had some idea of what had happened in her tavern after she'd left. Out of all the victims, neither the living nor the dead had provided any answers. The brainburned were being treated in Mistport's one and only hospital, but so far not one of them had responded to either drugs or espers. Their minds were gone. The autopsies on the dead all yielded the same result: death by heart failure. In the end, all deaths can be described as heart failure. Three days had passed since Cyder returned to find her tavern a charnel house, and still no one could tell her how or why it happened.

Or why the four guests on the first floor had been driven quite insane.

Something evil had come to the Blackthorn, and traces of its presence still remained. There was a permanent chill to the air despite the roaring fire. Even the quietest sound seemed to echo on and on endlessly. Oil lamps and lanterns filled the bar, but still the empty room remained dim and gloomy and the shadows were very dark. Cyder stared about her, and then put aside the broom she'd been pushing aimlessly about the floor. She had to face the truth. Even if there had been customers, she had little left to offer them. Nothing less than a total refitting could save the Blackthorn, and she didn't have that kind of money. Cyder turned her back on the deserted bar, and made her way to the private stairway at the rear. She'd have to speak to Cat. She'd put it off as long as she could, but there was only one chance left to her now, if she wasn't to lose everything. A chance she had to take, even if it meant putting Cat at risk.

She slowly climbed the winding flight of stairs up to the tiny attic at the very top of the Blackthorn, wondering all the way just how she was going to break the news to Cat. When she finally pushed open the door, Cat was waiting for her, already dressed in his white thermal suit. His working clothes. Cyder smiled, and shook her head wryly. There were times when she wondered if Cat was a secret telepath. He grinned slyly back at her, and jerked his head at the shuttered window, asking if there was a job for him.

"Yes," said Cyder. "There's a job for you, my dear. But this is going to be a tricky one, and I have to do some thinking first. Come and sit beside me."

She sat down on the bed at the far side of the room, and Cat came over to sit at her side. He slipped an arm round her waist, and she hugged him to her. More and more she found she needed the simple unquestioning support Cat offered her. Cyder had spent all her adult life looking out for herself, fighting off her enemies with ruthless skill, and making opportunities if there were none conveniently to hand. She never forgot a slight, and she never let a favour go unpaid. She trusted no one, cared for no one, was beholden to no one. It was a lonely life, but it was hers. And yet now all her vaunted cunning and business sense had come to nothing. Her fencing income had dropped to an all-time low, and her tavern was finished. What little money she had left dwindled day by day, and she was fast running out of options. Cat stared worriedly at her, and Cyder looked at him almost fondly. *My poor Cat,* she thought wistfully. *All this time you've depended on me to do the thinking for both of us, and now, when it really matters, I haven't a bloody clue what to do for the best.*

Cat sensed her despair, and gently pulled her head down onto his shoulder. He held her firmly in his arms and rocked her back and forth, as though soothing a worried child. He wished he had words of comfort to give her, but there was nothing in his throat but silence. He gave her what ease he could, and waited for her to find her strength again. Sooner or later she would work out what to do, and he would go and do it for her.

Cyder buried her face in his neck, her thoughts drifting tiredly from one vague hope to another. She needed money, and in a hurry. She could always send Cat out to do a spot of roof running, but she didn't like going into jobs blind. A successful burglary needed to be planned days in advance, with every danger weighed and allowed for. And even then, there were far too many things that could go wrong. If Cat were to get caught on a job, she'd be very upset. He was her main asset now. She frowned fiercely. She didn't like the direction her thoughts were heading in, but as far as she could see, she didn't have any other choice.

It was all Steel's fault, anyway. The only reason she'd been away from the Blackthorn when all hell broke loose was because she'd been trying to promote a little business with Port Director Steel. They'd worked well enough together in the past, but this time all he'd offered had been a chance at fencing some of the loot he expected to acquire from the *Balefire*. And even that would have to wait till it had cooled down a little. Cyder scowled. She couldn't afford to wait; she needed the money now. All Steel's fault; if she'd been at the tavern when things started to go wrong she might have been able to do . . . something. . . . She sighed regretfully. No matter which way she looked, she kept coming up with the same answer: the only remaining deal that could help her now. A deal not without its share of risks . . . She sat up straight, and gently pushed Cat's arms away from her. He saw the business look on her face, and obediently sat alertly beside her, waiting for instructions.

"I have a job for you," said Cyder slowly. "There's no risk involved, as long as you're careful. I want you to go and meet a man for me. His name's Starlight, Captain Starlight of the *Balefire*. At the tenth hour, you'll find him in the Gallowtree Gate cemetery, in the Merchants Quarter. He'll show you a sample of his merchandise. If it's a good enough quality, report back to me, and I'll set up a meeting to arrange the transaction. Now, watch yourself on this one, Cat. Legally speaking, Starlight won't be allowed to take anything with him from the *Balefire*; all valuables should have been turned over to the port as docking fees. So, anything Starlight has, he must have smuggled off the landing field. And since Port Director Steel is known far and wide as an extremely suspicious man, the odds are Starlight is being very carefully watched. The Captain assured me he could shake off any tail long enough for this meeting, but I don't want you taking any chances, Cat. If Steel discovers we're trying to cut him out, he'll have our guts for garters. If you spot anyone, anyone at all you don't like the look of, don't try and make contact with Starlight. Just get the hell out of there and come straight back to me. Got it?"

Cat nodded. All in all, it seemed a simple enough job, as long as he watched his back. He kissed Cyder goodbye, did it again because he enjoyed it, and then moved quickly over to stand before the shuttered window. He activated the heating elements in his suit, checked they were all working correctly, and then pulled the cowl up and over his head. Cyder unbolted the shutters and pushed them open, wincing as a blast of freezing air rushed into the room. Cat pulled on his gloves, ran his hands quickly over his body to check he hadn't forgotten anything, and then stepped lithely up onto the windowsill. He nodded to Cyder, and reached up and grabbed the two steel hoops set into the stonework above the window. He took a firm hold, flexed his muscles, and then swung out of the window and up onto the roof. The shutters slammed together behind him.

The sun had gone down into evening, but the real cold of the night hadn't begun yet. Cat padded cautiously across the snow-covered tiles to perch on a weather-beaten gable. He stared calmly about him, getting used to the cold and judging the gusting wind. The mists were heavy, and there was a feeling of snow in the air. Not the best of conditions for roof running. Cat shrugged, and grinned to himself. The worse the conditions, the better he was hidden from prying eyes. It all equalled out. He crouched thoughtfully on the gable, looking for all the world like a ghostly gargoyle. A thought came to him, and his grin widened. If he was going to meet Starlight by the tenth hour, he was going to have to cover a hell of a lot of ground in a short time. And there was only one sure way of doing that. . . .

Cat swung down from the gable, ran swiftly across the roof, and jumped the narrow alleyway to land easily on the next roof, casually disdainful of the long drop beneath him. He hurried on, passing from roof to roof like a drifting phantom, moving gracefully from gable to chimney to guttering as he headed deeper into the corrupt heart of Thieves Quarter. Some half an hour later he dropped down onto a low roof overlooking the docks area and perched precariously on the edge, staring out over the dark waters of the River Autumn.

Thin streamers of mist curled up from the sluggish waters as the River Autumn meandered into Thieves Quarter and out again. The river ran through most of the city, stretching from boundary to boundary and passing through three of the city's Quarters. Iced over as often as not, it was still the simplest method of transporting goods through Mistport. No matter what time of the day or night, there were always barges moving on the River Autumn. Cat watched happily as the coal-fired barges slowly nosed their way through the darkness, a single lantern burning on their sterns, glowing like dull coals on the night.

Cat swung down from a slippery buttress and dropped silently to the empty dockside. He faded back into the shadows and looked cautiously round. A dozen crates stood piled to one side, waiting to be loaded, but there was nobody about. Even this early in the evening, nobody braved the cold unless they had to. The dockhands were probably huddled round a brazier in some nearby hut, just as Cat had expected. Frostbite was an occupational hazard for those who worked on Mistport's docks. The pay was good, but then, it would have to be. Cat had never been tempted. He waited patiently in the shadows as the barges drifted unhurriedly past him, the long flat boats appearing out of the grey mists like huge floating coffins. Ice forming on the surface of the water cracked and broke against the steel-lined prows of the barges. Cat watched, and waited. Finally a barge passed directly by the dockside, and choosing his moment carefully, Cat darted forward out of the shadows and stepped quietly aboard the barge. With the ease of long practice, he ducked under the greasy tarpaulin that stretched half the length of the boat, found himself a comfortable hollow, and tucked himself away, out of sight of one and all. The barge drifted on, heading out of Thieves Quarter and into Merchants Quarter.

Cat lay back in the darkness, and let the quiet rhythms of the water soothe him. He liked travelling by barge. Roof running was fun, but this was so much more restful. As long as the barge crew didn't find him. He stretched lazily. The barge would get him to Gallowtree Gate in plenty of time. For once, his job seemed reasonably uncomplicated. He should be finished inside an hour, if all went well.

Gallowtree Gate cemetery was ill-lit and ill-tended, and not even the heavy incense from the neighbouring church could hide the graveyard stench. Tall gnarled trees lined the single gravelled path that wandered through the cemetery, their dark thorny branches stirring restlessly as the wind moved them. Overgrown grass lapped around the neglected graves and their markers, and the high surrounding wall was wreathed in ivy. Headstones and monuments gleamed brightly in the moonlight, looming out of the mists like pale, unmoving ghosts.

Late though it was, a small party of men were digging a grave. Wrapped in thick furs and thicker cloaks, they attacked the hardened earth with vigour, probably because the exercise helped to keep them warm. Captain Starlight watched them a while, and then turned away, bored. The thief was late, and the evening was bitter cold. Starlight pulled his cloak about him, leaned back against a tall stone monument, and glanced briefly at the timepiece embedded in his wrist. Nearly half past ten. He cursed Cyder and her thief, and sipped hot soup from his pocket flask.

The *Balefire* was a wreck, and with high tech rarer than gold on this misbegotten planet, Starlight was stranded. He'd let his crew go, and soon enough they'd disappeared into the city, which swallowed them up with hardly a ripple to mark their passing. The refugees were gone; taken care of, one way or another. Now Starlight was finally on his own, with no duties or responsibilities to anyone save himself. For the first time in his adult life he was free, and he hated it. He felt naked. He was also broke. His ship and all its technology was forfeit to the port in docking fees. All he had left was the jewellery and other loot he'd acquired from his passengers, one way or another. Starlight frowned. They had no cause for complaint, any of them. He wasn't a smuggler or a rebel, just a starship Captain caught in the wrong place at the wrong time. He'd saved as many people as he could, and lost his ship doing it. He was entitled to make some profit on the deal. Assuming the Port Director didn't rob him blind first. Starlight shook his head angrily. All that mattered was raising enough money to buy passage offworld on one of the smugglers' ships. From what he'd seen so far, Mistworld was a singularly unattractive place to be stranded.

Not far away, the gravediggers were singing a bawdy song to the rhythm of their shovels breaking the earth.

Thick streamers of mist curled among the headstones, palely reflecting the full moon's gleam. The wind whispered in the swaying branches of the trees. Coloured lanterns hung from the massive iron-barred gates, their parchment sides decorated with scowling faces to scare off evil spirits. Starlight looked at them, and didn't smile. Everyone needed something to believe in, even a Captain who'd lost his ship. He drank some more of his soup, hoping the hot, spicy liquid would help keep the night's cold at bay just a little while longer. He'd been here less than an hour, and already the heating elements in his uniform were hard pressed to keep the chill from his bones. He shifted his weight as he leant uncomfortably against the tall stone cross, and brooded yet again on the foul luck that had brought him to Mistworld.

Footsteps crunched clearly on the gravel path, growing louder as they approached. Starlight stoppered his flask and slipped it back in his pocket. About time Cyder's thief finally showed his face. Starlight stepped away from the monument and carefully adjusted his cloak to let his hand rest hidden on the energy gun at his side. A tall blond woman wearing a patched grey cloak came steadily out of the mists towards him. Her sense of purpose and calm, unwavering stare disturbed Starlight, and he moved back into the shadows to let her pass. She drew steadily closer, neither hurrying or dawdling, and then stopped directly before him. Her head turned slowly from side to side, as though she were listening for something only she could hear, and then she looked right at Starlight in his shadows, and smiled. He stepped reluctantly back into the moonlight, his hand still resting on his gun.

"Captain Starlight," said the blonde happily. "I've been looking for you."

Starlight nodded stiffly. "I thought Cyder said the thief would be a man."

The woman ignored him, her eyes searching his face with a naked hunger that chilled Starlight more than the night ever could. Her eyes seemed very large in her pale face. She was still smiling. When she finally spoke again, her voice was harsh and urgent.

"I want my sapphire, Captain. What have you done with it?"

Starlight's eyes narrowed, and he nodded slowly. "So. You're one of the refugees I brought in, aren't you?"

"My sapphire, Captain Starlight. I want it."

Starlight eased his gun in its holster. "I've nothing for you, lady. I don't know what you're talking about."

"That really is a pity, Captain." She giggled suddenly, and two bright spots of colour appeared in her gaunt cheeks. "Look at me, Captain Starlight. Look at me."

Their eyes met.

Cat crouched low on top of the slippery stone wall as the gusting wind swayed a tree's thorny branches against him. He glanced quickly around, and then dropped silently to the damp grass below. All was quiet in Gallowtree Gate cemetery. The shadows lay undisturbed, and no one walked the single gravelled path.

Cat stared about him suspiciously. There were supposed to be guards to discourage grave robbers from the body banks, but the rusty iron gates gaped wide, unmanned. Cat shrugged. More budget cuts, he supposed. He glanced up at the night sky and shook his head disgustedly. If he hadn't fallen asleep on the barge, he could have been here ages ago. As it was, he was almost an hour late. It wouldn't surprise him if Starlight had got tired of waiting and decided to fence his loot somewhere else. And Cyder wouldn't like that at all.

Cat shivered, not entirely from the night's cold, and moved off into the cemetery, padding down the wide gravel path like a stealthy ghost. Moonlight shimmered on his white thermal suit. He would have preferred to stick to the shadows of the walls, but the graveyard was littered with overgrown and unmarked graves, and Cat was superstitious.

He found Captain Starlight sitting with his back propped against a tall stone cross, breathing harshly, staring at nothing. Cat knelt beside him and waved a hand before the staring eyes, but they didn't react. Cat scowled, the hackles rising on the back of his neck. Brainburned, just like the ones he'd found at the Blackthorn. He swallowed dryly, and fought down an almost overwhelming impulse to turn and run. It was like being caught in a nightmare that followed him wherever he went. He quickly brought himself back under control, and searched Starlight's clothes with emotionless proficiency. All he found were a few silver coins and a small, polished ruby. He studied the stone with a practiced eye. Good stuff, but with Starlight gone there was no way to get at the rest of it. Cyder definitely wasn't going to be pleased.

He kicked the stone cross in disgust, and then froze as he caught a sudden movement at the corner of his eye. All his warning instincts suddenly kicked in, and he darted out of the light and into the shadows of the nearest wall, disregarding any graves he might be treading on. Whoever or whatever mindwiped the Captain might still be around, and the same white suit that hid him in the fog and the snow worked against him in the dark cemetery. More and more, Cat was coming to the conclusion that he should stick to the roofs where he belonged. He looked cautiously around him. A dim movement not far away caught his eye, and after a moment he moved stealthily forward into the mists to investigate.

Two men lay trembling on the ground beside a freshly dug grave, their heels drumming against the wet earth. One stared up at the night skies with unseeing eyes. The other had torn his eyes out. Brainburned. Cat edged closer, and peered down into the open grave. His hackles rose as he made out a still form lying on the uneven earth at the bottom of the grave, its neck twisted at an impossible angle.

Well, thought Cat crazily, *he's in the right place.*

He shuddered suddenly, and decided enough was enough. He faded back into the shadows, clambered over the high stone wall, and fled back to the more understandable evils of Thieves Quarter. He didn't know that the dead man had been an esper, and was already dying when he fell into the open grave.

Sitting under the tall stone cross, Captain Starlight stared unseeingly at the open cemetery gates through which Typhoid Mary had left. Guttering lanterns scowled at each other in reproach. Although Cat couldn't hear it, Starlight was whimpering.

CHAPTER THIRTEEN

Blood and Terror

THE Hadenman called Taylor was drinking wormwood brandy in the Green Man tavern when Blackjack found him. The Green Man stood on the boundary between Thieves Quarter and Tech Quarter, where the lowest of the low mixed openly with the rich and powerful. It was a place where deals were made and plans were finalized. Secrets were sold and traded, or openly discussed, and the devil take the hindmost. Deaths could be arranged, reputations made or destroyed. At any time of the day or night somebody would be making a deal, to somebody else's disadvantage.

Nothing cheap or nasty, of course. The Green Man boasted luxurious surroundings, first-class cuisine, and an excellent wine cellar. Rare and precious tapestries decorated the walls, and an oil-fired generator in the basement provided electricity for lighting and heat. There was a subtle perfume on the air, and no one was ever ill-mannered enough to raise their voices above a murmur. There were standards to be observed. The Green Man took a straight percentage from all deals made on the premises, and had never failed to make an extremely healthy profit at the end of each year.

Blackjack stood just inside the door, looking about him. It was early in the morning, with the sun barely up, but still some fifty or so patrons sat drinking at the exquisitely carved and polished tables. The Green Man never closed. Blackjack looked thoughtfully at Taylor, sitting alone in an alcove, with his back to the wall. The bottle of brandy before him was almost half empty. He looked up as

Blackjack made his way through the tables to join him,
and nodded politely. The mercenary pulled up a chair and
sat down opposite the Hadenman. Taylor shifted his chair
slightly so that Blackjack didn't block his view of the door.
The two men looked at each other for a while in silence,
each waiting for the other to speak first.

"Have you heard about Sterling?" asked Taylor finally.
His harsh, buzzing voice grated unpleasantly on Blackjack's
ears.

"I saw it happen," said Blackjack. "She broke his back
with her bare hands."

"Fifteen hundred in gold," said Taylor flatly. "I want it
by tonight."

"What's the rush?"

"Sterling gave Topaz my name. It's only a matter of time
before she finds me. Assuming the city Watch don't find me
first. It seems there's a price on my head. Even my friends
don't want to know me anymore. They're scared of the
Investigator. I'd known Sterling for almost nine years. He
was one of the finest gladiators ever to survive the Golgotha
Arenas, and that woman made him look like an amateur. I
always knew she was dangerous. You should have told us,
mercenary. . . . Investigators are no more human than I am.
Anyway, I don't plan to be around when she comes looking
for me. I don't know what fool killed her husband, but I
don't have a snowball's chance in hell of convincing her
of that. I've booked passage offworld on a smuggler's ship,
leaving at first light tomorrow."

"Such berths tend to be expensive," observed Blackjack.

"Fifteen hundred in gold," said Taylor. "If I didn't need
him to fly the ship, I'd break him into little pieces and dance
on the remains. Now, mercenary, I can get the money from
you in return for my silence, or I can get it from Port
Director Steel, as a reward for turning you in. I really
don't give a damn which."

Blackjack looked at the Hadenman thoughtfully. The
rasping, inhuman voice held few shadings of emotion and
never rose in volume, but deep in the golden eyes Blackjack
saw something that might just be fear.

"What's so special about this Investigator?" he asked slowly. "All right, I've seen her fight. She's good, very good. But you're an augmented man. You should be able to take care of yourself."

Taylor shook his head, and drained the last of his brandy. He stared down into the empty glass, his face grim, his eyes brooding. "You've never heard of Investigator Topaz? I thought everyone on Mistworld knew her story. She's a legend in the Empire. Mothers frighten their children with her name. She's a Siren, mercenary. When she sings, she can rip your mind apart. The Empire trained her to destroy whole alien civilisations. By all accounts she was very good at her job. And then one day she turned against the Empire, or it turned against her, and she went on the run. Sirens are rare, and the Empire wanted her back, under its control. I think even then she frightened people. The Empire sent a whole company of the Guard after her, five hundred fully trained warriors. They caught up with her on a little backwater planet called Virimonde. She killed them all with a single song; the most powerful esper there's ever been. Add to that an Investigator's training in gun and sword, and you've a warrior I've no wish to meet in combat. Nor would you, if you've got any sense. Now, how soon can you get me my money?"

"Forget it," said Blackjack.

Taylor looked at him steadily. "Perhaps I didn't make myself clear, mercenary; you don't have any choice."

"There are always other choices."

"Do you think I'm bluffing?"

"No," said Blackjack. "I don't think that at all."

Taylor threw himself sideways out of his chair, and the blazing stream of energy from Blackjack's gun missed him by inches. The Hadenman was quickly back on his feet, smiling grimly. Blackjack pushed back his chair and rose to his feet, sword in hand. Taylor started towards him, and the mercenary backed warily away, holding his sword out before him. There were frantic scrambling sounds all around as the Green Man's patrons hurried to get out of the way and under cover. At the rear of the tavern a table burned fiercely, having absorbed the disrupter's energy beam. Blackjack holstered his gun, and switched his sword to his right hand. By the time the crystal had recharged, the fight would probably be over, one way or another. He slapped his left wrist against his hip, and a glowing force shield sprang into being on his left arm.

Taylor slowly circled the mercenary, his golden eyes unwavering and unblinking. His movements were calm and deliberate, with a disturbing fluid grace. He didn't wear a sword or a gun. He didn't need to. Blackjack hefted his sword in his hand. He'd never fought a Hadenman before, but he had faith in his abilities. He circled slowly to keep facing Taylor, careful to keep the gently humming force shield between them. For a while the only sound in the tavern was their regular, controlled breathing and the quiet slap and scuffling of their feet on the floor. Blackjack feinted with his sword and then cut viciously at Taylor's exposed neck. The Hadenman ducked easily under the swinging blade and threw himself at Blackjack's throat. Blackjack got his shield up just in time, and Taylor slammed into it. Fat sparks spat and sputtered on the still air, and Taylor fell back, shaking his head. Blackjack staggered back from the impact, only just keeping his balance. He'd been lucky, and he knew it. He'd never seen anyone move so damned *fast*.

Taylor picked up a nearby table and tore it in two, the heavy wood groaning as it ripped apart. The Hadenman pulled at one of the legs and it came away in his hand, a yard-long club of ironwood. You couldn't cut ironwood with steel; it had to be trimmed and shaped with a laser. And Taylor had just demolished an ironwood table with his bare hands. *If he's trying to impress me,* thought Blackjack, *he's succeeding*.

Taylor moved forward, and swung the massive club at Blackjack's head. He brought up his shield, and Taylor changed the direction of the blow at the last instant. The club twisted in his hands and slipped under the glowing shield to hammer into Blackjack's side, throwing him back. He felt his ribs break under the impact, and had to fight to stay on his feet. He coughed painfully, and there was blood in his mouth. Taylor came at him again and he backed quickly away, holding his shield low to cover his injured side. Taylor swung his club with blinding speed, and only a lucky stumble saved Blackjack from a crushed skull. He felt a brief wind caress his face as the club swept past his head, and then, in the split second that Taylor was still off balance from the force of the blow, Blackjack brought his shield hard across against the club. The shield's glowing edge sliced clean through the ironwood, and Taylor was left with a short stub of wood in his hand. Blackjack stepped quickly back, and crouched behind his shield again. Taylor looked at the wooden stump in his hand, and then tossed it casually aside. He looked at Blackjack and smiled.

Blackjack circled slowly to his left, pushing chairs and tables out of his way. He needed room to manoeuvre. His broken ribs were a solid blaze of pain, but he ignored them. He couldn't afford to be distracted. Taylor lifted his left arm and pointed at Blackjack. For a moment the Hadenman held the pose, and then he lifted his hand in a curious gesture and Blackjack's heart missed a beat as he saw a stubby steel nozzle emerge from a slit in the underside of Taylor's wrist. He started to back away, and then brought his shield across to cover his chest just as a searing blast of energy spat from the Hadenman's disrupter implant. The energy beam ricochetted off the force shield and shot away to demolish a nearby overturned table. Taylor lowered his arm.

Blackjack swallowed dryly. He had to get in close and finish this while he still had a chance. There was no telling how many other surprises the Hadenman had built into his body. Blackjack moved carefully forward, and Taylor came to meet him. He cut at Taylor's unprotected ribs, and the Hadenman's right hand shot out to grab the sword. The wide, blocky hand clamped firmly onto the steel blade and held it tight, despite the razor-sharp edges. Blackjack could see the flesh part as he jerked the sword back and forth in the Hadenman's hand, and caught a glimpse of implanted steelmesh beneath the skin. He tried to pull the sword free, and couldn't. Taylor raised his other hand and reached unhurriedly for Blackjack's throat. The mercenary brought his force shield across to strike at Taylor's arm, and the Hadenman quickly released the sword and jumped back out of range.

They stood staring at each other for a moment, and then Taylor suddenly crouched and leapt into the air with a single graceful movement. His augmented muscles carried him clear over the startled mercenary, and absorbed the landing impact with hardly a jar. Before Blackjack could even start to turn, Taylor's leg shot out in a vicious karate kick, slamming into the mercenary's back. Blackjack's face contorted at the horrid pain and he fell heavily to the floor, dropping his sword and nearly cutting himself badly on the edges of his own shield. He rolled awkwardly over onto his back, fighting off the pain, and pulled a throwing knife from the top of his boot. Taylor stood watching him, smiling. Blackjack threw the knife straight for Taylor's heart, putting all his strength into it. The Hadenman snatched the knife in midair, snapped the steel blade in two, and threw the pieces aside. Blackjack's shield flickered and went out.

Taylor moved slowly forward, savouring the open desperation in the mercenary's face as he scrambled backwards across the thick carpeting. The Hadenman flexed his hands eagerly. Blackjack slammed up against the far wall, and knew there was nowhere left to retreat. He fumbled at the steel band on his wrist, to no effect. The glowing force shield did not return.

"You should have checked your energy level," said Taylor. "It'll be at least an hour now before the crystal recharges. A lot can happen in an hour."

He leant forward, grabbed the front of Blackjack's furs, and lifted him easily off the floor with one hand. Blackjack hit him in the gut. Taylor didn't even seem to feel it. Blackjack clawed at the hand so easily supporting his weight, and then reached out with both hands to take Taylor's throat in a stranglehold. Beneath the rough, scarred skin the mercenary could feel a thick layer of steelmesh. Taylor struck Blackjack casually across the face, and blood flew from his crushed lips. Taylor hit him again, and Blackjack felt his cheekbone crack and break under the impact.

And then the force shield sprang into being again on Blackjack's arm, and Taylor screamed briefly as the shield's upper edge shot up to slice deep into his throat. He dropped Blackjack and fell backwards, blood gushing from the wide cut that had nearly decapitated him. He rolled back and forth on the floor, grasping his throat with both hands, as though trying to hold the wound together by brute force. Finally the flow of blood lessened, and Taylor's hands fell limply away. Blackjack rose painfully to his feet, and turned off his force shield.

"A timing device," he said hoarsely to the unmoving Hadenman. "An old mercenary's trick. I was beginning to think I'd set it for too long an interval."

He moved cautiously forward and checked the Hadenman's pulse and breathing, to be sure he was dead. He took his time about it, but finally straightened up, satisfied, and looked around for something to drink. He felt very strongly that he'd earned a drink. He headed for the bar, walking slowly and carefully. He had at least one broken rib, probably more, and his back was giving him hell, along with his battered face. The Green Man's patrons slowly emerged from their hiding places, talking quietly but animatedly among themselves. There was even a smattering of applause. Blackjack wondered if he should take a bow. He'd just reached the bar, when the talk died suddenly away into silence.

"You did well against the Hadenman," said a cold voice behind him. "I'm impressed."

Blackjack turned painfully round to find a striking medium-height woman with close-cropped dark hair regarding him calmly from just inside the door. She wore an Investigator's cloak of navy blue. Blackjack knew without looking that there was a hole burned through the back of the cloak.

"Topaz," said Blackjack hoarsely. His eyes went to his sword, lying on the floor too far away, while his hand hovered over his holstered gun.

"You've heard of me," said Topaz, stepping elegantly forward. "Nothing good, I hope."

"You're taking a chance coming here," said Blackjack. "No one here has any love for the Watch."

Even as he spoke, he could see the fifty or so patrons moving forward. It was an unwritten law, enforced by the richer and more powerful patrons, that the Watch left the Green Man strictly alone. It was a small price to pay to avoid open war. It was also understood that any Watchman who entered the Green Man did so entirely at his own risk. No one there liked the Watch, and most had old scores to settle. There was a general rasping of steel on leather as swords were drawn from scabbards. Someone took a bottle by the neck and smashed it against a table. Light gleamed brightly on the jagged ends of the broken glass. The Green Man's patrons moved slowly forward in a pack, united by an eager, vicious anger. Topaz stood unmoving in the middle of the tavern, looking coldly about her. And then she opened her mouth, and sang.

The pack fell apart as the song washed over them, scrambling their nervous systems and screaming pain through their bodies. Swords, daggers, and broken bottles fell unnoticed to the floor as their owners staggered back and forth, hands pressed to their ears, unable to concentrate on anything but the awful sound that was tearing through their minds. Topaz stopped singing, and the sudden silence was broken only by the muted cries and groans of the Green Man's patrons. They turned away in ones and twos, and then there was a rush for the rear entrance. In the space of a few moments the tavern was empty, save for Topaz and Blackjack.

All through the Siren attack the mercenary had stood to one side, untouched. He watched, fascinated and horrified, as Topaz took on a murderous mob and routed it in a matter of seconds. Maybe that story about the company of the Guard hadn't been an exaggeration after all. He wondered for a moment why the song hadn't touched him. He had no immunity; nobody did, not even another esper. It could only be that Topaz had deliberately focused her song to avoid him. He didn't need to ask why she'd done it. She still needed information on her husband's death, and she meant to get it from him. As long as he was careful what he said, he might get out of this alive yet. He watched uncertainly as Topaz moved slowly towards him.

"I don't think we have a quarrel," he said carefully.

"Then you think wrong," said Topaz, coming to a stop a few yards short of him. "I've been keeping an eye on Taylor. I knew that sooner or later his master would send someone to shut him up. You did rather well, mercenary."

"Thank you," said Blackjack.

"You're welcome," said Topaz. "Now I want the name of your master. He can tell me who murdered my husband. Tell me your master's name, Blackjack."

"Leon Vertue," said Blackjack steadily. "He runs an organ bank."

"I know of him. He's a coward. He might order a murder, but he wouldn't have the guts to do it himself. He'd hire someone else to do it, someone like you. I'll deal with him, eventually. For now, I want the killer's name."

"I don't know it."

"Your voice tells me you're a liar. Sirens know a lot about voices. By any chance, Blackjack, did you kill my husband?"

"It was an accident."

"I did wonder," said Investigator Topaz. "He was wearing my cloak, and in the confusion of the fighting and the hounds and the mists . . . I did wonder. Michael died because of me. I'll kill you slowly for that."

"Of course you will," said Blackjack. "You esper trash never did have the guts for a fair fight."

Topaz studied him silently, her head cocked slightly to one side. "You're trying to anger me," she said finally. "You want me to throw away my advantages in a rush of emotion. But Investigators have no emotions. Surely you know that."

"You're different," said Blackjack.

"Yes," said Topaz. "I am. Michael taught me to be human again. And so, when he died, when you murdered him, I swore my husband the mercenary's oath of vengeance. I swore him blood and terror. You know what that means, Blackjack, don't you?"

The mercenary didn't answer. Topaz nodded slowly, her face cold and emotionless.

"Very well. A fair fight, Blackjack. Then, when I kill you, I will be able to savour it all the more. Pick up your sword, mercenary."

Blackjack moved quickly over to where his sword lay, and stooped down to pick it up. He caught his breath as his damaged ribs hurt him, and for a moment everything disappeared in a throbbing blood-red haze. He gritted his teeth and forced down the pain, shutting it away in the back of his mind where it couldn't reach him. He grabbed his sword and straightened up again. His injured side felt stiff and binding, but that was all. His mercenary's training would keep the pain at bay for as long as was necessary. He looked narrowly at Topaz, and took a firm grip on his sword. The Investigator had to die. She knew too much, and besides, he didn't like people who interfered in his business. Blackjack smiled slightly. She really should have known better than to agree to a fair fight. He'd never fought fair in his life, and he wasn't about to start now. Especially not against some damned esper freak. His smile slowly widened as he advanced on the waiting Investigator. No need to hurry this; he had time to mix business with a little pleasure. He'd show her the real meaning of blood and terror.

Topaz smiled at him and sang a single piercing note. Blackjack jumped, startled, as the steel band on his wrist suddenly shattered and fell away. He stared stupidly at the smoking wreckage of his force shield lying at his feet, and then looked back at Topaz. She was still smiling.

"You wanted a fair fight, didn't you? Now, it will be."

She took off her own bracelet and put it in her pocket, drew her sword, and started towards him. Blackjack hefted his sword and went to meet her. They circled each other warily, their blades reaching out to rasp briefly against each other, testing for strengths and weaknesses. Blackjack struck the first blow, and Topaz parried it easily. For the next few minutes the empty tavern rang to the sound of steel on steel as Blackjack used every tactic and dirty trick he knew to try and finish the fight quickly. He used every skill he'd learned in his long years as a mercenary, and felt a cold sweat start on his face as he slowly realised that, this time, those skills weren't going to be enough. Topaz was an Investigator. He fought on, not giving an inch, searching frantically for something that would give him an edge. He was already hurt and tired, and with his modified force shield gone the odds were too even for his liking.

He stamped and lunged, his blade whistling through the air in savage cuts and thrusts, but somehow Topaz's blade was always there to parry him. Step by step, foot by foot, she drove him back, her face never once losing its look of calm, thoughtful concentration. Blood ran from a dozen cuts on Blackjack's chest and arms, and he couldn't even get close to touching her. Fear and desperation put new strength into his blows, but still it wasn't enough. And then he looked into her eyes, and saw the cold remorseless fury that drove her, and knew he didn't stand a chance. He backed quickly away, switching from attack to defence as his mind worked frantically. When the answer finally came to him, he wondered how he could have missed it for so long. He drove Topaz back with a flurry of blows, and then threw his sword at her. She knocked it easily to one side, but in that short moment the mercenary was able to step back out of range and draw his gun from its holster. Time seemed to slow right down. Blackjack brought the gun to bear on Topaz. His finger tightened on the trigger. And Topaz opened her mouth and sang.

Blackjack froze in place, unable to move as the song washed over him, scrambling his nervous system. Try as he might, he couldn't move his finger the fraction of an inch needed to pull the trigger. Topaz's song rose and fell, roaring through his mind, and Blackjack watched in horror as his own hand slowly lifted the gun and turned it so that the barrel was pointing at his right eye. He couldn't even scream when Topaz's song moved in his finger and pulled the trigger.

Investigator Topaz stared at the crumpled body lying before her. *Blood and terror,* she thought slowly. *I promised you blood and terror, Michael, my love.* She turned away, and sheathed her sword. She felt strangely empty. She'd taken a fierce satisfaction in the moment of Blackjack's death, but now that was gone, and nothing had come to replace it. There was still Leon Vertue to be dealt with. He had ordered Michael's death. It might be interesting to ask him why before she killed him. But somehow she already knew that Vertue's death wouldn't mean as much to her as Blackjack's had. She looked tiredly about her. Her rage and need for revenge had been all that had kept her going since Michael's death. Now she had nothing left to fill her life, nothing to stop her from thinking.

Oh, Michael, what am I going to do now you're gone....

She left the Green Man without looking back, and disappeared into the mists. For a time her footsteps could still be heard, fading slowly away, and then even that was gone, and nothing remained but the cold and empty silence of the night.

✝

CHAPTER FOURTEEN

In Jamie's Memory

SNOW was falling heavily the day they buried Jamie Royal. Thick fog enveloped the cemetery like a dirty grey shroud, and a bitter wind moved sluggishly among the gaunt and twisted trees. Donald Royal stood beside the newly dug grave and watched silently as the snow-specked coffin was lowered into the waiting ground. Cold Harbour wasn't the finest cemetery in Mistport, or the most luxurious, but it was one of the oldest. Four generations of the Royal line lay buried at Cold Harbour; five now, with Jamie. Donald bent his head against the wind-swept snow, and tried to concentrate on the priest's words. The old traditional Latin phrases weren't as comforting as they once were, perhaps because he'd heard them too often in his life.

He raised his head slightly, and looked about him. He couldn't see far into the mists, but he didn't need to. He knew where his family lay. His wife, Moira, was buried in the shade of the great East Wall. He visited her twice a week; sometimes to sit and talk, sometimes just to sit and remember. Not far away stood a simple stone monument carrying two names; those of his son, James, and his wife, Helen. Both had died in the war against the High Guard, more than twenty years ago. Their bodies had never been found, but Donald had put up a headstone anyway. He felt they would have wanted it. His daughter, Catrina, lay buried close by, next to her mother. She had married twice, both times to scoundrels, but seemed happy enough for all that. Best damned cook he'd ever known. Her restaurant had been famous in its day. She'd deserved better than a knife in the back from some nameless cutpurse.

And now it was Jamie's turn. Donald stared silently at the small group of mourners beside the grave. He hadn't expected many to turn up, and he'd been right. Madelaine Skye stood at his side, unrecognisable in her massive fur cloak and hood. Next to her stood Cyder, the proprietor of the Blackthorn tavern. A hard bitch, by all accounts. Her face was calm and her eyes were dry, but earlier on Donald had seen her place a small bouquet of flowers on Jamie's coffin. Her hands had been strangely gentle, and before turning away she touched her fingertips lightly to the coffin lid, as though saying goodbye. Beside her stood John Silver, dressed in dark, formal robes and cloak that lent his youthful features an austere dignity. The esper stared down into the open grave with dark, brooding eyes, lost in his own thoughts or memories.

There was no one else to see Jamie on his way.

Donald sighed quietly, and hunched inside his cloak as the wind whirled snow around him. He'd expected Gideon Steel to at least make an appearance, but he hadn't come. With all the problems the Director had it was hardly surprising, but . . . At least he'd sent a wreath. The priest finished his prayer, signed himself quickly, and closed his Bible with a quick, decisive snap. He murmured a few words of sympathy to Donald, clapped him on the shoulder, and then hurried away to his next funeral. The beginning of winter was always a busy time for funerals. The two gravediggers stood a little way apart, waiting patiently for the mourners to leave so that they could get on with their job. Donald took a handful of earth and threw it down onto the coffin lid. It landed with a heavy thud; a harsh, final sound.

"Goodbye, Jamie," said Donald quietly. "Rest easy, lad. I'll get the bastards who did this to you, I promise. I promise."

He moved back, and watched in silence as one by one the others each took a handful of earth and threw it down onto the coffin. The lid had been closed throughout the service. Jamie's face had been badly burned, far beyond any mortician's skill to rebuild it. Donald hadn't wanted to see the body anyway. He preferred to remember Jamie as he was when he last saw him: young, handsome, brimming with life.

Madelaine Skye came over to him and took both his hands in hers. She squeezed them gently once, and then stood back a way as Cyder and John Silver came to pay their respects. Cyder glanced briefly at the mysterious figure with its hood pulled down to cover the face, and then nodded politely to Donald.

"I understand Jamie died owing money," she said gruffly. "I've got a few credits tucked away on the side. If you need any help putting his affairs in order . . ."

"Thank you," said Donald. "I have enough money to take care of all his debts. But it was kind of you to offer."

"I liked Jamie. You always knew where you were with him."

"Yes. I didn't know you and Jamie were friends."

"Neither did I, till he was gone. I'm going to miss him."

She shook Donald quickly by the hand, then turned and left, striding briskly off into the fog. John Silver stepped forward to take her place.

"I only knew Jamie a few years," he said quietly. "Looking back, it seems like I spent most of that time trying to keep him out of the hands of the Watch. Life's going to seem awfully dull without him around to liven things up."

"Have you any news on his killer?" asked Donald politely. He already knew the answer.

"I'm sorry, no. But it's early days yet."

"Yes."

"Director Steel sends his apologies. The way things are . . ."

"I understand. Please thank him for the wreath."

"Of course." Silver looked back at the grave. "Jamie was a good friend, in his way. I wish I'd known him longer."

He shook Donald's hand and walked away into the mists. Donald Royal and Madelaine Skye stood together beside the open grave.

"I always thought Jamie had more friends," said Skye quietly.

"No," said Donald. "Not real friends. Acquaintances, business partners, and drinking companions; he had plenty of those. But not many friends."

"I suppose that's true of all of us, in the end."

"Perhaps."

"What about the rest of his family?"

"There's no one else. Just me."

They stood together a while, thinking, remembering.

"Madelaine . . ."

"Yes, Donald."

"Did you love him?"

Madelaine Skye didn't look at him. "I don't know. Maybe. I didn't know him very long." She stopped suddenly as her voice broke. "Yes, of course I loved him."

"Did you ever tell him?"

"No, I never did. And now I never will."

"Why did you and he split up? You seemed to be doing quite well as partners."

"We were. We had an argument. One of those silly things. It seemed important at the time."

Donald took her by the arm and turned her away from the grave. "Let's go," he said quietly. "We've said our goodbyes, and now we have work to do. Someone has to pay for Jamie's death, and I think I know who."

"Donald, you can't just walk into Leon Vertue's office and demand to see him. He has a high-tech security system you wouldn't believe, just to keep out people like us."

Donald Royal warmed his hands at the crackling fire, grimacing as the cold seeped slowly out of his bones. Skye's office was taking a long time to warm up, and he'd been out in the cold for hours. Skye had been talking to him for several minutes, but if he heard her words, he didn't show it. He stared thoughtfully into the leaping flames, his mouth a flat grim line. When he finally spoke, his voice was calm and even and very deadly.

"I'm an old man, Madelaine. You should have seen me in my prime; I'd have made your eyes sparkle and your heart beat faster. To hear the way they tell it now, I was a hero in those days. I'm not so sure myself; I was so busy charging round Mistport trying to hold things together that I never really had the time to think about it. I only did what needed doing.

"Since then I've lost my wife and both my children, and today I watched them bury my only grandson. I've outlived all my friends and most of my enemies, and seen my past turned into a legend I barely recognise. Jamie was all I had left. He was a wild one, but he had style and a kind of integrity. I had such hopes for him. . . . And now he's gone. Someone's going to pay for that. I don't care if Vertue's got a whole stinking army to hide behind; I won't let him get away with what he's done."

And then he shrugged and smiled, and turned away from the fire to face Madelaine Skye. "You don't have to go along with this, lass. I've got nothing left to lose, but you're a young woman, with all your life ahead of you. Jamie wouldn't have wanted you to throw away your life on an old fool's schemes for revenge."

Skye smiled at him affectionately. "Someone's got to watch your back. Look, we can't be sure Vertue is our man. I've been doing a little quiet checking up on him, and there's not a lot to go on. It seems clear that Jamie was doing some kind of courier work for him, but no one seems too sure what it involved. Word is that Vertue might be in some kind of trouble. He's cut back his organ bank business to the bare minimum, and his bodysnatchers have been quiet of late. There's even a rumour that Vertue's been trying to arrange passage offworld on one of the smugglers' ships. It's hard to get any real evidence, one way or the other. People are afraid to talk about Vertue. After what happened to Shrike at the Redlance, you can't really blame them."

"Any word on who killed him?"

"Nothing definite. Chances are that Vertue's pet mercenary had something to do with it, but again nobody's willing to talk."

"Well then," said Donald calmly, "Since we can't get the answers anywhere else, we might as well go and ask Vertue."

"It's not going to be that easy, Donald."

"How right you are," said a harsh, sardonic voice behind them. Donald and Skye looked quickly round to see a great bear of a man standing just inside the open office door. Almost seven feet tall, and more than half as wide in his bulky furs, his broad face was mostly hidden behind a long mane of dark hair and a thick bushy beard. His eyes were dark and sleepy, but his smile was openly cruel. He looked round the poky little office, and sniffed contemptuously. Behind him, four husky bravos flexed their muscles and practised looking tough. Donald looked at Skye reproachfully.

"We're going to have to do something about the security in this building."

Skye nodded grimly, and glared at the newcomers. "Business hours are over. Now, who the hell are you, and what do you want here?"

"I'm Stargrave," said the giant cheerfully. "You've probably heard of me."

"Sure," said Skye. "Protection, blackmail, and a rather nasty variation on the badger game. Last I heard, there was a thirty-thousand-credit reward out on you."

"Fifty thousand, woman. Get your facts right."

"What do you want here, Stargrave?" asked Donald coldly.

The giant chuckled quietly. There was no humour in the sound, only menace. "I do so admire a man who likes to get down to business. Well, grandpa, it seems you and the young lady here have been poking your noses into things that don't concern you."

"And you're here to warn us off."

"Something like that, grandpa. You've both been naughty, so you both get punished. She gets her legs broken; you get a good kicking. Nothing personal, you understand."

Donald laughed, and Stargrave frowned as he recognised the genuine amusement in the sound. "You think I'm joking, grandpa?"

"Not at all," said Donald. "It's just good to know some things haven't changed. I'm going to enjoy teaching you the error of your ways."

"He's crazy," muttered one of the bravos. "Let's get the job done and get the hell out of here."

"Right," said Stargrave calmly. "Only I think we'll break one of grandpa's legs as well. I don't like to be laughed at."

He moved forward, and the four bravos sauntered into the office after him. Donald glanced unhurriedly about him, taking in the layout of the office furniture and checking for possible advantages and pitfalls. Even allowing for the odds, it felt good to be back in action again. One of the bravos looked curiously at Skye, still largely anonymous in her heavy cloak with the hood pulled forward. His face suddenly went pale, and he stopped dead in his tracks.

"You can't be. You can't be! Vertue said you were . . ."

He screamed and fell backwards, the hilt of Skye's throwing knife protruding from his left eye socket. There was a harsh susurrus of steel on leather and Skye leapt forward, her sword swinging before her in a bright silver blur. Another bravo fell to the floor, grasping desperately at the wide slash in his gut. Skye turned quickly away to face her next opponent, and steel rang on steel as she forced the bravo back with the sheer speed and strength of her attack.

Stargrave and the final bravo drew their swords and then made the understandable mistake of going after Donald, assuming him to be the weaker opponent. Donald backed cautiously away, his sword held out before him, and then darted behind Skye's desk, putting it between him and his opponents. Stargrave and the bravo shared a glance, and moved to opposite ends of the desk. Stargrave grinned. Whichever way the old man went, they were sure to get him. Donald looked from one adversary to the other, grabbed a handful of papers from the desk, and threw them in the bravo's face. The bravo automatically put up a hand to protect his eyes, and Donald skewered him neatly through the ribs. Stargrave stood and watched, frozen in place by astonishment as Donald pulled back his blade and the bravo fell limply to the floor. Donald grinned. That was one style of fighting they wouldn't find mentioned in his legend. It might spoil his image. And then Stargrave was upon him, and there was no time for anything but swordsmanship.

Donald backed away around the desk, ducking and weaving and meeting Stargrave's blade with his own only when he had to. He knew if he tried a full block or parry, the giant's sheer strength would force the blow home. Donald kept backing away, his mind working furiously. Even in his prime he would have been hard pressed to match Stargrave's power, and he was a long way from his prime. Already his arm was tired, his grip was weakening, and his breathing was growing short. Donald smiled suddenly, his eyes cold and grim. That just made it more interesting. It had been a long time since he'd had a real challenge in his life.

He ducked under Stargrave's sweeping blade and cut viciously at the giant's leg. Stargrave jumped back, startled at Donald's sudden switch from defence to attack, and then a slow, sullen fear crept into his heart as Donald pressed home his attack. Stargrave had never bothered to learn much of the science of swordsmanship; with his strength and reach he'd never needed to. But now this old man's sword seemed to be everywhere at once, striking from everywhere and nowhere, faster and faster, till the gleaming blade was just a blur. Stargrave backed away, step by step, unable to believe that this was really happening to him. And then he came up short against the desk, and realised that his retreat was blocked. He couldn't go back and he couldn't go forward, and the sword, the sword was everywhere. He hesitated as his mind worked frantically, and in that moment there was a sudden burning pain at his throat.

He hurt me, thought Stargrave incredulously. *I'll cripple him for that. I'll cut out his tongue and put out his eyes. I'll stamp on his ribs till they crack and break. He hurt me!*

His sword slipped out of his numb fingers and fell to the floor. Stargrave looked at it stupidly. Something warm and wet was soaking his chest. He put his hand to it and his fingers came away covered with blood. His vision blurred, and all the sounds in the office seemed to come from very far away. The strength went out of his legs, and he sat down suddenly. His eyes closed and his head dropped forward as the last of his life's blood pumped slowly out of his severed throat.

Donald Royal leaned back against the wall and waited patiently for his ragged breathing to get back to normal. An interesting opponent, but not very bright. He turned to see how Skye was doing, but she had already killed her man, and was busily searching through his pockets.

"Anything interesting?" asked Donald.

Skye held up a bulging purse and hefted it in her hand. It clinked musically. "I hate working for nothing," said Skye calmly. She straightened up, tied the purse onto her belt, and looked round her office. The five dead men had shed a lot of blood. Skye wrinkled her nose, and scowled. "What a mess. Why couldn't they have attacked us on the street? Ah well. We'd better get out of here before someone calls the Watch."

"Right," said Donald, pushing himself away from the wall. "You can stay at my place for a while. I've got plenty of rooms. Do you still have any doubts that Vertue is our man?"

"None at all."

"Good." Donald hefted his sword thoughtfully. "As soon as things have quieted down some, I think we'll pay him a little visit. I'm quite looking forward to speaking with Dr. Leon Vertue."

CHAPTER FIFTEEN

The Closing Trap

TYPHOID Mary stalked the city streets, hidden in the curling mists.

Mary wasn't really insane, just programmed. The Empire had altered her according to its needs, but Mary never knew that. As far as she knew, she was just another refugee, running from the Empire. Time moved for her in fits and starts, and memories from one day rarely passed to the next. The only constants in her shifting life were her terror of being captured and handed back to the Empire, and her need for the object she sought; the desperate, overwhelming need that kept her roaming the mist-choked streets and would not let her rest.

When she was a child on her father's estate, they'd called her greedy. Her mother said Mary had a sweet tooth; if she saw something pretty, she just couldn't resist it. Her father gave her a sapphire for her tenth birthday, because she pleaded for it so; a small polished stone with a heart of cold blue fire. It cost her father a great deal, since sapphires are very rare, but Mary neither knew nor cared. It was enough that it was pretty and she had wanted it. She hung it from a chain of rolled gold, and wore it always round her neck. The sapphire became her constant companion in good times and bad, through triumph and heartbreak. Now it was gone, and she wanted it back.

Someone had stolen it from her. She didn't know who or why, but ever and always a dark whisper in the back of her mind kept her moving, searching, hunting. From time to time it seemed to her that she'd found the thief, but somehow it never was, and she had to go on looking. Sooner or later, she would find her sapphire. She had to.

Scurrying from shadow to shadow, ever fearful of the Empire, Mary roamed the crooked streets and alleyways of Mistport. Deep within her, madness stirred. Behind her lay a trail of the dead and the brainburned, but she never knew that. Typhoid Mary had been programmed.

She hurried through the narrow streets, hidden in the mists. In the houses she passed, children woke screaming in the night and would not be comforted.

"People are dying by the hundreds, Investigator! I don't have the time or the patience to indulge your vendetta against Vertue any longer!" Steel hammered on the nearest console with his fist to make his point, and then growled under his breath as Topaz looked calmly back at him. Steel breathed deeply, and fought to hold onto his temper.

Behind her calm mask, Investigator Topaz felt deathly tired. It had all seemed so simple when she began. All she had to do was track down her husband's murderer and kill him, and then everything would be settled and she could carry on with her life again. Now Blackjack was dead, but nothing was settled. It might have been the mercenary's finger on the trigger, but Vertue had given the order. She didn't even know why. All she knew for sure was that Michael hadn't been the intended target. He died only because Topaz had lent him her cloak. He died because Blackjack had mistaken him for her.

Her first impulse had been to hunt Vertue down and kill him slowly, but she soon realised she couldn't do that. In the past few days she had given herself over entirely to death and destruction, and only Blackjack's death had shocked her sane again. It was the Empire that had taught her to think in such ways, the Empire that had taught her to kill and destroy. Over the years, Michael Gunn had shown her other ways to live, more human ways, and Topaz had thought her past was gone forever. Now she knew she'd only buried it deep down inside her. It was still there, and always would be, waiting to be called forth again. All she had to do was give up the humanity Michael had so painstakingly taught her. She couldn't do that, she wouldn't do that, not even to avenge Michael's death. He wouldn't have wanted it.

And so she had holstered her gun and sheathed her sword, and used her position in the city Watch to go after Vertue, using the law and all its slow-moving processes. It wasn't easy. As far as the law was concerned, Dr. Leon Vertue was a hard-working and honest citizen. Everyone in Mistport knew what he was and what he did, but there was no proof. Vertue saw to that. Those who enquired too deeply into his business had a habit of disappearing. But Topaz didn't give up easily. She fought on, step by step, working her way closer to Vertue and all his hidden dirty secrets, despite everything legal and illegal he could put in her path.

And all the time she thought how good it would feel to draw her sword and cut him down, and watch the blood flow from his dying body.

"Are you listening to me, Investigator?" Topaz jumped as Steel pushed his face close to hers. "Much as I sympathize with the loss of your husband, you can't spend all your time chasing after Vertue. It's not as if you had any real evidence against him."

"I have enough to satisfy me."

"That's not good enough, and you know it." Steel moved away and sat on the edge of his desk, which creaked complainingly under his weight. Steel ignored it, his gaze fixed on Topaz. "You haven't been here long, Investigator. In a place like Mistport, the Watch has to be above suspicion. There's always going to be a certain amount of graft and kickbacks; that's what helps keep the city running. But there's no place in the Watch for personal vendettas. We don't have many laws here, Investigator, but those we do have are enforced vigorously. They have to be. If they weren't, we'd fall into barbarism in under a generation, and the Empire would wipe us out. We survive because we're harder on ourselves than the Empire ever was. It's not easy being free.

"That's why I'm ordering you to leave Vertue alone. If he's broken the law, the law will punish him. Eventually. In the meantime, I need you here. Mistport's coming apart at the seams, and with the rest of the Council either dead or missing, I've ended up in charge of the whole damn mess. I can't handle everything, Investigator; I need people around me I can trust. That's why I went to so much trouble to keep you out of jail after you carved up Taylor and Blackjack. But if you keep going after Vertue, there's nothing more I can do for you. Vertue may well be as crooked as a corkscrew, but he's gone to great pains to hide it. He also has friends in high places. Very influential friends, who are presently doing their best to make my life even more difficult than it already is. You step one foot out of line, Investigator, and I'll have no choice but to cut you off at the knees. So, either you start pulling your weight, or I'll withdraw my protection and let the wolves have you. Is that clear?"

"Quite clear, Director. I had already come to the same conclusion myself; Vertue can wait. Acting under my instructions and your authority, the city Watch have sealed off Mistport. Nobody gets in or out until this plague's under some kind of control. Quarantine is enforceable on pain of death. Surviving victims of the plague are being held in isolation, and Mistport's medical staff are working round the clock to discover some common link between them. Now please be seated, Director, and kindly lower your voice. I don't care to be shouted at."

Steel scowled, and then reluctantly sank into the chair behind his desk. Outside his office, his staff worked furiously at their posts, struck silent by the thick steelglass windows that made up his cubicle. The plague had been running wild in Mistport for almost a week now, and they were still no nearer identifying it, let alone coming up with a cure. Even so, Steel couldn't help wondering where he'd found the courage to raise his voice to the Investigator. He was probably feverish from overwork and lack of sleep. He gestured for Topaz to sit opposite him, and she lowered herself gracefully into the stiff-backed visitor's chair. Steel's cubicle was designed for function rather than comfort, but from Topaz's relaxed air she might just as well have been reclining in her favourite padded armchair.

The Director looked down irritably at his crowded desk. His In and Out trays were swamped under overflowing piles of paper, most of them ostentatiously marked "Urgent." Steel hadn't bothered to read half of them. Of late all the news was pretty much the same, and he could only stand so much depression at one time. It was somehow typical that Mistport should undergo its first major catastrophe in years, and he'd be the one left in the hot seat. Darkstrom and the Bloodhawk were still wandering round the outlying settlements, Donald Royal had gone haring off on some dubious scheme of his own, and poor Suzanne du Wolfe was dead, one of the first victims of the plague. Steel sighed wearily. It was a sign of how desperate he'd become that he'd started to think he'd even welcome seeing the Bloodhawk again, if he and Darkstrom would just take some of the pressure off his shoulders. Steel came out of his reverie with a start as he realised the Investigator was talking to him.

"Director, what are the latest casualty reports?"

Steel punched up the answer on his command monitor, and glared at the result. "Worse than ever. Three hundred and forty-seven dead, and over two thousand brainburned. More cases are being reported every hour. And on top of that, dozens of buildings have been wrecked or burnt out at more than half of the sites where plague victims were found."

"We're under attack."

"I had worked that out for myself, Investigator." Steel turned off the monitor, and stared grimly at the blank screen. "The Empire's used us often enough before as a testing ground for new weapons, but there's never been anything like this. The nearest comparison would be the mutant virus they hit us with some twenty years ago, but whatever this plague is, the old vaccines don't even slow it down." He leaned back in his chair and rubbed tiredly at his aching eyes. Too much work and too little sleep . . . "None of it makes any sense, Investigator. The victims are always either dead or brainburned. No immunes, no in-betweeners, no recoveries. The survivors range from autistic to catatonic, but not one of them has enough mind left to respond to a psionic probe. We can't even discover how they contracted the plague."

"The Watch is undertaking preventative measures, Director."

"And a hell of a lot of good they've done. I've agreed to everything from quarantining victims' families to torching whole streets of houses, and still the bloody plague keeps spreading."

Topaz looked at him steadily. "We're doing everything we can, Director. If you've any other ideas, we'll be happy to implement them."

"I don't know what to do! I'm not even sure exactly what it is we're dealing with. The only clue we've got is that the first cases of the plague appeared soon after the *Balefire* landed. What's the latest news on that?"

"The field technicians are still tearing the ship apart, but so far they've come up with nothing."

"Great. Just great."

"Director, do you remember why you first called me in?"

"Of course. The port espers reported sensing something strange aboard the *Balefire*. But we checked every refugee to come off that ship, and every damn one of them was clean. We even broke open the sleep cylinders, but each and every body was where it should be, and as it should be. Unless there's some hidden compartment . . ."

"I doubt it, Director; the technicians would have found it by now. But we never did find an explanation for the espers' readings."

"You think that's significant?"

Topaz shrugged. "Who knows what's significant, at this stage."

Steel frowned thoughtfully, and clasped his hands across his belly. "The espers said they detected something strange, powerful . . . alien. Alien; could that be it? Some alien creature smuggled into the city, carrying an outworld plague?"

He stopped suddenly, and rubbed at his aching forehead. "No. It couldn't have gone undetected this long. Not in Mistport."

Steel and Topaz sat in silence for a while, each lost in their own thoughts. The monitor chimed suddenly, and the screen lit up to show the face of the duty esper.

"Director, I have a call from you. From Councillor Darkstrom."

Steel sat forward in his chair, grinning widely. "Great; put her through! I never thought I'd be so glad to see that grim face of hers again."

"I heard that," said Eileen Darkstrom dryly. The screen remained blank, but her voice carried clearly from the comm unit's speakers. "What's happened in Mistport while I've been away?"

"Death, plague, and devastation," said Steel succinctly. "I'm glad you're finally back; things have been going crazy here."

"Never mind that now," said Darkstrom briskly, "This is important. The Bloodhawk and I came across something very disturbing in the outer settlements. Communications between them and the city have been deliberately sabotaged, to prevent us from finding out that Empire agents have been herding the Hob hounds towards Mistport."

"Herding?" said Steel incredulously. "Are you sure?"

"Yes," said Darkstrom steadily. "I'm sure. Now, that was the bad news. The really bad news is that the Bloodhawk and I got here only just ahead of the main pack. We could see them, crossing the plateau; hundreds of the filthy creatures. They'll get here sometime during the next few days. You'll have to take every Watchman you can find and set them to guarding the boundaries."

"Darkstrom, I can't do that—"

"You've got to! Look, I can't stop and talk. I'm meeting someone and it's important. I'll see you afterwards, and you can fill me in on all the latest gossip then. Darkstrom out."

The speakers fell silent. Steel hurriedly punched a code into his monitor. "Duty esper, get Darkstrom back on the line. Now."

"I'm sorry, Director; she was calling from her comm unit implant. It's not a part of our comm net. We'll have to wait until she calls back."

"Damn. Very well, but I want to know the moment she calls."

"Yes, sir."

The screen went blank again, and Steel leant slowly back in his chair. "That's all I needed. First a city racked with plague, and now there are hundreds of Hob hounds headed straight for us. I should never have got out of bed this morning. Ah hell, maybe she's exaggerating."

Topaz shook her head. "Councillor Darkstrom is known for her rhetoric, but she rarely exaggerates when it comes to possible dangers."

"That's right, she doesn't. All right, take what men you can spare, and set them to watching the boundaries. We'll worry about the hounds as and when they make their appearance. Now then . . . oh hell, I've lost track of what we were talking about."

"The beginnings of the plague, Director, and its possible links with the *Balefire*. Captain Starlight was one of the first few victims, wasn't he?"

"Yes. He hasn't said a word since we found him. He won't eat or drink or sleep; just sits huddled in a corner, whimpering. If I didn't know better, I'd swear he'd been scared out of his mind. What kind of a plague is it where the living are worse off than the dead?"

"Where there's life there's hope, Director. My husband taught me that a long time ago, and I still believe it to be true. Given enough time, our medics might yet come up with a cure."

"Given enough time, the plague might wipe us all out."

"There haven't been many deaths so far. Not compared with the number of survivors."

"There have been enough, Investigator. More than enough. Most of us have lost someone to the plague."

Topaz looked at him curiously. There had been something in Steel's voice . . . "Who did you lose, Director?"

"A friend. His name was Jamie Royal."

Steel's voice was very quiet, and his eyes were far away, lost in memory. Topaz looked at her hands, folded neatly in her lap.

"I didn't know the esper was a friend of yours, Director."

"I liked him. Everyone did. Even his enemies." Steel sat slumped in his chair, his mouth twisted into a bitter grimace. "I couldn't even go to his funeral. Too much to do."

"I didn't think you had any friends, Steel," said Topaz quietly. "What was he like?"

"Jamie . . . was a gambling man. He owed money to everyone dumb enough to extend him credit, but he always paid his debts eventually. He never broke his word, and he never dealt from the bottom. And the only way anyone will ever remember him is as one of the first victims of this new plague. Not much of a legacy for a man like Jamie."

Topaz looked at him thoughtfully, then pushed back her chair and got to her feet. "We've done all we can for one day, Steel. Leave it for now. It's late, and we could both use some sleep."

Steel nodded goodbye without looking up. Topaz stared at his bowed head a moment, and then left, closing the cubicle door quietly behind her.

Eileen Darkstrom stood at the far boundary of Tech Quarter, staring out into the fog. All the time she'd spent trudging through the unrelenting cold of the plateau and the outlying settlements, she'd thought constantly of how good it would feel to get back to the warmth of Mistport. And now she was back, the first thing she had to do was hang about on the outskirts of the city, freezing her butt off. Darkstrom sniffed, and huddled inside her cloak. The fog was thicker than ever, with visibility no more than a few yards in any direction. The street lamps cast only shallow pools of light, and the mists muffled every sound. A heavy snow was falling, and the sinking evening sun was lost to sight. Another hour or so and it would be gone completely; night fell early on Mistworld as winter drew near. Darkstrom scowled, and kicked at the thick snow on the ground.

Where the hell are you, Stefan?

Darkstrom walked up and down before the boundary wall, stamping her feet to drive out the cold. The Bloodhawk had been very particular about her being on time, and here he was almost half an hour late. Typical. Not for the first time, Darkstrom wondered what the hell was so important that they had to discuss it out here in the freezing cold, so far away from everything and everyone. It had to be something to do with what they'd discovered about the Hob hounds. She'd intended to go straight to the Council and tell them everything, but the Bloodhawk had insisted that the two of them talk in private first. As if they hadn't had enough chance on the way home. Darkstrom smiled fondly, remembering.

There was a slight noise behind her, and she turned happily, expecting to see the Bloodhawk. There was no one there. She looked quickly around, but nothing moved in the thick grey mists, and silence lay heavily across the fallen snow. Darkstrom stirred uneasily, and dropped her hand to her sword. The hounds shouldn't be here for at least another forty-eight hours, but there was always the chance a few outrunners had got ahead of the pack. . . . Darkstrom drew her sword and glared about her into the mists. Her muscular blacksmith's arms flexed confidently, and her narrowed green eyes held an eager, dangerous gleam. She hadn't known much about the hounds until she'd visited the outer settlements. What she'd learned there had shocked and sickened her. Hob hounds attacked humans not because they felt threatened or hungry, but simply because they enjoyed it. They showed a distinct preference for weaker prey, like women or children. Particularly children. Darkstrom gripped her sword tightly. She thought she would enjoy evening the score against the hounds a little. She hitched back her cloak to give her arms more freedom of movement, stolidly ignoring the cold, and stamped her boots into the snow to get a good footing. Whatever was lurking out there in the mists was about to get the surprise of its life. She moved slowly forward, listening intently for the slightest sound. She quickly discovered that the only sound on the quiet was the snow crunching loudly under her boots. Darkstrom scowled, and moved quickly over to put her back against the boundary wall. No point in making it easy for the hound.

Her scowl deepened as she heard slow, unhurried footsteps approaching out of the mists. Whatever was out there, it wasn't a hound. It could be a footpad, or an Empire agent . . . Darkstrom hefted her sword and dropped into a fighting crouch. The footsteps drew steadily nearer, and then a tall slim shadow formed suddenly out of the fog. Darkstrom tensed, and then relaxed with a great sigh of pent-in breath as Count Stefan Bloodhawk came walking out of the mists towards her. He looked at her drawn sword, and raised an elegant eyebrow. Darkstrom laughed, and put her sword away.

"I know I'm a little late," said the Bloodhawk, reproachfully.

"Sorry, Stefan," said Darkstrom, smiling ruefully. "The mists have been getting to me." She moved forward into his arms and gave him a welcoming kiss, to show she forgave him for being late. "What kept you, dear? Is there some new problem about the hounds?"

"Yes," said the Bloodhawk regretfully, "I'm afraid there is." His right hand slipped the dagger expertly between Darkstrom's ribs, and she stared at him in silent horror before the light went out of her eyes and she slumped against him. He stepped back, and let her fall into the snow.

"I'm sorry, my dear," said the Bloodhawk calmly, "but I really couldn't let you talk to the Council. I want the hounds to be a surprise."

He sighed quietly, cleaned his dagger on a piece of rag, and sheathed it. It was a pity he'd had to kill her. He'd grown rather fond of her, in his way. But the Empire's orders had been most specific, and he couldn't risk upsetting his masters. Anything was worth it if it would finally get him off this stinking planet.

Now that Darkstrom was dead, the Council would have to face the hounds unwarned; or rather, what was left of the

Council would. Darkstrom and du Wolfe were dead, and he would be . . . missing. That just left Royal and Steel; an old man and a thief. The Bloodhawk smiled slightly. Everything was proceeding according to plan. He picked Darkstrom up and slung her over his shoulder. She was surprisingly heavy for such a small woman. The Bloodhawk walked unhurriedly back into the fog and disappeared among the mists. The sound of his retreating footsteps died quickly away, and soon there was nothing left to show that he had ever been there, save for a few scuffed footprints in the snow and a small patch of blood where Eileen Darkstrom had fallen.

CHAPTER SIXTEEN

The Wolf at the Gate

STEEL paced back and forth in his cramped glass cubicle, trying to wake himself up. He should have gone home and got some sleep while he had the chance. Now it was two in the morning, and it didn't look as though he'd be getting any sleep this night. His head was muzzy, his eyes ached, and his mouth tasted absolutely foul. He took another large bite from the candy bar in his hand, but it didn't help much. He glanced surreptitiously at Investigator Topaz, standing hunched over her computer console. She couldn't have had much sleep herself, but she looked disgustingly bright-eyed and alert. Steel growled under his breath. It wasn't natural to look that good this early in the morning. He moved in behind Topaz and peered over her shoulder as she keyed in a new series of codes. He watched the answers come up on the screen, and winced.

"Over five thousand and still rising . . . What the hell's happening out there, Investigator? We've got the strictest quarantine regulations Mistport's seen in more than twenty years, and still people are dying. How can everything have got out of hand so quickly? What the hell are we dealing with here?"

Topaz shook her head slowly, and stabbed at the terminal keys as though she could bully the computer into giving her the answers she wanted. "When the Empire creates a plague, it does a thorough job, Director. New outbreaks have been recorded all across the city. The actual death rate is still comparatively low, but there are so many mindwiped victims that we just can't cope with them anymore. The

174

hospital's already full to overflowing. If we don't come up with some kind of vaccine soon, in a few more weeks Mistport will be a city of the dead and the dying."

"I'm not even sure it is a plague," growled Steel, sinking into his chair. As usual, it groaned under his weight, and he cursed it absently. "It doesn't act like a plague, doesn't feel like a plague—" He took another bite from his candy bar and wiped his sticky fingers on his shirt front. The sugar gave him energy. "What kind of a plague doesn't have any symptoms? One minute the victims are fine and healthy, and the next minute they and everyone around them is either dead or mad. No plague works that fast."

"Could be a long incubation period."

"No. Our tests would have found something by now."

"Well what is it, if it isn't a plague?"

"I don't know! Some new Empire weapon, a rogue esper . . ."

"An esper? Be serious, Steel. What kind of esper could take out five thousand people in less than a week?"

"You once stood off five hundred Guards with a single song."

"Yes," said Topaz steadily. "And it nearly killed me. I'm the most powerful Siren the Empire ever discovered, and even I have my limits. No, Steel; it can't be a rogue esper."

"You can't be sure of that."

"We can't be sure of anything anymore, Director."

Steel and Topaz glared at each other helplessly, and then looked away as the command monitor snapped on.

"Director!"

"Yes, duty esper. What is it?"

"Sensors report a gathering of Empire ships off Mistworld, Director."

Steel gaped at the screen, unable to take the news in. *They've come. They've finally come.* He swallowed dryly, and shook his head slightly to clear it.

"How many ships?"

"Seventy-three and counting, Director. They're dropping out of hyperspace as we watch."

"It's the Fleet," said Topaz softly. "After all these years, the Empire finally thinks it's ready to destroy Mistworld."

Steel ignored her, and broke contact with the duty esper to key his monitor into the main system. The screen showed him a crowded radar image, with new contacts appearing every second. Overlapping voices from the command centre filled the cubicle.

Disrupter cannon don't answer to the computers. Get a team down there to check the systems.

Smuggler ships are powering up for takeoff. Ground crews please clear Pad Seven.

Where are the espers? We need the psionic shield.

Force shields are down. They don't answer to the computers.

Disrupter cannon are not on line. Repeat; disrupters are not on line.

The computers are dead! They don't hear us!

Where are the espers?

Steel cleared the screen, and the voices fell silent. He could feel his pulse hammering in his neck, and his palms were wet with sweat. Everything was happening so damned fast . . . He looked at Topaz, and her unruffled self-possession helped to calm him down a little.

"We've still got the smugglers' ships," said Topaz.

Steel shook his head. "They don't stand a chance against the Imperial Fleet, and they know it. They're going to die up there, just to buy us a little time." He sat back in his chair and stared dazedly round his cubicle. Beyond the glass walls, technicians were running back and forth, shouting and cursing silently. "The force shields are out. The disrupters are out. I can't believe our defences all fell apart so quickly. What the hell's happened to our computers?"

"The crystal!" said Topaz suddenly.

"What?"

"The memory crystal I delivered; it was part of the main defence systems, wasn't it?"

Steel swore softly. "Yes, it was. Your burglar must have had time to switch crystals before you discovered him. And what with all the excitement of the *Balefire* arriving, and the Hob hounds, and the plague . . . the crystal must have been installed without checking."

"And I never thought to check for myself."

"No reason why you should have; that was our responsibility."

A distant roar shook the control tower as the smugglers' ships threw themselves into the night skies, a dozen silver needles against the Imperial Fleet.

"Call them back," said Topaz.

"I can't. We need time to bring the espers together. Without our shields and disrupters, the smugglers' ships are the only other defence we've got left. Their names will be remembered as heroes."

"We're going to lose," said Topaz quietly. "I should have known. I should have known there was nowhere safe from the Empire."

Steel glanced quickly at her dark, brooding face, and then turned back to his command monitor and raised the duty esper.

"Gather the espers. We need the psionic shield."

"It's already up and holding, Director, but I don't know how long we can maintain it." John Silver's face was calm and controlled, but his eyes were grim. "Hundreds of espers have died from the plague."

"That's it!" Steel turned to his computer console, ignoring the startled esper, and tapped in a query. He nodded savagely as a stream of information flowed across the screen. "I should have seen it before; *only* espers have died from the plague. We were so busy looking for a physical common denominator we didn't think to check for any other links. Investigator, we've been set up. With our computers sabotaged, the psionic shield is all that stands between us and the Fleet, and the plague was introduced specifically to take care of that. And I was so proud of my cannon . . . I should have listened to Suzanne du Wolfe. Duty esper, maintain the shield. That has top priority until I tell you otherwise."

"Yes, Director, but . . . ."

"Just do it!" Steel broke off contact and stared thoughtfully at the blank monitor screen. "It's a carrier; has to be.

One of the refugees from the *Balefire*. I thought Starlight was lucky to escape from Tannim! Somewhere along the line the Empire must have smuggled aboard a carrier with an esper-specific plague."

"No," said Topaz abruptly. "That's not it." Steel looked at the Investigator in surprise as she paced back and forth before him, frowning. "You were right the first time, Director; it's not a plague, it's a rogue esper. A Siren, like me. When I sing, my voice and esp combine to work directly on the mind, boosting and scrambling the sensory imput. Take that too far, push too hard . . ."

"Brainburn," said Steel.

"Yes," said Topaz. "That's what happened to the five hundred Guards on Virimonde."

"And if you were to sing at an esper . . ."

"The weaker mind would self-destruct. The victim's talent would rage out of control, attacking both the victim and his surroundings. It's no wonder so many plague sites have been gutted by fire and violence; the victims must have included Pyros and Poltergeists. How could we have been so blind? The espers were the real target all along. The mindwiped survivors were nothing more than innocent bystanders; a blind to keep us from noticing that one by one those we depended on most for our defence were being murdered!"

Steel and Topaz looked at each other.

"You were the most powerful Siren the Empire ever had," said Steel finally.

"Yes," said Topaz. "I was. I destroyed five hundred minds, and they made me a legend. This new Siren has taken more than five thousand victims, in just a few days. I wonder if they'll make her a legend too. Probably not; she's more valuable as a weapon." Topaz shook her head slowly. "No wonder the port espers picked up strange readings from the *Balefire*. Director, we've got to find this rogue and stop her, while we still can."

Steel frowned thoughtfully. "It's not going to be easy, trying to find one woman in a city the size of Mistport. I take it we can be sure the rogue is a woman? If the Empire's finally produced a male Siren . . ."

Topaz shook her head firmly. "No, it's a sex-linked characteristic, like hexing or dowsing."

"Let's hope you're right, Investigator." Steel called the duty esper back to his monitor.

"Yes, Director?"

"How many espers can you spare me for a city-wide search? Emergency priority."

"Assuming everyone reports in, maybe a dozen; but that'll be most of our reserve."

"I'll take them. We're looking for a rogue esper, a very powerful Siren. You shouldn't have much trouble recognising her; she was responsible for the strange readings your people picked up from the *Balefire*. Report back to me as soon as you've found her, but no one's to approach her until I give the word. This rogue is dangerous. Got it?"

"Yes, Director."

"Is the shield secure?"

"For the moment. The Empire ships are in stable orbit, but keeping their distance. They know what will happen if they try anything."

"Stay with it, lad," said Steel gruffly, and John Silver grinned.

"With our shield or on it, Director."

The monitor screen cleared. Steel looked in surprise at his last piece of candy, melting forgotten in his hand, and popped it into his mouth. He chewed thoughtfully, his hands clasped across his belly. "The port espers scanned every man, woman, and child leaving the *Balefire*. There's no way the rogue could have got past them."

Topaz shrugged. "Empire agents must have got to her first, and spirited her off the landing field. This whole thing has been very carefully planned, right from the beginning."

"It's starting to look that way. But how far back does this thing go, Investigator? Did the Empire really scorch Tannim lifeless just to make sure we'd accept the *Balefire*'s refugees? A whole world?"

Topaz looked at him steadily. "They've done worse, Director. Much worse."

They sat in silence a while. Steel knew there were things he ought to be doing, but somehow he just couldn't seem to raise the energy. "Do you think they'll find the rogue, Investigator?"

"A dozen espers, to cover an entire city? They might get lucky, but I doubt it. We don't even know her name."

"Call her Mary."

"What?"

"Typhoid Mary. It's an old name for a fugitive carrier of disease." Steel smiled at Topaz's open astonishment. "A Port Director has to study many fields, Investigator."

He steepled his fingers and tapped them together thoughtfully. "As from now, I'm promoting you to Watch Commander. With the Bloodhawk missing, I need someone on the spot I can trust. You're probably the only one in the Watch who really understands what we're up against. Get all the Watch out on the streets and search the city, sector by sector. If you come across any espers apart from the rogue, I want them escorted here under full protection. We can't afford to lose any more espers. At least here we should be able to offer them some security."

Topaz nodded. "Sounds logical. Just one thing; what are my men supposed to do if they find the rogue?"

"They can't afford to take chances," said Steel steadily. "Keep her under surveillance, but don't approach her. I'll send men armed with disrupters."

"You're not going to give her the chance to surrender."

"No. I can't take the risk."

"With this many Watch out on the streets, we're going to need a cover story."

"Right. If the truth gets out there'll be a panic. Put a bounty on the rogue's head and tell everyone she's a plague carrier. It's true enough."

Topaz smiled slightly. "That should keep people off the streets. I'll lead a patrol into Thieves Quarter. I know the area."

"No! You're an esper, Topaz; I can't risk losing you to the rogue."

"I'm a Siren, Director. I may be the only real chance you've got of stopping her."

Steel hesitated, and then nodded curtly. He turned away and studied his computer console, and after a moment Topaz left the cubicle. Steel scowled at the blank screen before him. Damn fool woman was going to get herself killed at this rate. He wondered why that bothered him so much. He sighed wearily, and indulged in a long, slow stretch. He was so tired even his bones ached. He'd done everything he could, but he had a strong feeling it wasn't going to be enough. The Empire had been planning this for a long time. They wouldn't have left anything to chance. He blinked in surprise as his monitor screen suddenly lit up again.

"Yes, duty esper. What is it?"

"Hob hounds, Director! They're pouring into the city through a breach in the Guilds Quarter boundary. First reports are confused, but it seems clear there are hundreds of the beasts. The Watch on the spot are falling back, street by street. Without reinforcements, it's only a matter of time before they're overrun."

"Of course," said Steel. "The Empire can't risk us finding Mary too soon, so they provide a distraction. Logical."

"Director?"

"Take as many Watchmen as you need, but I want those hounds contained. It's vital they be stopped where they are."

"We've only got so many Watch, Director. We can't block off the hounds and maintain a city-wide search for the rogue esper."

"I know. Just . . . do the best you can."

"Yes, Director."

"What are the early casualty reports like?"

"Bad. The hounds are slaughtering everything that moves. The Watch are slowing them down, but that's all. Still, it could have been worse."

"I don't see how."

"At least the Watch was there, Director. If you hadn't posted men to watch the boundaries, the hounds would have taken us completely by surprise. There's no telling how many they would have killed, running unstopped through the city."

"Yes. I suppose so. We've got Councillor Darkstrom to thank for that. I take it there's still no sign of her or the Bloodhawk?"

"Not so far, Director."

"And Donald Royal?"

"Still missing, sir."

"That just leaves me. The last Councillor. Ironic, in its way, I suppose."

Steel sat in silence for a while, staring at nothing, his eyes far away. John Silver waited patiently.

"Duty esper."

"Yes, Director?"

"I'm going home. Re-route any messages, and . . . let me know if anything happens."

"Of course, Director. Not much else we can do now, is there?"

"No. You look tired, lad."

John Silver smiled. "I think I'll stay a little longer. I couldn't sleep anyway."

Steel nodded. "I'll see you later."

"Goodbye, sir."

The screen went blank. Steel rose slowly to his feet and looked about him. Beyond the glass walls, the technicians sat unmoving at their posts, tense and silent. Steel looked away. He'd done everything he could. "I did my best," he said softly. He hesitated a moment, as though waiting for an answer, and then he turned and left without looking back.

Twelve espers lay side by side on comfortable couches, and spread their thoughts across the city, searching.

Tarpaulined barges drifted down the River Autumn, steel-lined bows breaking through the newly forming ice. Outleaning timbered buildings bowed to each other like tired old men, upper stories no more than a hand's-breadth apart. Watchmen patrolled the lamplit streets, shivering in their furs. Cats darted along the low stone walls of a back alley, appearing and disappearing in the thick fog like dusky phantoms.

The espers found Mary in less than an hour, and made contact with her mind. She killed them all.

Typhoid Mary had been programmed.

CHAPTER SEVENTEEN

Heroes and Villains

THE building itself was quiet and unassuming, almost anonymous, and the sign above the door said simply BLACKSMITH. Donald Royal smiled grimly. He knew better. During his many years on the Council he'd read a great many reports on Dr. Vertue's body bank. It was one of Donald's old familiar angers that he'd never been able to raise enough evidence to close the place down. He should have tried harder. If he had, Jamie might still be alive today.

Donald sighed quietly and pulled his cloak tightly about him. The fog was thick and heavy, the snow had been falling for hours, and it was still barely morning. It was going to be a hard winter. Donald glanced at Madelaine Skye standing next to him, unrecognizable as usual in her thick fur cloak with the hood pulled well forward. She seemed calm enough, but Donald could tell from the set of her shoulders that her right hand was resting on her sword hilt. He wasn't surprised. He'd heard the open rage in her voice on the few occasions she'd spoken of Dr. Vertue.

"Well," said Donald. "This is the place."

"Yes," said Skye. "I know."

"You've been here before, then?"

"Yes."

Donald waited a moment, and then sniffed when he realised Skye wasn't going to say any more. He had a strong feeling there were things going on that Skye wasn't telling him about. It didn't really matter. If it was important, Skye would tell him eventually. Vertue was all that mattered now. Donald Royal looked at the closed door and felt a slow, cold anger build within him. Leon Vertue knew how and why Jamie had died, and one way or another Donald was going to learn the truth. He glanced quickly at Madelaine Skye.

"Ready?"

"Ready."

"Then let's do it."

Donald stepped forward and tried the door. It wasn't locked. He pushed the door open and moved cautiously forward into a quietly tasteful lamplit hall. Skye stepped quickly in behind him and pushed the door shut. It felt good to be in out of the cold. Donald pushed back his hood and beat the snow from his cloak as he looked about him. The short, narrow hall was completely empty, and ended at the only other door. Donald started towards it, Skye at his side. He took off his gloves and tucked them into his belt. He flexed his hands slowly. Gloves just got in the way when you used a sword. He checked the walls unobtrusively as he passed. He couldn't see any security cameras, but he assumed they were being monitored. Both the walls were covered with ostentatiously expensive paintings and tapestries. Donald smiled suddenly as he recognised a forgery. He knew it was a fake, because he owned the original. His smile slowly faded. At least, he'd always assumed he owned the original. He arrived at the end door in a thoroughly foul state of mind, and scowled fiercely when the door handle wouldn't turn under his hand. He hammered on the ironwood door with his fist and waited impatiently. There was a hiss of static from a small comm unit set into the door frame.

"Dr. Vertue thanks you for calling, but regrets to announce that he is unavailable today. We apologise for any inconvenience this may cause."

"Get that recording off the line and talk to me," growled Donald. "Or so help me I'll call in a company of the Watch and have them turn this door into kindling. I am Councillor Donald Royal, and I have business with Dr. Vertue."

There was a pause, and then a hesitant female voice issued from the comm unit. "I'm sorry, Councillor, but the doctor left strict instructions that he wasn't to be disturbed for any reason."

"Your boss is already in trouble," said Donald coldly. "Unless you want to join him, I suggest you open this damned door. Now."

The door hummed quietly to itself, and then swung smoothly open. Donald smiled grimly, and stalked forward into the doctor's reception area. So much for the first line of defence. A gorgeous redhead was rising nervously from behind a huge steel-and-plastic desk. Donald nodded briskly to her, and glanced about him. There was no sign of Vertue. Highly polished ironwood wall panels gleamed richly under the overhead lightsphere, and the carpet was thick enough to hide a good-sized snake. Any other time Donald might have been impressed, but right now he wasn't in the mood. He had other things on his mind.

"Vertue," he said bluntly. "Where is he?"

The secretary tore her eyes away from the bulky, fur-wrapped figure of Madelaine Skye, and glanced quickly at the closed door to the right before answering Donald. "I'm afraid you can't see him just at the moment, Councillor; he's in conference. He was most emphatic that he wasn't to be disturbed. If you'd care to wait . . ."

"He'll see us," said Donald, and headed for the right-hand door.

"I'm sorry, Councillor," said the secretary, and something in her voice made Donald stop and look back. The secretary had a disrupter in her hand, pointed carefully midway between him and Skye. Donald stood very still. The secretary had them both covered, and he had no doubt she'd use the gun if she felt at all threatened. He thought about the throwing knife in the top of his right boot, and then thought better of it. He needed a distraction. . . .

The secretary looked quickly from Donald to Skye, frowning thoughtfully. "If you really had a company of the Watch, you'd have brought them in with you. And if you don't have the Watch's backing, that means you don't have a warrant. So I can throw you both out any time I feel like it. But you wouldn't have come on this strong if you didn't have something you thought you could hurt us with. I don't think I can afford to take any chances with you, Councillor. Or your mysterious friend. Unbuckle your sword belt, Councillor. Slowly, and very carefully. And you, in the furs; push back that hood and let me take a look at you. I'm sure I know you from somewhere."

Donald fumbled at his sword belt, taking his time about it without being too obvious. The secretary seemed more interested in Skye than she was in him. If he timed it just right . . . He knelt carefully down and dropped his scabbard onto the floor. The secretary's eyes flickered from Skye to him and back again. Skye slowly lifted her hands, and then jerked her hood back to show her face. The secretary's eyes widened with horror, and her gun hand started to shake.

"You can't be. You can't be! I saw your body in the tank!"

Donald pulled the knife from his boot and threw it under-hand, putting all his strength behind it. The knife slammed into the secretary's shoulder, spinning her round. The disrupter fired, discharging its energy harmlessly into the ceiling. Skye stepped quickly forward, sword in hand. The long blade flashed once, and the secretary fell limply to the floor. Skye knelt beside her to be sure she was dead, and then sheathed her sword. Donald picked up his sword belt and buckled it on again.

"Nice throw," said Skye.

"Thanks. Why did she spook like that when she saw your face? And what did she mean . . ."

"I'll explain later. Come and take a look at this."

Donald sniffed, and moved behind the desk to crouch down beside Skye. His knees protested loudly, but he ignored them. Skye gestured for him to study the secretary's face. He did so, frowning, and then reached out to gently touch the flawless skin with his finger-tips. It was just a little bit too taut, and he could feel the telltale little scars behind her ears and under her chin. Somewhere along the line, the redhead had

undergone extensive skin grafting in order to retain her
stunning good looks. Donald wondered briefly what had
happened to the woman who'd donated the skin, and
then he grimaced as he realised he already knew the
answer. He took a firm hold on the hilt of his throwing knife, and pulled it out of the secretary's shoulder.
He wiped the blade clean on her blouse and slipped
the knife back into his boot. He had a strong feeling he might need the knife again before the morning
was over.

He rose awkwardly to his feet, wincing as his knees protested again. There were days when he wondered just whose
side his body was on. Skye moved over to the right-hand
door and tried the handle. It was locked. Donald reached
into his pocket for his lockpicks.

"Don't waste your time, Donald," said Skye. "It's an
electronic lock. Vertue thinks of everything." She scowled
thoughtfully at the tiny security camera built into the door
frame. "We can't afford to waste any more time. We've
probably set off all kinds of alarms, and there's no telling
how long they've been watching us. Try the desk; maybe
there's a hidden switch or something."

Donald nodded, and searched the desk drawers one by
one. It didn't take him long to find a simple remote control
unit, hidden in an empty candy box. He tried the various
buttons at random, and after he'd turned the lights on
and off a few times, the right-hand door hummed loudly
and swung open revealing a long, narrow passage. Donald
tucked the remote into his pocket, and moved quickly over
to stand beside Skye. He noticed she'd pulled her hood
forward to cover her face again, but he decided not to say
anything. She'd tell him when she was ready.

The corridor stretched away a good thirty feet and more
before turning a sharp corner. Lightspheres had been set
into the ceiling at regular intervals, but only one was working. There was a strong smell of antiseptic. Skye moved
slowly forward into the corridor, and Donald followed her.
He couldn't see any security cameras, but he knew they
were there. Their footsteps were eerily loud on the quiet

echoing hollowly back from the bare, featureless walls. There was a quiet rasp of steel on leather as Madelaine Skye drew her sword. Donald couldn't help noticing that her hand was shaking slightly.

Leon Vertue glared at his master, standing calmly before him on the other side of the reclamation tank. He'd been shouting and blustering at the man for the best part of an hour, and little good it had done him. Nothing that Vertue could say seemed to have any effect on Count Stefan Bloodhawk. *I should never have got involved with the Empire*, thought Vertue sourly. *Once they get their claws into you, you're theirs for life.* He fought hard to hold on to his temper. Mistport was going to hell in a handcart, Blackjack was dead, Investigator Topaz was on his trail, and now some damned fool had let Hob hounds into the city. One way or another, his life here was finished; he had to get off Mistworld and start again somewhere else. It didn't matter where. There was always a demand for body banks. What did matter was how much of his stock and equipment he could take with him. He had to take some of it, and it was up to the Bloodhawk to help him. The Empire owed him that much. Vertue glared at the Bloodhawk, who stared calmly back at him.

"You've got to get me out of here!" snapped Vertue. "While you've been hiding safe and sound in the outer settlements, that damned esper of yours has gone crazy; she's been mindblasting everything that moves! I don't know what happened between her and Royal, but that rotten bitch of yours has been out of control ever since she got here. You never told me she was so powerful! She'll destroy the whole city before she's through."

"Do stop whining, my dear doctor; it doesn't become you in the least." The Bloodhawk brushed an invisible fleck of dust from his sleeve. "The lady in question is not out of control; she's doing exactly what she was supposed to. She did make her start a little earlier than was intended, I'll admit, but that was your fault. You should have told me this Jamie Royal was unreliable."

"I had no way of knowing that! All the signs were that Blackjack had him thoroughly terrorized. I still don't know why Jamie disobeyed his orders."

"Why isn't important. The fact remains that he led Mary straight to another esper. No wonder her programming took over."

Vertue shook his head angrily. "That's all irrelevant now! Blackjack's dead, and too many people are starting to tie me in to what's been happening. It's only a matter of time before one or all of them come after me. You should have let me kill Topaz, as I wanted."

"No. Once the initial attempt had failed, we couldn't afford to draw attention to her. Someone might have realised she was dangerous to our scheme because she was a Siren. Like our dear Mary."

"Look, you got me into this mess, Bloodhawk; it's up to you to get me out."

"Or?"

"Or I'll go straight to what's left of the Council, and turn myself in."

"They'd lock you up and throw away the key."

"At least I'd still be alive."

"Just another rat deserting the sinking ship," said the Bloodhawk sadly. "My dear Leon, you must know I can't possibly allow you to upset my plans. Not at this stage."

"And just how do you plan to stop me?" Vertue stepped back from the reclamation tank, grinning wolfishly. The Bloodhawk raised an eyebrow at the disrupter in Vertue's hand, but said nothing. "You've got a ship somewhere," said Vertue tightly. "A private ship. You're going to help me transfer my equipment to that ship, and then we're both going to take a little trip off-planet. As soon as we reach the nearest starport, we both go our separate ways. That's fair, isn't it?"

"You can't hold a gun on me forever," said the Bloodhawk.

"I can give it a bloody good try," smiled Vertue. "Now let's go. We've wasted enough time talking."

"More than enough," said Donald Royal.

Vertue and the Bloodhawk spun round to find Donald standing in the doorway, leaning lazily against the door-jamb, a throwing knife poised in his hand. Skye stood beside him, sword in hand, anonymous as always in her furs.

"Your security really is appalling, Vertue," said Donald mildly. "Now put down that gun. You even try pointing it in my direction, and I'll put this nasty little dagger right through your left eyeball."

Vertue stared at him, clearly weighing his chances, and then carefully put the gun down on the closed lid of the reclamation unit. Donald nodded his thanks, and walked unhurriedly forward into the vast chamber. He glanced quickly about him, taking in the great walls of shining crystal and the bulky reclamation tanks that took up most of the chamber. The air was freezing cold, and the stench of cheap disinfectant was almost overpowering. Skye moved silently at Donald's side, her eyes fixed on Leon Vertue. Donald finally came to a stop before Vertue and the Bloodhawk, carefully keeping a few yards distance between them. Donald stared steadily at the Bloodhawk.

"I thought Vertue didn't have the brains or the guts to pull something like this," he said quietly. "And I always thought you were too good to be true. How long have you been a traitor, Bloodhawk? How long have we had an Imperial agent sitting at the heart of our Council?"

"Almost from the beginning," said the Bloodhawk calmly. "As soon as I saw Mistport, I knew I'd made a dreadful mistake in coming here. Such a pitiful, squalid little place. Totally uncivilised. It quickly occurred to me that since . . . what I'd done hadn't really been all that bad, the Empire might possibly be interested in reacquiring my loyalty. After all, I could do a lot for them. For the right price. It wasn't difficult, making contact, even then, and the Empire wasn't slow to see my potential. I've done rather well, over the years. There's even been some talk the Empire might give me a medal for my services."

"No one gives medals to traitors," said Donald. "Not even the Empire."

The Bloodhawk shrugged, unperturbed. "Be that as it may, with the Empire's help it wasn't difficult to get myself elected Councillor. And after that . . ."

"Yes," said Donald. "It all starts to make sense now. No wonder we were never able to keep anything secret from the Empire."

"Quite," said the Bloodhawk. "You know, you really should be surrendering to me. When all is said and done, I hold all your lives in my hands."

"Run that by me again," said Donald. "I think I missed something."

The Bloodhawk smiled. "My dear Donald, even as we speak the Imperial Fleet is gathering above our heads."

"What?" Vertue looked sharply at the Bloodhawk. "You never said anything about the Fleet coming here. You never said anything about the Fleet!"

"Do be quiet, Leon. It wasn't necessary for you to know. Now, Donald, within a matter of hours, the Fleet will move in and scorch the planet lifeless. Just like Tannim. Your only hope for survival is to surrender to me and throw yourselves on my mercy. I know what you're going to say, Donald, but I'm afraid you're wrong. Very soon now, every esper in Mistport will be dead, and without the psionic shield, Mistworld will be defenceless."

"The disrupter cannon . . ."

"Are out of commission, along with the force shields, thanks to a little discreet sabotage. By now Port Director Steel should be discovering that his precious computers aren't listening to him anymore. It's really quite amazing what you can do with one carefully programmed memory crystal in just the right place. You do remember how I convinced the Council that the defence computers needed a new memory crystal?"

Donald looked at him for a long moment. "How long have you been planning all this?"

"Years," said the Bloodhawk. "Allowing for a few small hiccups, I don't think things have gone too badly."

"Who are you?" said Leon Vertue suddenly, glaring at the silent, hooded figure standing beside Donald Royal.

"Why do you keep staring at me?"

"You know who I am." She pushed back her hood, and Vertue's face went white, his eyes wide and staring like those of a trapped animal. "You and I have a debt to settle, Vertue."

"You're dead!" said Vertue loudly. "Blackjack killed you, and I put you into the reclamation tank myself! I saw you torn apart by the blades and the saws!"

"No," said Madelaine Skye softly. "Unfortunately, your mercenary got it wrong. He arrived while I was out. The only woman in my office was my sister, Jessica. She'd come to pay me a surprise visit. I'm told she looked a lot like me. Your man cut her down in cold blood, and then brought her back here to you and your reclamation tanks. You used my death to force Jamie to work for you. The poor lamb never was very brave without me to back him up.

"I found out what had happened soon enough, and decided to stay dead until I could find out what was going on. I knew there had to be somebody behind Vertue, and the whole thing had the Empire's smell about it. I couldn't even tell Jamie I was alive. I needed to be sure just whose side he was on. By the time I was sure, it was too late. He was dead. I never even had a chance to tell him I loved him."

"You can't blame me for his death," said Vertue quickly. "It was the Bloodhawk's idea. He gave the order; I just passed it on to Blackjack."

The Bloodhawk raised an eyebrow. "He's lying, of course."

"Of course," said Skye, "But then, both of you would say anything to save your skins, wouldn't you?"

"I've got money," said Vertue. "Lots of it. I'll give you half, if you'll let me go."

"You gave my sister to the knives," said Madelaine Skye. "And there isn't enough gold in the Empire to make up for what you did to my Jamie."

Vertue looked into her cold green eyes and saw his death staring back. He whimpered faintly, and then snatched up the disrupter lying on the reclamation unit. Skye's sword flashed up and down in a silvery arc, and severed Vertue's hand from his wrist. He just had time to scream, and then he fell back as Donald's throwing knife sprouted from his throat. Blood flew on the freezing air, and Vertue fell dying to the floor. Donald and Skye turned quickly to face the Bloodhawk, only to stop suddenly as they saw the disrupter in his hand.

"You didn't think he was the only one with a gun, surely?" said the Bloodhawk. "Please put away the sword, Madelaine. I assure you, you're not going to get a chance to use it."

Skye sheathed her sword, being careful to make no sudden movements.

"Very good, Madelaine. Now, both of you unbuckle your sword belts and let them drop to the floor."

Donald and Skye did so. The scabbarded swords made a heavy, hopeless sound as they hit the floor. The Bloodhawk gestured for Skye and Donald to move back from the reclamation unit, and they did so. The Bloodhawk glanced at Vertue's disrupter lying on the floor, and kicked it out of reach.

"That was a nice throw, Donald," he said appreciatively. "A direct hit on the carotid artery, from a very tricky angle."

"It wasn't that good," said Donald. "I was aiming for his eye."

"Dear Donald, modest as ever. You realise I can't let either of you live. You know far too much. As far as everyone else is concerned, I am missing, presumed dead, and I fully intend to stay that way until I'm safely off this stinking planet. Don't make this any more complicated than it has to be. Just take it quietly, and I'll kill you quickly and cleanly."

"Like you killed Darkstrom?" said Donald suddenly.

"Exactly."

"Bastard."

"Really, Donald . . ."

"She loved you!"

"She was useful."

Donald Royal stared grimly at the Bloodhawk. "There's two of us, and only one of you. Shoot me, and Skye'll get you before your gun can recharge."

"Quite possibly," said the Bloodhawk. "But she won't risk your life, any more than you'll risk hers. And neither of you is desperate enough to throw away your own life on the chance the other will get me. No, you'll just go on doing as I tell you, hoping that I'll make a mistake and you'll be able to turn the tables on me. You'll find some rope over there in the corner, Donald. Go and fetch it. Don't even think of trying something heroic, or I'll kill Madelaine."

"Rope," said Donald, not moving.

"You're going to tie her up, and then I'm going to tie you up. Then I can shoot you both quite safely. Now, don't say any more, Donald. I don't really have the time to kill you as slowly as I'd like, but give me even the slightest excuse, and I swear I'll find the time. I hate you, old man. I've always hated you. If it hadn't been for you and your example, Mistport would have fallen apart years ago, and I would have been free to leave this squalid little planet. Time and time again I set up schemes and you wrecked them. You kept the Council honest, and fought corruption in the Watch. You're the reason I've been trapped here all these years!"

He started towards Donald, his face twisted with rage. His gun hand shook in the intensity of his emotion. And in that moment, while his attention was fixed solely on Donald, Madelaine Skye drew from her pocket the disrupter she'd taken from the dead secretary in the reception office. The Bloodhawk caught the movement out of the corner of his eye, and started to turn. Donald stepped quickly forward and hit the Bloodhawk with a left uppercut to the chin. He put everything he had into the blow, and the Bloodhawk staggered backwards, his gun hand swinging wildly back and forth. Skye chose her moment carefully, and shot him through the heart. The searing energy beam threw the Bloodhawk back against the reclamation tank. He stood spread-eagled against it for a moment, and then slid lifeless to the floor.

Skye looked at him for a moment, and then put away the gun. "That was for you, Jamie," she said softly. She turned to Donald Royal, who was nursing his left hand gingerly. "Are you all right, Donald?"

"I think I've broken every bone in my hand."

Skye laughed. "My hero. Come on, it can't be that bad if you can still flex your fingers like that."

Donald sniffed, but had to smile. "We didn't do too badly in the end, did we?"

"Not bad at all. We made quite a team." She stopped and looked at Donald thoughtfully. "Donald, how would you like to make it permanent? I could use a partner like you."

Donald looked at her. "Are you serious? At my age?"

"I said partner, not husband. We work well together. My skill, and your experience; it's a natural."

Donald thought about it, and then grinned suddenly. "What the hell. I was getting bored with being a Councillor."

They grinned at each other. Donald put out his hand, and Skye shook it firmly.

"Now what?" said Madelaine Skye.

"Well, first I suppose we'd better get back to the command centre and see if that bastard was telling the truth about the Imperial Fleet. I have a strong feeling we don't know the half of what's really been going on."

CHAPTER EIGHTEEN

Songs in the Night

WITH so many Watchmen roaming the streets most thieves decided that discretion was after all the better part of valour, and retired from their normal lives for a while. The patrols had been out in the bitter cold all morning with hardly a break, and were growing increasingly tired and touchy. They'd arrest anyone, on the slightest suspicion, just to get off the streets and out of the cold. Thieves stayed indoors, and waited for better days.

All save the roof runners.

Perched high up on a weather-beaten gable like some ghostly gargoyle, Cat rested his chin on his white-gloved hand and sighed quietly to himself. It was almost three days since the unfortunate affair at Gallowtree Gate, and Cyder was still furious at missing out on Starlight's loot. Cat had been in such a hurry to get out of the cemetery that he'd even forgotten to take the Captain's disrupter. Such guns were rare on Mistworld, and therefore valuable, and Cyder was still giving him hell for having left it behind. Today had been no better than the day before, and so Cat had decided to take to the roofs for a while, until Cyder calmed down a little and stopped throwing things. Fresh movement caught his eye, and he peered interestedly down into the mists below, where a patrol of the Watch were halfheartedly searching a garbage-filled back alley while their leader reported in.

Investigator Topaz shifted her weight from one numbed foot to the other and pulled her heavy cloak about her as she waited for the command centre to re-route her call to

Steel's apartment. *Typical,* she thought sourly. *My men are out here risking pneumonia, and he's sitting at home with his feet up in front of a nice warm fire. There's no justice. Or at least none we can learn to live with.* She glared about her into the thinning fog. A low wind had sprung up, dispersing the mists, but it only made the cold bite deeper. Even with her Investigator's training, Topaz was beginning to feel the cold. *I must be getting soft. I'll be needing eight hours of sleep a night next.* She shook her head sadly, and then looked down as static whispered from the comm unit in her hand.

"Yes, Investigator."

"Sector Four clear, Director; no trace of the rogue. Any news your end?"

"A few sightings, but none confirmed. The twelve espers I set looking for Mary must have found her. They're all dead. I daren't risk trying that again."

Topaz swore under her breath, so as not to alarm her men. Right now, the last thing they needed was more bad news to discourage them. "What's happening with the Fleet? Have they moved against the shield yet?"

"No. They're still up there, waiting. We may have something on the rogue. One of her first victims after the Blackthorn was Captain Starlight. There's some evidence to suggest she deliberately hunted him down."

"Evidence?"

"I was . . . having him watched at the time. I suspected him of trying to smuggle valuables off the landing field. Most of my watchers lost their minds along with Starlight, but one of my men had left earlier on. It's only now that what he had to say is starting to make sense. . . . Anyway, it's possible the rogue thought Starlight had something she wanted, something smuggled off Tannim. Among Starlight's effects we found a single blue sapphire, apparently acquired from one of the refugees. Such gems are increasingly rare throughout the Empire, and are especially prized on Tannim."

"Who has this sapphire now?"

A fat chuckle answered her.

"Of course, Director. I should have known."

"Quite. It seems to me there might be some connection between the rogue and the sapphire. I've sent for a courier to take it to the port laboratories. Maybe it'll tell them something. Looks like just another gem to me. Anyway, we should have their report sometime this afternoon. Assuming we're all still here this afternoon."

"Very well. Let me know the results when you get them."

"Of course. Topaz . . ."

"Yes?"

"Donald Royal finally turned up at the control tower. I was just talking to him when you called. It seems Leon Vertue is dead. He was shot, while trying to kill Donald."

"I see."

"No doubt we'll get all the details later. I thought you'd want to know."

"Yes. Thank you, Steel. I'm moving on to Sector Five now. Topaz out."

"Steel out."

Topaz slipped the comm unit back into her pocket and called for her patrol to re-form. The Watchmen emerged from the back alley shaking their heads and brushing rotting garbage from their clothes. Topaz accepted their report, and then led them off into the mists.

Cat watched them go from the gable's shadow, and scratched thoughtfully at his pockmarked cheek. What he'd been able to read off Topaz's lips both intrigued and worried him. The Empire hadn't moved directly against Mistworld in almost two hundred years; not since the Fleet first smashed itself against the psionic shield. But now it seemed they were back. . . . He worried his lower lip between his teeth, scowling. He'd better tell Cyder, and see what she made of it. If nothing else, it might take her mind off losing Starlight's loot.

Cat padded softly away across the snow-covered roofs. As he disappeared into the rising mists, a tall blonde with faraway eyes emerged from the shadows of the alleyway below. She'd thought for a time that the Watch were going to find her, but they hadn't looked very hard. To be exact, they hadn't dug deep enough. The garbage had been very unpleasant, but Mary had hidden in worse places. Anything was better than being found and handed back to the Empire. She'd found Topaz's conversation very interesting. So, Port Director Steel had her sapphire, but he was going to give it to somebody else. She couldn't have that. She'd have to find Steel first, and make him give her back her sapphire. This woman, Topaz; she'd know where Steel was. Mary moved off into the thickening mists, following the Investigator and her patrol.

Even the best programs can be diverted.

Cat hung upside down from the Blackthorn's guttering and frowned worriedly as he saw that the attic room's shutters stood slightly ajar. It wasn't like Cyder to be so careless. He pulled the shutters open, grabbed the steel hoops set above the window, and swung down and into the attic room.

Only one of the lamps was lit, and there was a chill to the air. Cat pulled the shutters firmly together. Cyder was sitting in a chair before the fire, staring into the leaping flames. She looked tired and bitter and just a little lost. There was no loot for her to fence, and the Blackthorn was still closed. Cyder had worked hard at repairing what she could, but there was a limit to what she could do with her resources, and she'd pretty much reached it. To be poor in Mistport was a crime, often punished by death in the cold and unforgiving streets. Cat scowled fiercely. He was still a roof runner, and a good burglar could always make money. One way or another.

Cyder looked round as she heard him approaching and gave him a warm smile, but her eyes were vague and absent. She got up to greet him, and Cat put his arms around her. For a moment she leant against him, happy just to be held and comforted, and then she pushed him away, her face falling back into its usual hard, controlled lines. She smiled at Cat's disappointed face, and kissed him warmly.

"It's about time you got back. Where've you been?"

Cat laboriously spelt out in fingertalk what he'd learned from the leader of the Watch patrol. He was puzzled; Cyder seemed strangely calm as she watched his fingers, almost distracted. When he'd finished, she kissed him quickly and then moved away to inspect her face and hair in the mirror on the wall. Cat watched her lips in the reflection.

"Don't worry about the Imperial Fleet, my darling. As long as the esper shield's up, they can't hurt us. As for the plague carrier, I know the price on her head is tempting, but we're thieves, not bounty hunters. Leave such work for those with a taste for it. All right?"

Cat nodded reluctantly.

"Good. Now then, I've got a job for you. I'm going to see Port Director Steel."

Cat raised an eyebrow, and Cyder laughed.

"Don't worry, darling. Steel and I have been business associates from time to time in the past. He recently acquired a rather fine sapphire, and I have a buyer for such a gem. I had made arrangements with Steel to purchase the sapphire from him, but when I contacted him an hour ago, he broke our agreement and refused to sell me the jewel at any price. In fact, he was quite short with me. Now we can't have that, can we? I was depending on that deal, Cat. The profit on reselling the sapphire would have gone a long way to helping us out of our present difficulties. Now we've got nothing, and it's all his fault. So, I am going to invite myself to dinner with Steel. It shouldn't be difficult; dear Gideon does so love showing off his culinary skills, and we usually enjoy each other's company. And that's where you come in, Cat. While I keep him occupied, you're going to break into his apartment and steal the sapphire."

Cat smiled politely. He'd have been better off staying on the roof.

"I knew you'd approve," said Cyder.

The mists filled the narrow streets as Topaz waited impatiently for her patrol to catch up with her. The fog pressed close about her, leaving a sheen of moisture on her hair and cloak. Visibility was poor, the high stone walls around her little more than dim shadows. A single street lantern glowed bravely against the encroaching fog, a pool of amber light in a sea of endless grey. At least it had stopped snowing.

Vertue was dead. Topaz smiled slowly. With him gone, her vengeance was finally complete. She would have preferred to kill him herself, but it didn't matter. It was enough that he was dead. She felt as though a great weight had been lifted from her shoulders, and yet . . .

What do I do now? I need . . . something in my life; something to give it shape and purpose.

For a long time that had been Michael. Then there had been revenge. Now . . . what? She frowned slightly. She was a Commander in the Watch. Michael would have found that amusing, but Topaz had already found a kind of comfort in the Watch. Right from the beginning they had accepted her, despite who and what she was, and what she'd done in the past. Perhaps, through the Watch, she could repay Mistworld something of the debt she owed it, for having taken her in and given her sanctuary from the Empire.

Slow footsteps broke the silence, and Topaz looked quickly around. Her men were going to have to do much better than this if they were going to cover all the sectors in this Quarter before nightfall. And then Topaz frowned as she realised there was only one set of footsteps approaching. The harsh, crisp sound of boots on snow carried clearly on the still air. Topaz turned to face the sound, one hand moving automatically to the gun at her side.

Typhoid Mary came walking slowly out of the fog, wrapped in a filthy, tattered cloak. Her gaunt face and hands were bare to the cold, and already showed clear signs of frostbite. She was smiling, and her eyes were very bright. Topaz knew who she was. One Siren can always recognise another. Topaz saw the power that burned in the rogue like an all-consuming flame, and felt her mouth go dry. For as long as she could remember, she'd always known she was the most powerful Siren there'd ever been. Now she wasn't sure that was true anymore. Even through her shields Mary's mind blazed like a searchlight. Deep within Mary's mind Topaz could see the Empire's handiwork; a dark and savage conditioning that writhed among Mary's thoughts like maggots in a fallen apple.

Topaz glanced back the way she'd come, and saw nothing but the mists. And even if her patrol did get to her in time, there would be nothing they could do. Cold steel was no defence against a Siren's song. Topaz knew she stood or fell alone, just as she had once before, when she'd faced an entire company of the Guard and destroyed them with her song. She could still hear their screams. Typhoid Mary stood before her, still smiling. Topaz carefully moved her hand away from her gun. It couldn't help her now.

"Mary . . ."

"That's not my name."

"I can help you."

The tall blonde shook her head slowly, her dead-white face as empty as a mask. Her smile was a grimace, and the light in her eyes was cold and deadly. "I thought Mistworld at least would be free of bounty hunters. Save your breath, Investigator. I won't let the Empire take me again."

"I'm no bounty hunter. I just want to help you."

Mary laughed harshly. "I've seen the Investigator's cloak before. I know your kind. I know what you are, and what you do. You're as inhuman as the aliens you walk with. You want to take me back to the Empire."

"Listen to me," said Topaz, stepping forward.

Mary opened her mouth and sang.

The street lantern shattered. Topaz staggered back as Mary's song roared in her mind, and she raised her own voice in defence. Topaz and Mary stood face to face, unmoving, and the force of their combined songs whirled the fog and snow around them in a slow, churning maelstrom. The two minds smashed against each other, neither giving an inch, but Topaz felt a slow fear stir deep within her as she realised the rogue was using only a fraction of her power. Topaz summoned her strength. If she lost, then all of Mistworld went down with her. She reached deep inside herself, and drew upon the vast well of power she'd sworn never to use again. *Five hundred men, screaming. Their eyes, so dark and empty.* Topaz drew upon her strength, made it a part of her song, and threw it at the rogue esper. Mary didn't even flinch.

The rogue's song rose effortlessly over Topaz's, striking past the Investigator's defences with contemptuous ease. All Topaz's shields fell away, and Mary howled through her mind, searching ruthlessly for the information she needed. It only took a moment, and then Mary's voice rose in triumph as she finally discovered the location of her precious sapphire. Topaz fell limply to the ground. She never felt the impact when she hit.

Mary fell silent, and stood thoughtfully over the unmoving Investigator. The churning snow dropped back to the ground again, and the fog slowly grew still. A slow excitement welled up within Mary as she thought of regaining her lost sapphire, but there was also a dark, quiet voice whispering at the back of her mind. The voice had been there a long time. It told her where to look for her sapphire, who to approach, and what to do when they lied to her. Now the voice was telling her about the Mistport command centre. It told her there were lots of espers there, waiting for her; waiting for her to sing for them. Mary wanted to sing for them, but even more than that she wanted her sapphire. She hesitated, confused, torn between the two conflicting poles of her conditioning, and then she smiled and relaxed again as the answer came to her. First, she would go to Steel's apartment and reclaim her lost jewel. Then, once the sapphire was safely hers again, she would go to the command centre. Mary smiled brightly as she walked away into the curling mists, and her eyes were very dark.

Typhoid Mary's program was nearing its end.

CHAPTER NINETEEN

A Final Sacrifice

CAT crouched uncomfortably on the flat asphalt roof of the building overlooking Steel's apartment, and waited impatiently for Cyder's signal. Port Director Steel lived right in the heart of Tech Quarter, a high-income high-tech area that Cat usually had enough sense to stay well clear of. The buildings were mostly bleak slabs of concrete and glass left over from the original Empire colony. They offered no easy hand- or footholds, and were lousy with security devices. Even worse, they all looked the same and Cat kept getting lost. He scowled about him at the thickening mists. He'd be glad when this job was over and he could get back to the more familiar timbered and gabled roofs of Thieves Quarter.

The heating elements in his gloves had cut out again, and he pounded his fists together to keep the blood flowing. At least the thick mists and the recent heavy snow meant he could blend easily into the background. For once his white thermal suit was actually earning its keep. He glowered down at Steel's apartment, but there was still no sign of the arranged signal. Cat thought of Cyder and Steel reclining at their ease before a blazing fire, sipping mulled wine and discussing the sumptuous meal they were about to enjoy. His stomach rumbled loudly. He sighed, and peered resignedly through the thickening mists at the brightly lit window below.

Steel's ground-floor apartment was warm, comfortable, and bedecked with carpets of an impressive thickness. Tapestries and rugs covered the walls, less to keep out the cold

than to ward off the chill inspired by the blank white walls
and ceiling. Colony buildings were designed to be easy to
erect and proof against the elements, but that was all. Since
they were never meant to be lived in for long, it didn't
matter that they were hardly pleasant on the eye. Frills
and fancies could come later, when there was time. It said
something about Mistport's short and troubled history that
buildings originally intended for temporary shelters were
not only still standing hundreds of years later, but were
still preferable to any of the stone-and-timbered buildings
that had followed them.

Pieces of high tech and *objets retrouvés* lay scattered
casually across Steel's spacious living room, side by side
with small statuettes of gold and brass and silver. Steel
fancied himself a collector, though his taste was frankly
appalling. The various chairs and couches were smart and
elegant, whilst still being sturdy enough to cope with Steel's
weight. First and foremost, the Director was a practical
man. The single great window had the faint bluish tinge of
steelglass, but Steel's other security measures were politely
inconspicuous. Even the window was mostly hidden behind
heavy curtains.

Cyder let Steel take her cloak and hang it up, and strolled
admiringly round the room. Every time she paid Steel a visit
he seemed to have acquired some new expensive trifle. It
was a pity she'd only come for the sapphire. . . .

"What are you doing here, Cyder?"

She turned slowly to face Steel, knowing she looked
stunning in her gown of red and gold satinet, tightly laced
across the bosom.

"I wanted to talk to you, and you wouldn't answer my
calls. So, here I am. Aren't you glad to see me, darling?"

Steel smiled suddenly. "Yes. Yes, I am. I could use
some company. I'm just preparing dinner. Would you care
to join me?"

"Are you sure there's enough for two?"

Steel chuckled, and patted his stomach. "My dear Cyder,
I always have enough for two."

"Then I would love to join you for dinner. You are, after all, still the finest chef in Mistport." Cyder stopped, and looked at Steel curiously. "Is something wrong, Gideon? You look . . . tired."

Cyder was being polite, and they both knew it. Steel looked ghastly. His face was drawn and haggard, and his eyes were deep-sunk with exhaustion. Overweight though he was, Steel usually gave the impression of being light on his feet, but now all his weight seemed to have caught up with him, and his movements were slow and ponderous.

"It's been a long day," said Steel, smiling faintly.

"I heard about the gathering Fleet."

Steel looked at her for a moment, and then chuckled admiringly. "Now how the hell did you find out about that?"

"I have my sources," said Cyder, smiling demurely.

"I'm sure you have," said Steel. "Don't worry about the Fleet, my dear. The esper shield is up and holding. Donald Royal's keeping my seat warm at the control tower. There's nothing really for him to do there, but . . . Hey, I was sorry to hear about the Blackthorn. The damage sounded pretty bad."

Cyder shrugged. "It wasn't good. Still, we're slowly picking up the pieces. We'll be open for business again almost before you know it."

"That'll cost you an arm and a leg. Are you all right for money, Cyder?"

"Of course. I have my savings, and I should be collecting on a debt I'm owed quite shortly."

"Good. Well, make yourself comfortable while I see to the dinner. It won't be long now."

He moved off into the adjoining kitchen, and Cyder poured herself a stiff drink from the most impressive of the decanters. She hadn't thought it would be this easy. Something was worrying Steel, and it wasn't just the Fleet. The plague carrier? Cyder shrugged, and sipped slowly at her wine. Excellent vintage. If nothing else, she would give Gideon an evening of good talk and company, and make him smile. It was the least she could do. They were, after all, old friends.

But fond as she was of Steel, business was business. She strolled over to the window, pushed back the heavy curtain, and drew a pencil torch from her voluminous sleeve. Outside, the fog was thicker than ever. She switched on the torch and waved it back and forth, hoping Cat could see it. He shouldn't have any trouble breaking in, assuming her information on Steel's security was up to date. If it wasn't, this was going to be a most embarrassing evening. She turned off the torch and slipped it back into her sleeve. She glanced at the kitchen door, to be sure Steel was still safely occupied, and then pulled the curtain back into position and turned away from the window. She looked about the room, mentally pricing a few of the more expensive items, then wandered towards the kitchen. Something smelled nice. Out in the street, someone was singing.

The window exploded inwards. Flying slivers of steelglass sprayed across the room, amid an inrush of freezing air. Cyder was thrown violently to the floor and lay sprawled on the carpet, her ears ringing. Not far away, a chunk of steelglass had been driven deep into the side of a chair, and other slivers had gouged deep holes in the carpet. Cyder slowly raised her head, and rivulets of blood ran down her face. She couldn't feel her legs. She was shivering violently from the cold, and her head ached horribly. She fought to sit up, but her legs wouldn't obey her. She finally raised herself up on one elbow, and turned her head painfully slowly to look behind her. And there, standing among the wreckage of the window, was a tall blonde wrapped in a tattered grey cloak. She was smiling, and her eyes were not sane.

Thick streamers of fog rolled into Steel's living room through the shattered window. If the blonde felt the cold, she gave no sign of it. She looked at Cyder, and moved slowly towards her. Cyder tried to drag herself away, and couldn't. Blood ran down her face in a steady stream. The blonde loomed over her, still smiling.

"Where is he?" she said calmly. "Where's Steel?"

"Here I am, Mary," said Steel quietly. "Now get away from her."

Steel stood just inside his kitchen door. His face was pale, but his hands were steady. He and Mary studied each other for a while in silence.

"How did you break my window?" said Steel finally.

"I'm a Siren. A good singer can always shatter glass."

"But that's steelglass."

The rogue shrugged. "Glass is glass. Where's my sapphire."

"Mary . . ."

"Don't call me Mary! That's not my name."

"It is now. You're a rogue esper; Typhoid Mary, the killer."

Mary shook her head impatiently. "I haven't killed anyone."

Steel stared at her. "What are you talking about? You've killed hundreds, and mindwiped even more! Why do you think we've been searching for you?"

"You want to hand me back to the Empire! I know you; I know your kind. I'm not going back. I'll kill you first. I'll kill you all before I let you send me back!"

Steel saw the madness in her eyes, and licked his dry lips uncertainly. The rogue had all the signs of someone who'd been conditioned by the Empire mindtechs. Reason would only affect her within the limits of her conditioning. And even then, he had to be careful. There was no telling what might set her off. Say the wrong thing, and he could quite easily sign his own death warrant.

"Mary, please let us help you. The Empire has been using your song to murder other espers. . . ."

Mary laughed contemptuously. "Don't waste my time, Steel. Your lies don't interest me. You have something of mine, and I want it back. Where is it, Steel? Where's my sapphire?"

"Mary . . ."

"Where's my sapphire!"

Steel looked at her for a moment, and then nodded at a smart little desk by the front door. "It's locked in one of the drawers."

"Get it."

Steel moved slowly over to the desk, followed all the way by Mary's unblinking gaze. He took a key from his pocket, careful to keep his movements slow and deliberate, and unlocked one of the desk's drawers. He reached in and brought out a small leather pouch. He pulled open the drawstrings and took out a small blue gem, no more than half an inch in diameter.

"Is this it?" he said slowly. "Is this what it's all been about? One stupid little jewel?"

"Give it to me," said Mary eagerly. Steel put the pouch and the jewel on top of the desk, reached into the open drawer, and took out a disrupter. Mary looked at the gun, and smiled.

"You killed Jamie Royal," said Steel.

"Give me my sapphire."

"He was a friend of mine, and you killed him. You want your sapphire? Come and get it."

Mary sang a single piercing note and Steel convulsed, the gun flying from his hand. He fell to the floor and lay there helplessly, shivering violently.

Cyder tried to sit up further, so she could see where the gun had fallen, and her arm gave out. She fell forward onto the bloodstained carpet, and lay trembling in the silence. Somehow she'd never thought it would end like this. To die in the middle of a petty burglary . . . it just wasn't fair. She coughed, and her ribs hurt, but she couldn't move to ease them. One of her eyes was gummed shut with drying blood. She was cold, and so very afraid.

Cat crouched helplessly outside the shattered window. There was nothing he could do. The woman was obviously a very powerful esper, and he didn't even have a weapon. Taking on a rogue esper with his bare hands would only get him killed. If he just stayed where he was, hidden from sight, there was a chance he could still get out of this alive. He didn't have to risk his neck. Cat shrugged suddenly, and pulled himself up onto the jagged window frame. He couldn't run away. Cyder needed him.

He crouched on the ironwood frame a moment, getting his balance just right. The rogue had her back to him. Cat gathered his strength and threw himself at her. The rogue must have heard something at the last moment. She started to turn, but Cat still slammed into her with enough force to send them both crashing to the floor. They rolled back and forth on the bloodstained carpet, Cat trying desperately to get a stranglehold on her. She brought her elbow back hard into his ribs, driving the air from his lungs, and his grip loosened. Mary pulled herself free, and turned to face him. Cat struggled up onto his knees. Mary opened her mouth and sang.

Cat froze on his haunches as the song washed over him, searing through his muscles. His senses blurred in and out, twisted and jumbled. A tearing headache bent him in two, and then was suddenly gone. Mary was the most powerful esper Cat had ever encountered, and for the first time since he was a child, Cat could hear again.

There was the sound of his own rasping breathing, and the scuffing of his hands and knees on the carpet. From out beyond the shattered window came the never-ending sounds of the city, muffled to a murmur by the thick fog. From all around him came the simple, wonderful, everyday sounds of life and living. And over and above everything else, he could hear Mary singing.

Her voice was sweet and true, rising and falling like a single petal tossed on the wind. It filled Cat's mind, and nothing else mattered. Mary knelt singing before him, face to face. Cat swayed to the song's slow rhythm, glorying in his freedom from silence. He felt himself growing steadily weaker, felt the darkness gathering in around him, and didn't care at all.

He looked past Mary, and saw Steel sitting slumped against the far wall, his hands clapped to his ears, staring at nothing. Lying on the floor between Mary and Steel was

Cyder. She lay stretched out on the carpet, bloodied and broken and very still.

Cat rose shakily to one knee, took careful aim, and lashed out at Mary. The last sound he ever heard was his fist slamming into Mary's chin. Mary fell backwards, and lay still.

Cat cried silent tears, and moved slowly over to cradle Cyder's bloody head in his lap.

CHAPTER TWENTY

Starting Over

TOPAZ handed Steel a mug of steaming coffee.

"Steel, you've got to be the luckiest man I've ever met. If your mysterious friend had waited just a little longer to punch out Mary, you'd all have been brainburned."

"And don't think I'm not aware of that, Topaz." Steel warmed his shaking hands on the mug, and nodded his thanks to the Investigator. The coffee smelled delicious. If he hadn't known better, he'd have sworn it was the real thing. "The Watch Sergeant told me you had a run-in with Mary yourself, on the way here."

Topaz smiled grimly. "Seems I was lucky too. My Investigator's training protected me from the worst of her song, and she didn't wait to finish me off." She looked at Steel narrowly. "Did you really stand up to Mary, armed only with a handgun?"

Steel shrugged, embarassed. "I was too mad at her to be scared. I knew I didn't stand much of a chance, but . . . I couldn't let her get away. I had to give it a try, didn't I?"

Topaz laughed. "Steel, there's hope for you yet."

They shared a grin, and Steel sank back in his chair and sipped gingerly at his coffee. It was real coffee. Where the hell had she found real coffee? He decided not to ask. It would only embarrass her. He sighed contentedly. He hadn't felt this good in ages. The crisis was over, he was still alive, and Mistport was safe. It had been a bloody close thing, but they'd come through, and that was all that mattered. He glanced about him, and smiled wryly. He hadn't come out of it entirely unscathed. His living room was a mess, with blood and glass everywhere.

Someone was on the way to replace the shattered window, and he hated to think how much that was going to cost him. For the time being he kept the curtains closed and tried to pretend he couldn't feel the cold. Thinking about it, Steel was surprised to find he didn't really give much of a damn. He was alive, and the port was safe . . . He'd been thinking about redecorating anyway.

The Watch had taken Mary away, still unconscious. The hospital would keep her safely sedated, until the port espers could work out some way to defuse her programming. She wasn't to blame for all the things she'd done; Mary was just another Empire victim. There were lots of those on Mistworld.

On the couch opposite Steel, a somewhat revived and repaired Cyder was sitting with her arm round Cat, who was cheerfully nursing the heavily bandaged right hand he'd broken on Mary's jaw. Steel studied the young burglar thoughtfully, and Topaz followed his gaze.

"Know anything about him, Steel?"

"Not a damn thing. Roof runner by the look of him, but he hasn't said a word so far. Just appeared out of nowhere and saved all our lives by flattening Mary. I suppose he's entitled to the reward."

"I'd forgotten about that."

"I'll bet he hasn't."

"Be that as it may, Steel; right now I'm rather more interested in what one of Mistport's most notorious fences was doing here in your appartment."

Steel glanced briefly at Cyder, smiled weakly, and became very interested in his coffee. Topaz glared at him, and moved over to stand before the couch. Cat studied her warily, while Cyder smiled graciously and nodded a polite hello.

"How are you feeling, Cyder?"

"I'll live, Investigator. In the meantime, I am this young man's agent. When can he collect the reward?"

"He'll get it, but first I want a few answers from him. He looks remarkably like a burglar who once stole a memory crystal from me."

Cat smiled innocently, and Cyder hugged him to her.

"I'm afraid we'll never know, Investigator. Unfortunately he's a deaf mute, and can't answer questions."

Topaz turned away, shaking her head in disgust. Steel chuckled softly, caught Cat's eye, and dismissed him with a wave of his hand toward the door. Cat shook his head, grinning. He rose quickly to his feet, padded over to the shattered window, pushed back the curtains and disappeared out into the thick fog. Steel raised an eyebrow, but Cyder just smiled back at him, unperturbed. Topaz decided not to ask.

"If it's all right with you, Gideon," said Cyder, "I'll be getting back to my tavern. I want to get these bloodstains out of my dress before they set."

"Of course. I'm sure Topaz can find you an escort."

"Thanks, that won't be necessary."

Cyder got to her feet, wincing slightly as her cracked ribs protested. Steel levered himself out of his armchair and escorted her to the door. He wrapped her cloak about her shoulders, and opened the door for her. Cyder paused a moment in the doorway.

"Goodbye, Gideon. It would have been a lovely dinner, I'm sure."

"Thanks for keeping me company."

"Any time."

Cyder blew him a kiss, and left. Steel shut the door quietly behind her. He went back to his chair and sank gratefully into it. Topaz plumped up his cushions for him with a rough efficiency.

"Drink your coffee, Steel. It's getting cold."

Steel picked up his mug again and sipped obediently at his coffee. He sighed appreciatively, and then looked round his ruined living room with an abstracted air.

"What's wrong, Steel?"

"Mary's sapphire; what happened to it?"

"Is that all you can think of? Don't you want to know what's happened to the Imperial Fleet?"

"I imagine they've realised by now that the esper shield isn't going to fall, and they've all dropped quietly back into hyperspace."

Topaz nodded. "They left one ship on sentry duty, but no doubt that'll be gone tomorrow. If it isn't, I'll let the Poltergeists play a few practical jokes on it."

"So, we've weathered another storm. What were the final figures from the hospital?"

"More than twelve thousand brainburned; eight hundred and thirty dead."

Steel sighed. "Not much of a victory."

"We stood off the Imperial Fleet and survived," said Topaz calmly. "I'll settle for that."

"To hell with the Empire; where's that damned sapphire? I put it on top of the desk, but that got knocked over when Mary sang. She didn't have it when they carried her out, and neither did any of the Watch. It's got to be here somewhere, but damned if I can find it."

"Cyder; she must have taken it."

Steel shook his head firmly. "No. The sensors built into my door frame would have detected the jewel even if she'd swallowed it."

"The roof runner?"

"I had his suit checked while the medics were treating him. No sapphire."

"Then who's got it? That jewel's worth a small fortune."

Steel shrugged, then relaxed suddenly and sank back in his chair. "What the hell; it's only a sapphire."

Topaz looked at him. "Are you sure you're feeling all right, Steel?"

Steel laughed. "Perfectly all right, I assure you."

"Good." Topaz leaned forward suddenly to stare him straight in the eye. "Because the next time we meet, Director, I'm going to find the evidence that will nail you once and for all."

"You're welcome to try, Investigator. You're welcome to try."

Topaz laughed, and left. Steel grinned, and sipped his coffee.

In the dark, overshadowed alleyway opposite Steel's apartment Cyder leaned wearily against the rough stone wall and waited for her head to settle. She was sweating heavily, despite the freezing cold, and her hands were trembling. The Watch medic had done a good job strapping up her cracked ribs and putting a few stitches in her torn scalp, but she'd still lost a fair amount of blood from her various cuts and gashes. She felt awful, but she hadn't dared stay any longer in Steel's apartment. There was no telling when they might start asking awkward questions. The medic had wanted her to spend the night at the hospital for observation, but Cyder had curtly refused. She had a morbid fear of hospitals, and besides, they were expensive. She leant her head back against the cold stone wall. Half killed by a rogue esper, and all for nothing . . . She jumped despite herself as Cat dropped out of the fog to land beside her. He frowned as he took in her condition, and moved quickly forward to take her arm.

"I'm all right," she insisted, but let him help her away from the wall. Her legs seemed a little steadier now she wasn't alone. "Are you all right, Cat?"

He smiled, and nodded.

"After all we've been through, I didn't even get the sapphire. Still, the reward money will come in handy. . . . What are you grinning at?"

Cat opened his mouth, reached in, and took out a small blue jewel. Cyder stared at the sapphire a moment, and then started to laugh. It hurt her ribs, but she didn't care.

"Of course; there were no sensors left in the broken window! Cat, my love, I'll make a master thief out of you yet." She hesitated, and studied him searchingly. "Nobody ever risked anything for me before; you risked your life to save me. I'll have to think about that. Now let's get back to the tavern. There's still a lot of work to be done before we can open for business again."

Cyder leaned heavily on Cat's supporting arm, not wholly through weakness, and slowly, together, they disappeared back into the ever-curling mists of Mistport.

MICHAEL MOORCOCK

"A major novelist of enormous ambition." — *Washington Post*

THE CLASSIC ELRIC SERIES!

Elric, cursed and beloved of the Gods, follows his black hellblade Stormbringer across the myriad planes of Earth and Time—and to the countless hells that are his destiny!

___ELRIC OF MELNIBONE, BOOK I	0-441-20398-1/$4.50
___THE SAILOR ON THE SEAS OF FATE, BOOK II	0-441-74863-5/$4.50
___THE WEIRD OF THE WHITE WOLF, BOOK III	0-441-88805-4/$3.95
___THE VANISHING TOWER, BOOK IV	0-441-86039-7/$4.50
___THE BANE OF THE BLACK SWORD, BOOK V	0-441-04885-4/$3.95
___STORMBRINGER, BOOK VI	0-441-78754-1/$4.50

And THE FIRST ELRIC NOVEL IN 12 YEARS
THE FORTRESS OF THE PEARL

___0-441-24866-7/$4.50